Tentacles
OF
CORRUPTION

Alvin S. Berger

Copyright © 2023 by Alvin S. Berger.

ISBN 978-1-960753-74-8 (softcover)
ISBN 978-1-960753-75-5 (ebook)
ISBN 978-1-960753-78-6 (hardcover)

All rights reserved. No part of this book may be reproduced or transmitted in any form or by any means, electronic or mechanical, including photocopying, recording, or by any information storage and retrieval system without express written permission from the author, except in the case of brief quotations embodied in critical reviews and certain other noncommercial uses permitted by copyright law.

This book is a work of fiction. Names, characters, places, and incidents are the product of the author's imagination or are used fictitiously. Any resemblance to actual locales, events, or persons, living or dead, is purely coincidental.

Printed in the United States of America.

CHAPTER 1

Charles Barlow sat with a thump in his dusty, cluttered office, waiting for his phone to ring. He hadn't had a new case in two weeks. The world must be in equilibrium, he thought. The sun's rays danced on the scattered papers strewn across his desk. He had been in the detective business for only three years and solved more cases in that short time than most of his peers. Maybe it was his steely chin that made the ladies flock to him, or was it the way he spoke to his clients, both male, female and all of the genders in between? He smiled with a slight upturned edge of his lip. He could engage a woman with charm, or a man with a macho facade. It was almost metrosexual. He loved with a passion all who entered his sanctuary, except Denise Florio. She drove him bonkers.

It all began in September of last year. The door chime announced a new body, the lovely, sensual Denise Florio. She wore a hot pink sweater with a gold chain that dangled just above the cleavage that she knew would bring all eyes to her. She stopped in front of the door as it slowly closed behind her so she could make a spectacular entrance. She wore black high heels that clicked on the weathered wooden floor. Charles wondered why she did not just walk in instead of posturing. He'd know soon enough as she sauntered toward his desk, her hips swinging rhythmically side to side. Her full lips began to move ever so slowly as the words slipped out.

"Are you the detective?"

"Yep, and who might you be?" He smiled inside.

"I'm Denise Florio. I need some help with my husband who is cheating on me." She grimaced as she tried to keep from crying. "I know he sees other women on his frequent trips." Her eyes narrowed to slits as she waited to see his reactions. She didn't have to wait long to see him rise slowly out of his old office chair.

He stood at all of his six foot one inch, and towered over her diminutive frame. He walked around to the front of his desk, took her hand into both of his warm hands and spoke softly with compassion.

"It's a pleasure to meet you, Denise. Oh, may I call you Denise?" He said.

"'Of course. May I call you Charles?"

"Yes. Now that we have the formalities over, please tell me everything and leave nothing out. I want to trust you and will only help you if I know for certain that you are truthful." He released her hand and looked into her bright green eyes. Her attributes called, but he contained himself as only a thirty eight year old man could: difficult, but necessary. She calmed visibly as he leaned against the desk.

"Please sit and you can tell me the whole truthful story." Charles always doubted his clients and felt that they usually had something to hide. He wanted this case on his terms.

She sat quickly and crossed her leg, her skirt shifted midway up her thigh.

"I don't know how to begin. My husband is a real character and does business all over the world."

"Okay, go on. How do you know he cheated on you?" Charles responded.

"Oh, I found a receipt in his jacket for diamond earrings that he did not give me. He must have bought them for his other woman." She was visibly shaken. An act, he thought.

"They might be yours as a surprise." He needed confirmation of her accusation. "No, he just bought me a nice car for our tenth anniversary."

"That was really thoughtful," he replied.

"He's very good to me, but I still think he's fooling around." Charles needed to get to the crux of this before she repeated the same thing.

"So, what does your husband do for a living?"

"He sells military hardware, like rifles, bazookas, grenades and that kind of stuff. He reps for a few companies. He works in Washington with various committees in the Senate and House. He loves political maneuverings."

"Does he have a real connection to the top people?" Now, he thought, they were getting to the fine points of this triangle: love, politics and corruption. He knew that all of these things fit neatly into the package of the Washington swamp.

"Oh, yes, he is right in the middle of that. He loves to showboat. I guess it makes him feel important." She was noticeably colder as she described her husband.

"Do you have a picture of him? I like to see who I'm tracking." The Google search was not far away.

"Sure. Here, and this is the family. My husband is really charming, and my two children adore him. Actually, I love him, too." She spoke with such admiration that he had difficulty understanding her angst. Charles asked,

"Tell me more about his business. Maybe that will shed some light on what you found."

She frowned briefly to show her disapproval of what he did. "He's away a lot from the family, but does check in often to make sure we are doing okay. I know he has lots of contacts with the Speaker of the House who helps him often. He has shared that with me. Montrose Fairchild yaps a lot and regales us with his pompous tales of successes, both political and with his feminine conquests. I know some of his ladies. He also has some dealings with the new President, but she stays pretty distant from him. From what I've heard, she is very smart and does not enter into his pushy style." She sighed and peered into his eyes as if she was trying to invade him. He was perfectly aware of her intent, and it made him even more concerned about her motives. She was almost on the hunt.

"So, thanks for that insight into your husband. Tell me more about your knowledge of our new President, Mallory Cranston. How do you and your husband interact with her?" He waited patiently, and watched her body language.

"Oh, she and I attended some political meetings before she announced her candidacy. Really nice woman. I'm glad she won. My husband, Andy, knew her longer than I did. He was friends with Matt Cranston when they were in the service, and when she married Matt he sent them a gift. My Andy is a really good guy." She then looked quizzically and said " So why would he buy jewelry for some bimbo?"

"I have no clue about that. Maybe it was not for a woman friend of his, but for a gift for a male to give to his friend. Have you ever thought of that?"

"Actually, I did not." She smiled.

It seemed that she was now unsure of her whole complaint and her reason for coming to see him. "I'm so sorry to have wasted your time, Mr. Barlow. I'm embarrassed". She blushed.

"Forget it. Chalk it up to a misunderstanding." He then thought that it was his time and money she wasted. He actually wondered for whom Andy bought the diamonds. "Can I ask you a question before you leave?" "Sure", she replied.

"Do you have the receipt?"

"Yes, here it is." She reached into her purse and held it out for him.

He looked at it carefully and he saw that it was bought in Virginia, not in Washington. What the hell was he doing there so out of the way from where they lived or where he worked. Maybe she had something, but not what she thought.

"Denise, I think that you might have stumbled onto something, not related to some bimbo, but to a deeper motive for Andy. I know this jeweler, and he is not known for being very scrupulous. If you don't mind I'll take this case if you want me to pursue this."

She perked up as he spoke. Maybe her Andy was in over his head. "I'd be happy if you'd take the case. What kind of cost will there be?" She looked relieved.

"I hope you're prepared for a big number. I think that we should work together on this project so let's say just a five thousand retainer, and then it is two hundred an hour. If I find out anything that will help both of us I can actually drop most of the fee. Are you willing to do that?" He hesitated because it was his first big fee in a while. Would she take the bait?

"Done!" Denise reached into her Gucci pocketbook, took out her checkbook and wrote quickly. "Anything after your name?"

"Nope, just me." He glowed inside and grinned outside. "Please share all of your info with me. Just text it to my phone. I have some research to do before our next meeting. I need to see this jeweler first. I'll let you know what I find out and set up our meeting either here or another quiet place. Don't say anything to anyone about your visit here. You never know who's listening or watching." His demeanor changed from jovial to serious.

"Thanks again for your help. I hope that you will discover something to make me regain trust in Andy. Talk to you soon. Be careful." She admonished..

Denise turned slowly, turned back at Charles, opened the door and walked out. Charles looked out the window and wondered where all of this might end.

CHAPTER 2

Charles checked the map of Virginia and realized that the jeweler was in Alexandria, only about twenty minutes outside of D.C. So many unrelated thoughts ran through his mind. Was this purchase for a real bimbo for Andy, or for a high ranking politician? Where in high places does Andy go and who does he know? This iceberg of politics only showed one tenth above the water line. So, the underbelly had the secrets to be uncovered. It might be more than he could ever imagine. He got into his aging Toyota Sonata and slowly drove through the heavy traffic on I-495 to Morton's Jewelers on Fairfax Street. He had done a routine Google search and realized that the owners have been in business since 1951. Jack Morton started the business in a small store and gradually built it into an international empire. He passed away in the late nineties and his son, Jason, became its president and a big muck a muck. He knew that Jason was the link to whatever might happen with these earrings. He parked in the public garage next to Morton's Jewelers. His mind percolated with so many scenarios. It was show time as he walked into the store filled with the art of diamond treasures. He approached the fair blond woman at the first counter. She smiled at him with sparkling veneered teeth and asked politely,

"May I help you?"

"Yes, Ma'am. I'm looking for Jason Morton."

"So, you have an appointment?"

"No, I don't. Do I need one to see him?"

"No, I'll get him for you." She walked toward the back of the store, and then looked back as if to say don't stare at me. He was, actually. Why waste a chance to admire the perfection of a woman?

Jason walked rapidly toward Charles. He extended his arm in greeting. He spoke first.

"Hi, I'm Jason Morton. And you are?" His grin belied his inward insecurity.

"Hello, my name is Charles Barlow. I'm a private investigator representing a local woman. I hope you can help me." Jason's jaw dropped slightly and his grin turned into a frown.

"I'm not sure that I can help you." His stance became more erect, and his voice hardened.

"I'm also not going to give you private information about people who come into my store."

"I certainly understand that, but I just need you to tell me about this receipt that I have. It's a really sensitive issue for my client, and I would appreciate it if you'd help me so that I can allay her concerns." He oozed charm, and was genuinely pleasant to Jason. "May I show you the receipt?"

"I'll take a look." He softened slightly, and put on his reading glasses. "Well, this is a receipt for a pair of Graff earrings that I sold to a long standing customer. What's the issue?"

"I need to be honest with you. My client is his wife, and she never received those earrings. So, I really need to know for whom he bought them. I know that he is involved with many high up political 'friends'. I would appreciate your help. Please."

"You seem very sincere. It is not unusual for Mr. Florio to buy items here for many people. Actually, I have no idea about the recipient. He just comes in and pays for them. Sorry I could not be of more help. Anything else?"

It felt like he was hiding something. Charles answered quickly.

"No, thanks for your help. I guess I'll meet with Mr. Florio and tell him that you were very helpful"

"Wait!" was Jason's immediate response. "Why do you need to go to him? I've told you what I know." His face turned a light pink, and he shifted onto his right leg. It was a sure sign of fright.

"Look, I know that you're fudging. Andy is known for being involved with many high up political figures. You think I'm naive? Either you tell me the information I need, or I'm going directly to Andy and get it from him."

"Okay, okay. Let's go to my office to talk. There are too many prying ears and eyes here." He practically lost his balance as he turned abruptly to go to the rear of the store. Charles followed exactly in sync with Jason, but perfectly balanced. As they approached his office, one of the staff stopped him to quietly ask Jason a question. Charles could not understand what she said, but Jason's face puckered as if to say, 'Shut the hell up.' This was a new part of the puzzle. Why does a staff member produce such a gut reaction? Jason motioned Charles into his office and shut the door quickly. He sat behind his oak desk and blurted,

"I don't want to get Andy or me into any kind of trouble. What do you want from me?" He talked quietly, but sadly.

"I want the truth. No BS, and just who did Andy buy the earrings for?" Charles sat forward in the chair, and leaned on the front of the desk with both hands. Yes, confrontational.

"You must assure me that Andy will never know that I said anything. He is more than just a customer. He has contacts in many unusual places, if you know what I mean! He paid cash for these earrings, in hundreds. They sold for sixty six thousand. I'm pretty sure they were for a Senator who had some extracurricular activities. Andy gets favors from many political people and, in return, they do nice things for him. I get paid and that's all I do. Honestly, that's all I know, and I keep my mouth shut." The beginning of beads of sweat formed on his furrowed brow. Charles knew that Jason was only in the loop to a small degree. Yep, just a cog in the dirty wheels of scum in Washington politics. Charles raised his hands from the desk and stood erect. It was a good beginning to find out who got the earrings.

"How did Andy get rewarded?" Charles spoke with clipped tones. "Well, that sounds like you're in the midst of a scandal. I hope that you are prepared for more questions from me or another source. So far, we're on the same page."

Jason stood quickly and stretched his hand toward Charles. "I'm sorry I couldn't help more. Call me if you need anything else."

Charles took that sweaty hand, shook it, and turned to the door, thinking that this was the beginning of the end for someone up high.

As he opened the door the woman who whispered to Jason was standing adjacent to the door. Did she know anything? Just ask!

"Hi, I just met with your boss to ask a question about a recent purchase. Maybe you could help me, too. Oh, my name is Charles Barlow. And yours?" He was as caring as he could be.

"Hi, I'm Clara Denoit. I don't know if I know anything more about the gift from Andy." She was very direct.

"How did you know it was about Andy? I never mentioned it."

"I heard it when you walked in to talk to Jason. Actually, Andy bought many nice pieces here. I guess for his wife." Charles knew that she was lying.

"That was so generous of him. Did he tell you to send them to a specific address?" He looked at her hoping to probe her more.

"Well, we did send a few to his wife, and then some to another address in D.C. That's information that I cannot share." She was toying with him. Charles knew that he had better go back to see Jason immediately. He thanked Clara, took her hand in both of his and reopened the door to Jason's office. Jason was on the phone, and appeared shocked to see Charles so soon. He hung up abruptly saying a quick 'bye'.

"I hate to be played for a sucker. This time you had better be truthful" Charles boomed. "Who did you send the pieces to and why?"

"I only do what I'm told! Andy told me never to say anything to anyone about the articles I send out. He was adamant. Now I'm in between him, you and the Senator." The sweat flowed freely now. Charles knew that Jason was in a no-win situation.

"Clara told me that she was not allowed to tell me to whom you or she sent the gifts. I saw that you were on the phone as soon as I left you. I assume it was to the recipient. Now, you're going to tell me who it is, or I'll bring in the police, and that will not be good for you or this store." He was backed into a corner. "Tell me now or I'll go to the next step!" His voice went from loud to a staccato.

Jason's hands trembled, and his face was a brighter pink than before.

"I told you that I am just a middle man. I sent the gifts to the Speaker of the House, Montrose Fairchild. I have no idea what will happen after that." He was in tears. The thought of losing the business forced its way into his mind.

"Okay, then who else gets these things? Do not think that I'll let you off the hook this time. One is not the limit!" Charles yelled at him.

"On another occasion Clara sent gifts that Andy bought for two Senators. She will have to give you that information." Without skipping a beat, Charles slammed his fist on the desk and demanded that Jason bring her in.

He picked up the phone and called the front desk, "Please send Clara to my office."

The door opened slowly, and Clara walked in. She was a woman in the middle forties with delicately coiffed blond hair. She approached Jason's desk and she asked politely,

"What can I do for you?"

Charles never let Jason speak. "Just a few minutes ago, you gave me a non-answer. Jason gave me lots of information, and you need to clarify some of that information. First, what gifts did you send to Montrose Fairchild, and who else got gifts from the store? I told Jason that either you people fess up, or I bring in the police. Yes, I'm a private investigator, so I do have leverage!"

Clara looked at Jason, and he nodded. "Yes, you can tell him. We have a lot to lose if this gets out in a bad way."

Clara was calm and unruffled. She spoke with assurance which seemed out of place since there was so much riding on it.

"When Andy comes in we allow him lots of time so that he can privately choose what gifts he can send. He gives me the name and address of the person, and I send the gift out. That's all I know."

Clara looked at Jason for his approval. Again, he nodded. She continued.

"You have to understand that we are in real jeopardy after we confide this information to you.

Those people are not what you'd call nice guys." She looked again at Jason who was shaking.

"I'll give you the names of the two Senators to whom I have either sent or hand delivered items from the store. Roland Smathers from Texas, and Emil Chartoff from California are the ones that I know personally. Maybe Jason knows of others."

Jason squirmed impatiently hoping that he might just disappear into the ether. The words tumbled out as he unfolded more unusual tales of bribery from these defective servants of the people.

"Yes, we have sent out a few other nice items to other members of the House, among them Speaker Fairchild, as well as Tom Beauford from Virginia. These Senators or House members help Andy when he is in a bind for government contracts. Andy says that one hand washes the other, especially in Washington. I think there might be others, too. I can't remember them now. Please, I beg you, don't tell anyone that Clara and I have given you this information."

"Your discussions are secure with me. I'll do my own research based on this information and will contact you when I need your continued cooperation."

He got what he came for and turned without any further discussion. He got into his car and promptly drove off. He thought that there was so much more than just gifts to be uncovered. What did those Senators trade for some piddling diamonds? He needed to touch base with Andy Florio to see the real operation.

He asked Siri, "Call Denise Florio, cell."

"Hello Charles, What's up?" She sounded really happy to hear from him so fast.

"I spoke to the jeweler and have some questions for your husband. I actually would prefer seeing him rather than on the phone." Although Denise was the client, he felt that she had other motives. They were not clear to him, but his gut was usually right.

"Oh, his office is on 17th and Pennsylvania Avenue, near the White House. I'll call him and set up a time for you to see him. He actually knew that I was going to see you since we had a big fight over the receipt. Yes, I brought it up to him." That detail pissed Charles off. He held his temper in check.

"Denise, you never told me that you confronted him. I told you when we first met that you needed to tell me everything, but why did you leave that out?"

"Oh, I guess I forgot to mention it." He knew his gut was right. "So, anyway, I'll set up the appointment for today, close to three. I'll call him now. Bye, Charles." This was a very different Denise Florio, one who was conniving, devious and probably the reason that Andy looked for other women. He'd get to her later.

The drive to Andy's office took about thirty minutes. He had so many questions to ask, but he knew that it would be a challenge to get any useful information. The Executive Office building was a magnificent structure that portrayed class and importance. It was a perfect place for Andy Florio to conduct his business, legit or otherwise. He parked as close as he could, and walked briskly to the lobby. Andy's office was on the fifth floor. It was a really cozy place, which surprised him. He assumed that it would be large, roomy and elegant. The woman at the reception center asked those normal questions. Charles answered respectfully.

"Yes, Mrs. Florio did call to set up this appointment with Mr. Florio."

She responded cheerfully, "He'll be with you shortly, Mr. Barlow. May I get you a refreshment?"

"No, Ma'am, I'm okay. I'll just have a seat and wait. Oh, has Texas Senator Smathers stopped in today? I heard that he was in the area." He hoped that she'd take the bait.

"Oh, no, he didn't stop today. He was in on Friday of last week. He's such a sweet man." Effervescent and dumb was what he thought. This was better than talking to Andy. He continued.

"I was talking to the good Senator about some of my contacts at the Department of Defense, and he told me that he had some dealings with a few smart people there. I wonder if Andy knows some of them, too. Andy sure is a smart man." He sounded so sincere, like honey dripping from his mouth.

"I don't know about those people. I just know how we deal with the people at the military area of the Pentagon. They are very helpful to us. Andy, I mean Mr. Florio, sees them a lot." She was genuinely happy to talk about her work.

The time with her seemed perfect for the information he needed. It was now more important to see Andy and get a real sense of what was going on with Denise and the military intrigue. Maybe getting closer to this receptionist would be just as fertile. He had to be politely inquisitive as to her availability. He leaned closer to the desk and said quietly,

"You are so kind. Do you have children?"

"No, no, I was married, but divorced now." She broke into a wide smile.

"Well, someone is missing out on a real smart woman." He mirrored her smile, and felt a twinge of inner glee.

"You're too nice, Mr. Barlow. Oh, Mr. Florio just alerted me that he's ready for you. Enjoy your time with him." She looked up and smiled again. This time he knew she meant it. He beamed back at her.

Andy Florio opened the door to his office and motioned for Charles to enter.

"To what do I owe this pleasure?" He was very sure of himself.

"I wanted to ask you a few questions about your wife, as well as some of your business encounters." He minced no words. It was just business.

"That's pretty direct. I like that, Mr. Barlow. Okay, talk to me."

"Your wife came to me because she was pissed that you bought diamond earrings that she never got. I assume that you wanted to buy it for her, but you somehow got sidetracked. Okay, I'm being a bit obtuse. Sorry." He actually felt comfortable talking frankly to Andy.

"Well, you aren't subtle, are you! I like that. So tell me what's really on your mind, Chuckie!" He leaned back, very secure in himself.

"I'd really like to know about your dealings with some of the Senators, or the people in Congress. Do you ever get to play with women there, or just men?" He was toying openly, and he had a huge grin. It was locker room fun that he loved so much.

Andy sat upright, and his confident attitude morphed into a sly, cunning, defensive posture.

"What makes you think I have so many dealings with the legislative branch? Where did you get that information? You know, Charles, our time here is getting short, so let's not delve into my professional matters." He stood quickly, reverted to his caustic self. "We have nothing else to discuss. Have a nice day." With that curt announcement, the discussion was over and Charles turned to leave. He had his 'in' with that receptionist, and did not need Andy. She would be his eyes and ears. It was obvious that he'd get no pertinent information from good ol' Andy. All of the information would have to be discovered from many other sources, especially the most obvious one: her. He walked to the desk and did his best to enter into a normal conversation.

"You know, I never got your name." He said pleasantly.

"Oh, I'm Brenda Williams. I already know who you are, and also what you want from Andy." She was all business now. He needed to change his approach after feeling nearly rejected. He wondered if she had listened to their conversation.

"Nice to meet you, Brenda. I could not help noticing your delightful accent. You from Georgia? You sound like my fifth grade teacher who was from Macon." He had to engage her so he could wine and dine her.

"No, Charles, I'm actually from Newton, right near the Florida border. I actually thought my accent was gone, but I guess not. Where do you hail from?" She smiled demurely, doing the woman- man mating dance. She was as clever as he was manipulative.

"I'm from New Haven, Connecticut. Yes, you might have guessed that I went to Yale. I'm not sure I have a Yankee accent. Do I?" It was obvious that they both knew that game, and played it very well.

"Nah, you speak just like all of the other northerners I've met. You sound fine. I've never been to New Haven, nor to Connecticut for that matter. Someday, maybe!" She hesitated briefly and said, "Are you an attorney?" Her effervescence teased him.

"Yes, I am. I got tired of doing that, and decided to go into private investigating. It's more enjoyable for me. Hey, we can continue this conversation over coffee, or even dinner. How about it?" He saw the twinkle in her eyes, and thought she'd agree.

"I don't usually date clients, so I'm not sure if it's a good idea." She knew his response already. He was that transparent.

"Technically, I'm not a client since he just threw me out of his office. So, again, let's do dinner." He smiled and knew he was her date.

"Okay, you got me there. Pick me up at eight and we can do dinner and things." Her lips curled into a grin and Charles beamed. "Oh, let me text you my address. See you tonight."

"I'm looking forward to our time together. I think this is the beginning of a beautiful friendship" His adrenalin kicked in and he felt like a schoolboy again.

"Brenda, I'm laughing at what I just said about a beautiful friendship. That is the great line from Casablanca. You're too young to remember it." He laughed again, even heartier.

"Of course I know that line. I've seen that movie many times. Rick waved as Louis walked to the plane. We'll have many interesting things to talk about." She got up and walked to Charles and kissed him on his left cheek. "See you later, friend."

"We sure will. Bye." He walked away, stepped into the doorway, and turned to see if she was looking at him. They both smiled.

Charles thought of how he could separate his new found feelings for Brenda from his desire to get more information from her. She might be turned off if he brought it up too quickly. He needed to do this carefully. It was a conundrum. The ride back to his office brought up many conflicts with relationships: first with Denise who was his client and then, now, to Brenda whose information he needed. He might have to alienate one to satisfy the other. Who? He'd figure it out as he went along, but it was just business, not personal. Right? The day had passed fast, and he needed to get home to rest, shower and get ready for his date.

His house was a few blocks from his office, and it was his place of peace from the hustle and demands of work. The sound of the key unlocking the door brought barks of joy from his golden retriever, Spade. He named him after Sam Spade, the detective from the books of his youth. Maybe that's why he gravitated to being a PI.

He hustled into the bathroom and quickly showered, shaved and wondered how he'd manage business with pleasure. His character was to be forthright, honest and above reproach. Was this the beginning of a new Charles? It gnawed on his psyche. There was that proverbial deceitful devil that sat on his shoulder, and on the other shoulder sat a figurehead that warned him that he should not compromise his honorable convictions. Twas a tug of war. He dressed with care to impress her with his manly features, and then to invade her pliable mind, so he thought. The colored shirt and carefully knotted tie made him feel that the figurehead on his good shoulder might actually be the predominant one.

He looked at the clock next to his closet. He still had time to check his computer to see anything special about Brenda Williams. There were a few Williams so he narrowed it down to one special lady. She graduated from University of Denver in Colorado with a degree in Political Science and was married and divorced. She began working for Andy Florio with no date mentioned. Okay, now he had some idea about her. He was just looking for a soft spot so that he might get her to talk freely. He punched in her address and off he went with a brisk step down to his trusty car. It took only twenty minutes to arrive at the appointed hour of eight. She opened the door to her apartment looking magnificent in her burgundy dress, gold hoop earrings and a smile that was very welcoming.

"Wow, you look incredible. I'm impressed!" He effused.

"'Well, thanks. That was certainly joyful." She was animated, and beamed at Charles.

"Let this be the start of a great night. Ready?" He was almost at a loss for words. That devil on his shoulder tried to be in the forefront, but that push was not going to work.

He reached for her arm to guide her down the few steps, and she took it gladly. He gallantly held the door for her as she slid into her seat. Charles rushed around to his door and jumped in anticipating the sparks that would fly. He didn't have long to wait.

"Charles, this is such an unexpected evening. I'm just happy to be with you." She cooed.

"Wait 'til you see where we're going. Fancy, fancy for our first date of many, I hope." He pulled away and put The Capital Grille into his GPS. He had his credit card close at hand for this expensive treat. The trip was filled with the generalities that people needed to get to know each other, but he still felt insecure about how to handle her. He hated that he had put himself into this situation. He really liked her. They arrived safely and the valet took the car. He'd probe soon enough. The booth was perfect for them: dim lights and near the back of the room.

"How about a nice glass of 1997 Ste. Michelle Merlot? It's one of my favorites." He needed it to prepare for the subtle questions he had to ask, or maybe just forget it tonight and enjoy the evening. He never had to even think about it since she began the conversation with a startling statement.

"So, you thought you'd wine and dine me for information? Charles, I'm not stupid. I'm happy to dine with you, but do not ask me for private information about our clients." She didn't smile.

He was unnerved and embarrassed. Now what could he say?

"You're an amazing woman. Okay, you got me. Yep, I was trying to soften you up, but now there is no need to play this game. I guess this is now just a date, and you can forget my inquisition. I never should have underestimated you. My apologies." He was sincere, and flushed.

She grinned along with a hearty laugh thrown in for good measure.

"I'd appreciate it if you'd just be honest with me. I can be a good friend or a very difficult enemy. Now that we've finished with the not so subtle quest for answers, we can move on." She said firmly.

The evening passed without any further questions. Charles tried to control his other emotions that always seemed to get in his way, like most other men. He had not given up on her being a good story teller. She knew much of those intricate details about Andy Florio and Senator Smathers that he needed. It might take some prodding, but he'd find out one way or another.

CHAPTER 3

Andy Florio tapped the desk with his pencil and looked out the window trying to analyze his next productive move. He was angry that his wife brought in that idiot PI to snoop on his business. She knew exactly what was going on, but was just being her normal pain in the ass. What was her motive? Get information for a divorce and hang him out to dry, or horn in on his lucrative congressional business. "This business is mine, not hers," he said aloud. He smiled as he said it since there was no one to hear him or respond. Brenda was safely ensconced in the outer office. He grabbed the phone and tapped in the number for Senator Smathers, his good, honest buddy.

"Good morning, Senator Smathers office. How may I direct your call?" She said blandly

"Hello, this is Mr. Florio. Please let me talk to Smathers." She certainly knew his voice. She never even responded, but clicked into the Senator's private line.

"Hello Andy. What can I do for you today?" He quipped. It was just his normal insincere opening to their usual discussions about military sales and Andy's "commission."

"Hello Smathers, I have a new proposition for you. I have a connection with some acquaintances in another country. They need some HIMARS Rocket systems that just arrived this week. I know that your 'friends' in the defense department are available to discuss some adjustments to their inventory. You can make it happen, and it would be good for our bank accounts."

Those disrespectful words grated on him.

"Well, Mr. Florio, I'm sure that I can make some inquiries to my friends in that department. It might take me a day or two to check it out. I can figure out the total cost and my fee for an introduction. I don't discuss your bank account. Delivery is also not my department." He never let Andy say anything else. He hung up abruptly, called his secretary and yelled into the phone,

"Call Barney Turpening at the military supply depot." He morphed into a hardnosed procurer. She called immediately. The phone rang only once, and the southern accented voice announced,

"Yes, boss. What can I do for you now?" It was a normal destructive conversation from one crook to another.

"Never call me boss. I'm Senator Smathers, and don't forget it. Got it?" He fumed. He also knew that he was the boss of this ingrate, and he'd never let him forget that! He continued.

"I know that you just got some new MIMARS Rocket systems that have surpassed our old ones. When can I take a look at them for my Senate Armed Services committee?"

"Well, Senator Smathers, They have just arrived and most of them are already assigned to various sectors outside the country. I'm getting the shipping orders now as we speak. So I'm not sure how I can help you." He sure knew the drill, and how to wheedle the most out of this scum bag, Smathers.

"That's not what I wanted to hear, Barney. I know that you can find some extra ones for my personal showing. Right?" He played the game as well as Barney, and he held all of the right cards.

"I guess I can figure something out. Since you need to see them for your committee, then let's do it tonight, say, around eight? I'll make sure that we are not bothered by my staff." It was the beginning of another round of price haggling, how to make it secretive, and down the wormhole of Washington deceit. The Senator responded in kind.

"Okay, I'll be there at eight sharp. Stay focused on this deal for my committee."

He smiled. It would be another sizable addition to his government 'pension'. He put away his pocket recorder in the secure compartment in the top drawer of his desk. It was his insurance just in case he needed proof that Barney tried to oust him. He had to be careful of those other crooks. He was just looking out for his Committee. The afternoon slipped by without much else for him to do, so he called Maurine at the front desk and told her that he was leaving for the day, and she should close the office.

"Yes, Senator. Thanks. I'll leave now. Have a good night." She was her usual charming self. She had been with him from the beginning of his term, just six years ago. She was faithful, sincere and knew everything about him. She was an employee who knew him very, very well.

Smathers sat back pensively to concoct the story for the three characters. Him: He was the Chair of the Committee so he had to have this contact, even at a late hour so it fit into his schedule. Barney: He needed to help another group of people who needed this equipment and would pay handsomely to get it. The government need not know all of the details, other than he had been a great help for them. Florio: What the hell was his job? Hmmm, he was the contact with the other group, and he had their best interests at heart. Yes, that would be what he could say, if they ever asked him. He doubted that they would ever know what happened. Barney knew all of the loopholes, and he'd been through this many times himself.

The swamp was filled with many carnivorous creatures. This trio was just one of many similar groups in Washington. It was the feeding trough for favors, money and perversions. No one was immune. It only took a hint of money, or that unnerving desire of a woman to bring those men into the circle of corruption. Roland Smathers thought he was going to be pure as he strode into Washington on that proverbial white horse. He'd change those immoral beasts into great statesmen, and he'd win over those who might have doubted him. Sad to say, he succumbed to that scent, and the lure of filthy lucre. It took only one or two calls from that beast, Florio, to show him the ways of the swamp. He veered from the original righteous path to the nasty trail of debauchery. First, it was Florio telling him that he needed to see a wonderful, powerful woman to show him the sights of Washington. That was a joke. She bedded him on that first night, and she made sure that she had videos of him in the act. Florio never missed a beat, and had Smathers by the short ones. She was paid, and Florio had Smathers. It was the way of the flesh, and of the weakness of some men. A wave of disgust flowed over him as he recounted the errors of his ways, but he was not ready to dissolve the contacts with Florio or change his modus operandi. He lived high, so he had to play hard. Someday he'd repent. Maybe!

He heard the door close and adjusted his chair. The phone rang. The ID showed his wife, Sharon.

"Hello, my sweet. What's up?" He reverted back to nice.

"I got an invitation to a ladies dinner tonight, so you're on your own tonight. I hope that's okay." She was unusually polite to him. She had been out of sorts as of late. He never knew how she'd behave. Maybe she was going to file for divorce. She knew about some of his philandering, but not all. She was prepared to dismiss them as part of her price to remain in Washington society. Without him as a shield, she'd be back in Texas doing mundane projects.

He needed her as his way to remain respectable among his peers. It was a symbiotic curse. He responded as casually as he could.

"Oh, have a great time. I have work to do tonight, and will grab a bite at Loco's, that Mexican joint. See you later tonight by about ten. If you're late, don't worry, we can catch up tomorrow, and you can tell me all about the lady's adventures." He didn't know if he was placating her, or giving himself some kind of morality. His white steed gradually slipped away as he sank deeper into the mire. He quickly discarded the thought of Sharon and her meeting tonight, or maybe it was an assignation. No matter, their connection was damaged long ago. He reconnected with the matter for tonight.

The drive to Fort Belvoir was always a crap shoot with uneven traffic on some days and grid lock on others. It took him almost an hour just to get to the Fort exit and another twenty minutes to its entrance. He dutifully gave the Sergeant at the gate his ID and was saluted as he drove through. The supply building was immense, and Barney was at the customary position near his desk. There was the usual hustle even at night, but Barney had assigned a few men to do the nightly routine away from them. Smathers hesitated briefly, looked around to see if there was anyone he knew, and walked quickly to Barney.

"Good evening, Senator. Nice night for negotiations." He went right to the point.

"Well, now, aren't we in a productive mood!" He liked fast results without playfulness.

"Here it is in a nutshell. I can get you four of the products you requested. My cut is ten K per item. Take it or leave it." He was firm and in no mood to negotiate.

"Okay, that's your usual cut. I can take it off your hands tomorrow night." He put out his hand to seal it. "I'll have a marked trailer truck here tomorrow night at nine. I'll have your cash, and you will have my four items. He never even blinked. Barney managed to make his vig, and now it was time for the honest broker to get his. He drove back home quickly and got Andy on the phone. The price? Twenty five thousand per item. He wanted them? He'll pay.

"Hello, Senator." Andy's voice was always chipper as he engaged him. "What's up?"

"I have confirmed your specific need to be picked up tomorrow night at Fort Belvoir. Nine is the best time. Please get your U.S. Army trailer for the items. I just need one hundred K for that assistance, and an additional forty K for my other assistant. You can work any number from your clients. Please bring me my fee tomorrow in my office before you go on your assignment." He wanted his cash before Andy did his deed. Trust? Never, ever trust him.

He slid into his couch near the window and poured himself a full tumbler of Jack Daniels with a splash of water. He contemplated how his bank account would swell from just a few hours of work. It was better than the travails of litigation in a court. He lost his passion for law as he entered the lucrative world of Washington politics. It was so easy to find buyers and sellers of anything. Just let the filthy fingers find you, and it took such a small effort to gain so much. How could anyone resist that, he thought, while sipping on that heavily taxed alcohol. He sighed as his assets increased while sitting in his office like a spider baiting its web. He did have a problem that always confronted him. Where to put the cash? Bank, nah! Into the shoeboxes in the basement with all of the other filthy greenbacks? He could no longer buy stocks for cash or even deposit more than ten thousand into an account, or the feds would check it out. So, the next place is jewels, and that's easy to trade cash for diamonds. He sure knew where to do that. Andy always told him about Jason Morton.

He used him as a depository for money. He could do the same. First things first: Get this money from Andy and then worry about what to do with it.

Maybe even buy Sharon a gift with some of it. That would make her happy, and he'd have a reason to go to see Jason. The double edged sword would be good for both of them. He'd do it as soon as Andy brought him the one hundred forty thousand. He often wondered who would be the recipient of those military items. Maybe they'd be used against us, or pointed against our friends. The mere thought caused him grief, but not so much that he'd stop doing this money maker.

Smathers thought about Barney's brief encounter with a wide grin that quickly turned to a frown as he contemplated how far he had dropped into the treachery of this game of trading his patriotism and the country's goods for money. He'd never get it out of his mind even as he accepted this act of treason against the country for whom he had pledged honor and duty. It was that devil who won every time. His shoulders slumped. He realized that even this car that he used was this government's largesse. He abused all of it while those who paid taxes got no such thing. It drained him. Someday he'd repent, but not now.

Alvin S. Berger

CHAPTER 4

Charles always knew that the slippery slope of greed and the Washington swamp would lead to him again. He was like a magnet for those slime dwelling creatures. It was no wonder that even those who touched those rich and connected denizens of the deep state fared no better. It was like touching grease, and then shaking hands with those people closest to you. The corruption was contagious. As those thoughts cluttered his mind the phone's chimes jolted him back to reality.

"Hi, Mr. Barlow. This is Brenda Williams. I'd like to see you as soon as possible to talk to you about something private."

"Hi Brenda, nice to talk to you again. What's up?"

"I need to talk to you about something that's on my mind. Can I see you at twelve thirty. I'm working so that's the only time I can get away."

"Sure, See ya then."

Now, he thought, what the hell was so important that she had to see me today? She gave no information when they were out together, so what now? Maybe it was about Smathers, that crooked piece of Washington garbage, or even Florio. Okay, settle down. Maybe she had something on him. Could be yes, or not. 'Tis a puzzlement. He smiled to himself as he mentally saw himself standing, naked on his chest, with his hands on his hips, like Yul Brenner.

He did the usual busy work of the day, searching for new clues and trying to understand how each of these new people fit together. He understood how the Mortons converted cash for jewels, and how many in the political arena did those conversions. How did Denise Florio play into this scenario, and was she a legitimate complainant? Was she complicit in any way? He always tried to delve into their psyche. Those human frailties often overlaid the facade they tried to portray. He knew people, and they often underestimated him. He stared out the window contemplating how he'd screen Brenda again. .

The time passed slowly. It seemed that he did his best detective work when he was hard pressed for time. The appointed hour intruded on his feckless meanderings.

In walked Brenda Williams, statuesque, coiffed and confident.

"Good to see you again, Charles," she said confidently.

"My pleasure, Brenda," he said. "After our recent dinner I thought you were done with the Washington gossip. Have you changed your mind?"

"I have some information that I no longer can keep to myself." She quickly announced without even blinking.

"Is this a national security issue?" He was firm, yet open to listening.

She lost some of her composure and reached into her handbag to get a tissue. "Yes, it is a combination of national security as well as graft. I hate Smathers, and he's not a good Senator." She wiped her eyes.

"I guess you'll have to start from the beginning. Here's another tissue." His curiosity was piqued.

"How can a man, a Senator, say that he's working for the country, and then take money under the table?"

"How do you know that?"

"I know everything that happens in that office. Andy's office and theirs are closely connected. When we had dinner, I didn't know if I could trust you. I contemplated what I should do regarding us as friends, and then I realized that this issue was more important than our friendship, or maybe more."

"I understand your reticence in trusting a perfect stranger. I appreciate that you and I have gotten over that hurdle." He reached out to touch her hands. She smiled briefly and continued.

"I was so conflicted when we were out together. I wanted to say something, but just couldn't! The knowledge that I had was so damning for Smathers that I hated to tell anyone, especially a man whom I had just met. Forget that you said you were a PI. Anyone can say that, and I trust no one at this point." Her smile had faded into a frown, and the tears flowed faster.

"Thank you for sharing your innermost feelings. That's hard to do. So now you trust me?" He said.

"I do." She was soft, open to him and calm. "So let me begin by saying that, right now, this is between us and no others! Agreed?"

"For sure. So tell me what's going on."

"Smathers is selling our military supplies to Andy Florio. He gets cash from Andy, and Andy gets weapons or anything else that he wants. He then sells those items at a huge profit to someone in the world market. I know all of this from direct knowledge. I see it as it happens in Florio's office. They think that I'm stupid, and don't see anything that happens right under my nose." She became stringent in her demeanor and in perfect control. Her tears dried as she spoke with animation, her arms moving in cadence with her words.

"That, dear Brenda, is a scathing rebuke of the Senator. Do you have any documented proof, or is this just your observations?" He knew she'd get cantankerous by his remark.

"Are you kidding me?" She fumed. "Of course, I have proof. Do you think I'm an idiot, too?"

"I didn't mean that at all. I just want to be sure that you, we, can prove this, or there might be very dangerous repercussions from Smathers or Andy or others in the loop. When there is money involved, or when the powers that be try to neutralize these perpetrators, they become vicious. No life matters to them, only their own. Get it?"

"Yes, Charles, I know exactly what you mean. This is more than just bringing them to justice, it is a matter of putting our lives on the line. Yes, I got it."

"Now that we are in sync, we can begin this journey. We need to have each other's backs. Once you and I open this door there's no turning back. Be forewarned, those outside forces will never let us live unless we can bring them down quickly. Are you ready for this?" His voice lowered and was decisive. "Did you hear me?"

"Yes, I know, and am willing to do it. So, listen! I have recordings as well as personal knowledge of what Smathers is doing. In fact, he went to a military base today looking at new rockets to sell, and he gets a hefty sum for just making contact with Florio. He's a crook. Period!!" She described the happenings of the day concisely and without stumbling over her words. She was determined to convict him and the others involved.

"I'd like to listen to any of the recordings that you have made over any period of time. Also, do you have any signed papers from Smathers?" He was very careful in his approach to her, sensing that she was getting very tense and worried about potential repercussions. She bristled as he spoke. She shifted in her seat and became more agitated as she tried to stay in control. Charles knew that she was torn between doing the right thing, and wondering if she had bitten off too much, even for both of them. The challenge was to bring this to a head rapidly so that Smathers could be punished and Florio put into jail.

Brenda spoke without hesitation, "I have them at my apartment. It's time we spend some quality time together and read what I have, and listen to all of my recordings. No funny ideas either, Charles. This is business, not pleasure. Got it?" She even had a dazzling smile. Her demeanor had changed, he thought, just like a woman. He reached for her hand, mirrored her lightened mood and said happily,

"Yep, I got it. Work with no pleasure or happy ending!"

"Okay, you made me laugh. Let's hustle and get this done. My apartment tomorrow night at 7.

I'll make a snack for us while we work."

She stood quickly, shook his hand professionally and turned toward the door. He jumped from his swivel chair and ran to intercept her. She stopped as he blocked the door. He embraced her, kissing her sweetly. It was just a friendly, new partner kiss.

"What was that, Charles? I told you no fooling around." Another grin lit up her face as she returned the friendly kiss with even more passion. "Maybe fooling around after we do our work." She laughed playfully.

"See you tomorrow at seven." She pinched his cheek, opened her eyes very wide and said with a wink,

"Never believe a woman when it comes to romance." She walked out the door, and left Charles with an impish grin, a flushed face and a raging hormone imbalance.

CHAPTER 5

Andy Florio trusted no one, especially that scumbag, Smathers. He knew, however, that he was the only one who could get him into that base to get rockets for his contact in Taiwan. Son Wu Kim was even more secretive in the operation than he. Kim was determined to get these items to undermine any Chinese possibility of intervention into Taiwan sovereignty. He was part of a group of local Chinese businessmen who hated Chairman XI and never wanted China to annex Taiwan. Smathers had no clue who finally got these rockets. His only motive was that almighty dollar dripping into his government protected crime schemes. It was as if he deluded himself into thinking that no one would care if "someone" got these rockets that could kill hundreds, maybe even Americans. He was just one of those five hundred and twenty five members of both houses of Congress that were similarly motivated by the government's protection as they squeezed donations from anyone who might need a favor. Sure, give them a million and a new dam can be placed near an Indian reservation and starve them. Who cared? Not them. Andy Florio picked up the phone to check in with Smathers.

"Good afternoon, Senator Smathers office." Maurine's pleasant voice was not what he cared about.

"Get me Smathers." He bellowed into her ear. She said nothing after that, and called the Senator to inform him that Florio was on the phone. Her neatly painted lips turned into a sneer.

"What's up, Andy?" He knew that Andy needed to give him the treasure before he got the goods. There was irony in his voice. Up the dollars, and down with Andy.

"You piss me off. All you care about is the money. I need those rockets pronto. What kind of truck will get me into the base?" Sure, Andy only knew about the rockets and that he needed them. Money? He was beyond money. The recipients had called for an early delivery and cared zip about his problems with money or trucks. They only wanted performance or heads might roll. Yes, that's what they said. He worried about his head and maybe even the Senator's. They made Andy an offer he couldn't refuse.

"I told you the last time we spoke that you needed a large trailer truck with base markings. What's with you, Florio?" Smathers had no patience for stupidity, or men who would not pay.

"Okay, cool it. I'm under a lot of pressure from my sources. They aren't in the mood for any delays and made it clear that we could be in jeopardy if we delay this order." He spoke rapidly and breathlessly. It was almost a plea for help.

"Why are you so crazy? Who the hell are these people? I'm sure I can handle them with help from my government's men and women. Relax, man." Smathers was reassuring, but there was a sense of urgency that unnerved him "You don't know these people. Look, just get me in tonight. I know you, Smathers, I'll bring the gifts in an hour or so." He calmed slightly. This actually might be his last venture. Nothing is worth losing one's head for a few bucks.

Andy never considered that Kim knew more people in Washington than he did. Dirty dealings with dirty players never worked out well for the people on the lower totem pole. He had to talk to Kim again without delay. The danger was too great to put on the back burner, He used the throwaway phone that he had purchased online. He called Kim's private number and steeled himself for the first confrontation.

"Hello, who's this? His faint accent always bothered Andy.

"It's Andy Florio, Mr. Kim. I just wanted to confirm our agreement. I'm getting the merchandise tomorrow night and I expect payment on delivery. I also do not want anyone else at our meeting. Is that clear?" He felt secure warning him from afar. Bullets don't go through the phone, nor do swords.

"So, Mr. Florio, you sound rattled today. Do you not trust me?" It was an obvious attempt to intimidate Florio. It was right out of the Sun

Tzu playbook of point counterpoint with one's enemy. Kim understood the enemy and knew each and every move. It was human chess, and it was not just a checkmate. It was live or die whenever Kim decreed. Florio knew how that game was played, but he was never fully vested in it to be its proponent. He often wavered in implementing anything with Kim, but it was his move now.

"Of course I trust you, or I wouldn't be in this with you. I just want to be clear in our agreement." He spoke in a metered cadence. It was obvious to Kim's keen observance that Florio was, indeed, flustered. It played into Kim's next move.

"Mr. Florio, we initially agreed on one hundred thousand per item. I think that is not a good number for me now. I am changing our number to eighty thousand per item. Take it or leave it! You need to think hard about your terrible position here. I know many people who might be willing to discuss your selling these government properties to a foreign group. That puts you in jeopardy. Are we now agreed on this adjusted price?"

"You are playing with the wrong person. I also know many people who are not happy with foreign countries using our products even with a helping hand from a U.S. citizen, so don't fuck with me, Kim!" Florio knew that he couldn't back down. He rather not do the deal than to succumb to this asswipe screwing with him.

"The price is still one hundred ten thousand per item. I have an added person to pay. You wanna play this game? Take my number or I'm not delivering." He finally got his backbone up and delivered a strong message to Kim. He knew Sun Tzu, too.

"You are a difficult man, Mr. Florio. I, too, am in a difficult position and now even more so since you upped the ante. You have forced me to agree to your price. My position is untenable with my superiors."

They played the game of gorillas beating their chests in mock battle. The deal was now almost complete. It was now getting the trailer truck and picking up the items.

There was no time to delay the truck procurement from his friends at the motor pool.

They all loved to be a part of the payments to their government assisted hidden piggy banks. It seemed fair to them. Who did it hurt, they imagined? The truck was just a loan for an evening to a nice man. Sergeant Wayne Chambers, the procurement chief, already had the signs painted on the side of the trailer. The bright white letterings were standard so no one would question anything when it pulled into the compound. Sergeant Chambers would make six month's pay, and he could get a new small car. All would be right with the world again. No one cared what happened after the rockets were delivered. It was just business.

Son Wu Kim also knew what was right in his world, even though he was beaten by Florio this time. He was the procurer for the shadow government in Taiwan. Not only did he obtain these rockets, he was on the verge of getting a RQ-7 drone from his other sources in the United States. His contacts fed him subtle connections to others who might help him. He was so secretive that no one above him even knew that the contact existed. He only knew the code name. It was "Money." They had never met, but there was one telephone expression of interest. The voice was computer generated so he had no idea of the gender or nationality. The contact had secrets, too. He smiled at the thought of being played by an internal spy operation. He needed to be overly cautious. No one was safe from the prying eyes of any government. He decided to open another conversation with "Money". The only communication was by that one number. He punched in the number and waited patiently, strumming his strong fingers on his desk.

There was a double beep and a garbled answer.

"Whhhaaat dooo you waannt?"

"Hello, Money. I want to discuss a matter that we touched on in our last brief talk. When can we meet?" He hoped there would be some kind of detente between them.

"Never." The computer voice modulated. It continued, "What is your interest?"

"I am interested in a drone, specifically the General Atomics RQ-7. I need it in two weeks. Can you get it for me? I'm willing to pay top dollar for it, or even crypto." He was brief and concise. He put himself in danger as well as the whole operation, not knowing with whom he was dealing. It was worth it to get this valuable drone.

The muffled, indistinct, computerized voice replied after a pregnant pause.

"That is a huge request. I will have to do a search for it and get back to you very soon. I know your number." It hung up without further comment. Kim was still puzzled by this secrecy. What was to be gained by not knowing who it was? Did he know this person? Was the voice in a super-secret government position? It was the drone he wanted, not the person, but it still gnawed on him. He never liked to have issues unresolved. He went back to his immaculate desk to continue his research on this valuable drone. He saw that it sold for about fifteen million dollars. His only concern was acquiring it, no matter the cost. He touched the iPhone on the desk and asked Siri for his boss, Major Chong.

"Major Chong's office, Who's calling?" The man's pleasant voice asked politely in his native language.

"It's Son Wu Kim. This is important so please connect me immediately." He never knew that his boss had a male secretary. That seemed unusual, especially in Taiwan, but times were changing even in that patriarchal society. He wondered if Chong's wife had anything to do with that office adjustment.

"Kim, I hope that you have done your assigned job." Precise and formal was his custom.

"Yes, Major Chong. All is in order for our last assignment. I need approval to obtain a RQ-7 drone from a source in the States. I suspect it will be over twenty million US dollars. The source is being very secretive. I don't have a specific timeline for delivery yet, but will get that done as soon as you give your approval." This was a typical request, but he sensed a reluctance from Chong even before he spoke.

"What do you mean, 'secretive'? You don't know your contact? That is unacceptable!" He screamed. "Either get information on this person, or it's off." He hung up.

That didn't sit well with Kim. Now he was stuck without approval and without knowing the contact. He had better resolve this or the deal would be off and Chong would still want the drone. How to initiate a real personal contact? Threats? Nope, that would not work. What did the contact have to lose except a twenty million dollar deal. He thought that he could entice 'it' to at least speak directly to him. It was worth a try. He went to recent calls and punched it. It answered in one ring.

"Hello, Mr. Kim." Announced that annoying, irritating computerized voice.

"Hello, person! I need to clarify our relationship. I have no idea if I can trust a computerized voice. I don't even know if you are real or a bot. You must identify yourself or you can kiss the twenty mill out the window." He left no room for ambiguity.

"You can be sure that I am real. What difference does it make who I am if I can get you your item? Okay, I am human and that's all I will ever say to you. I will tell you how and where to get this item when you deposit the agreed upon money into a bank account number that I'll give you after we agree that this is a done deal. No other discussions, period." The human was unwavering, and the irritating voice changed to a very moderate computerized voice.

"You're shitting me, right? I'm not a fool to give you the money without even seeing the drone. No drone, no money! Here's the deal: You tell me where the drone is for me to pick up and you make that arrangement. Then I'll make the deposit when I actually get the drone. Deal?" He was not a novice at this and the unknown human knew it.

"Agreed. The exchange of money will be synchronous. I'll be in touch by tomorrow." The asexual computer sounded sweet. Hmm, computer sweet?

Now he had to convince Chong that this was a real person even though he had not met it. He grimaced at the thought of confronting Chong again, but he had to do it.

Sweat flowed under his arms as he hit the recent call button.

""What now Mr. Kim?" It was that terse voice that always unnerved him. Now the sweat percolated from his brow. It was as if he began the first round of a boxing match. His seemingly confident attitude speaking to this grand master of conflict masked his tension and uncertainty.

"I have determined that this computerized individual has access to the drone and I've made arrangements to see the drone, pick it up and then deposit the twenty million into a specific bank account. It will not do this any other way. I feel that this is the best way to achieve our goal of getting this valuable asset." Kim had no doubt that this was the right path even though no personal contact was made. He knew of no other way to get this drone. He strained his mind to try to determine why this person wanted to cloak its identity. Was it a member of the government or one of the various spy agencies? If its identity was known would it change the relationship with Taiwan and the United States? He only wanted results. The person would ultimately be found out either by him or those nasty CIA people. He actually smiled at that thought.

CHAPTER 6

It was almost dusk when Charles Barlow walked out of his office into the crisp air in Virginia. He had a hard day at the office preparing his report for Denise Florio. She wanted anything that would give her incriminating information about her husband, Andy. She wanted to know about his business dealings and with whom he worked. Did he have assignations with ladies? Play with foreigners? Have hidden bank accounts? She wanted the real dirt on him, and Barlow was supposed to do it, or not get paid. He wondered how she was able to stay with him even though she had such bad feelings about him for a long time. Maybe it was her idea of torturing him by being a vengeful bitch of a wife. Why was she so intent about deposing him? What did she have to gain knowing all of his secrets? Charles could not understand that dynamic. All she needed to do was get a divorce and collect half of his money, both hidden and observable, plus a lifetime of monthly payments. As he got to know her, his gut feelings began to distrust her and her motives.

The appointment to meet Denise was in just an hour, so he casually drove to the Silver Spoon and parked in the lot next door. He sent her a text to say that he had arrived. She responded that she was already at a table near the door. He quickly made his way there. She smiled broadly as he approached her and she stood, reached for his hand and kissed his cheek. Not very professional, he thought.

"Welcome, Charles. Good to see you. I hope you have lots of valuable information for me." She said without that gleaming smile. His instincts reared it ugly head.

"Hi, Denise. I do have some information for you. I hope it's valuable to you, but you'll have to evaluate it."

"Do you have any of his bank accounts, or his contacts?" She probed even before they looked at a menu. Strange, he thought. What was her rush?

"I do have that information. Don't you want to eat first? I'm hungry." He was testing her. It was that same cat and mouse game that intrigued him.

"Give me the info. Then we'll eat." She wasted no time on chit chat, and food was really not on her agenda, so why meet at a restaurant?

"Your husband has multiple bank accounts, some of which are offshore. I don't have their numbers, but I do have the banks in which they are located. He has made multiple calls to various people at a nearby military base, and I do have those numbers. Don't ask me how I got any of this material. That's what I do! He is also involved in some kind of bartering system with someone at that military base. I do not know the person or what was traded. That's above my pay grade. I hope you know that this can be a dangerous game you're playing. People who are involved in these transactions may not be very polite either to you or me. I'd advise you to keep a low profile and maybe even just forget this whole matter." He became serious, and reached out to hold her hand in a fatherly manner.

"I know what I'm doing, so I need no advice from you. I pay you to find answers, not to judge me." She morphed into a demanding interrogator who was neither in the mood to eat or play the game of chit chat. She pulled her hand away and then regripped him hard.

"If you want any kind of reward from me, you'd better get your facts together."

He grabbed her hand and unhinged it. He could not understand her hostility. He thought it was an act to push him harder to find more information, but why alienate him this way? He spoke without equivocation,

"Behave yourself. You're not my boss, nor my friend. I gave you information and I don't need your attitude. Fire me now and pay me, but keep yourself in line. I don't appreciate your attitude!" He left no room for discussion. She was taken aback by his response.

"Charles, I'm sorry. I've had a tough day and I apologize. Let's start over." She seemed genuine, but he was even more convinced that she had something to hide and was not who she appeared to be. He was even more wary now.

"I have no qualms about quitting. You can do this yourself without any more input from me. Pay me now and I'm outta here." He braced his back against the chair when his voice roared.. Every head in the restaurant turned toward them. It was not a pretty sight. He stood abruptly, slammed his fist on the table and said,

"You need another person to do your dirty work."

"Charles, please wait. Please," she said with heartfelt emotion.

His angry inner voice said to go, but that docile, sweet sincere counter voice overrode that protective one and he sat quietly, distancing himself from the anger he felt.

"You are creating a scenario that makes me very unsettled and pissed. This is the first and last time we will ever have this discussion. I'm not your trash boy, nor am I your servant. I work for myself. You pay me for my time. Don't try to push me. Got it?" He gradually calmed as he berated her. Tears welled in her eyes. She turned in her chair.

"I'm truly sorry. I think that this whole episode with Andy has turned me into a nasty shrew. I beg your forgiveness, please." He heard the words, and knew she meant it for the time being, but he was also now certain that she was just playing him. He would not forget this, and be on heightened alert from this time forward.

"I may forgive, but am not forgetting this. Be cautious of how you treat me. I'll leave no stone unturned to help, but I will also treat you very badly if you mess with me again." His anger subsided as she looked at him with a tearful expression.

"Thank you, Charles." It was more of a dutiful mea culpa than a real "sorry".

"I'm no longer hungry so let's pack this in, and I'll keep you informed as I find out more information. Also, please give me a check for my time thus far. I think that this might be near our final discussion." She realized that she went too far and was now in a desperate place with him. She would need to use her feminine wiles to keep him in her grasp. Men, she thought, were an easy mark to be played. Him? Maybe a more difficult task, but still a man with needs and pliable hormones.

"Charles. I see that you are still upset with me. Can I please treat you to dinner, or even bring something to my apartment?" A simple suggestion that most men would see as an open door to action.

He knew exactly what that meant, and never, ever thought of her as a playful partner.

His response was a pure rebuttal.

"I have no interest in having another meal with you, nor do I want to see you at your apartment. You and I are on different pages. We are client and investigator. Nothing more. We can meet at my office next time. Please bring another check for services rendered." It was a short, accurate response to a manipulative woman who was, in fact, a real bitch. He stood abruptly and walked away, leaving her at the table, speechless. Every head in the restaurant turned again to them as his chair gripped the floor and squealed. Denise squirmed in her seat with embarrassment. She pulled out her wallet, left a crumpled ten dollar tip, rose silently, looked straight at the door and walked with slumped shoulders out to that same crisp air. She knew her place with Charles. Sad!

Chapter 7

It was seven thirty on a rainy Tuesday morning as Charles walked into his darkened office. He switched on the overhead fluorescent light only to see papers strewn along the floor and the safe torn open. He knew that this was the beginning of a scenario that he had dreaded. Someone either listened to his conversations, or one of them ratted him out. This was now a new ballgame for all of them. He wondered why anyone would want to harm him or seek information. Was it Denise? Brenda? Jason? His security camera was the answer. His loss of serenity left him depressed. That bitch began this as she darkened his door. Yes, Denise, that's who.

The flash drive was intact in the closet near the camera setup. He saw the red light blinking so it was still in use. His mind churned as he tried to understand what was happening. Was he or she in danger? What clandestine information was written in his files? None!! Now he knew for sure that there was a lot more to this than he knew or understood, and he was the center of this crazy case. He took out the flash drive and put it into his laptop. Nothing on it. He looked at the camera. Damn, a piece of tape over the lens. They sure knew how to mess up his security system. He looked carefully at the amateurish system, but smiled to show that they only saw what he wanted them to see. He looked at the painting of Thomas Jefferson hanging above his desk, and saw the red glint in his right eye. Funny how smart people are immune to other ways of observing. The camera was nestled behind that roving eye. He moved the camera, pulled out the active flash drive and plugged it into his laptop. There it was: a masked person rifling through his files and opening up the safe. He had no clue who it was. The files seemed the same as before, just strewn around the office. Everything in the safe was intact. He whispered to himself, "This is just a warning shot to keep me silent. That's not going to work."

There was no need to call the police. He had printed out a picture of the intruder even though there was no definitive facial feature. He'd scour it later to see if there might be an identifying mark. The police would ask too many questions for which he had no good answers. He did have questions for many others whom he had contacted.

It was now a puzzle he had to solve alone. He had no reason to call Denise Florio because she was too out of touch with what he was doing. He gave a passing thought to Brenda. Why would she want him scared off? Nope, not her. His feelings about her became trapped in a more romantic mode, so that warped his usual rational thinking. Jason? Nah, too frightened to act like this, and not in his wheelhouse. His thoughts focused on Andy Florio. He wasn't very helpful when confronted at the office. Well, even if it was him, what good would it be to call him or even talk to him: a futile effort!

Sometimes it is better to let things simmer, watch for an emergent clue and then act. Battles were never won by hasty actions. It was the careful planning and predictable actions that won wars. He'd wait and listen carefully.

Now that his thinking was clearer he began to clean up the mess. The ceiling light cast dark shadows on the floor as he tried to put the papers in order. He still felt it was strange that apparently nothing was stolen. Then he saw a pen under a piece of paper next to the safe. Would robbers leave a calling card? His mind played multiple tricks on him as he tried to understand why anyone could be so stupid, or was it supposed to be that way? One look at the pen and he laughed. It was from Morton's Jewelers. No way would that wimp try to steal anything from him. He was sure that it was just a planted cute, funny clue. Would there be a fingerprint on it? Doubtful. Did 'they' think he'd be so foolish to go after Jason Morton? Then he thought of Jason's assistant. Could she have done this? Was she more than just a store manager? All things percolated in his racing thoughts. He took out the flash drive to see if he missed anything, and there it was! A bracelet peeking out from under the sweater. Gold and diamonds telling him that it was a woman who was toying with him.

It was just a ruse to get him to stop, nothing more. It was another part of the puzzle that annoyed him. Did Jason come back into the picture as a participant of this treasonous behavior, using his assistant as that vehicle?

He had to go back to Morton's Jewelers and confront Jason and Clara Denoit, the store manager. Was she so involved with Jason that she'd be stupid enough to fake a robbery? She seemed to know a lot of what was going on and Jason was a creepy wimp. It was back into his car to confront them. He felt like he was in this alone and that Denise was just a bystander now. Well, maybe Brenda was along for the ride. He knew the way to Morton's Jewelers, and tried to think of how to confront them. It was Clara who was at the forefront in his mind. He then wondered if she acted alone and Jason wasn't involved. Charles pulled into the parking spot next to the store and walked in, holding the flash drive. He strode through the front door as if he owned the place and walked directly to Clara's place in the center of the store. She looked at him with wide opened eyes and said ,

"Welcome back, Charles." She shifted her stance, waiting for his next action.

"I love your bracelet, Clara." He enjoyed playing with her, and seeing that she actually had on that same bracelet. She shifted again, and he reveled in her discomfort.

"The next time you're in my office, you should try to hide it, or better yet, tell me that you're coming and we can do lunch as you rifle through my safe and papers. Oh, how did you open my safe?" Her face turned as pink as her nail polish. She tried to murmur a rational reply but all that came out was a soft, "Charles."

She wanted to explain her position, but he interrupted her.

"Now, please tell me why you messed up my office, opened my safe and left your calling card? You better give a smart answer or the Washington police will be here next." It was now or never for her response. He pushed forward on the counter filled with precious stones. They meant nothing to him, and actually annoyed him for being a symbol of that Washington swamp culture. Clara tried to speak, but nothing came out. It was as if she was so frightened that she shut down. Really? he thought: a clever thief, unremorseful and faking fear.

"I don't know what you're talking about, Charles." She gave him an insincere smile as she fidgeted with her pen. "I never went to your office."

"Here's the video of YOU tossing papers and opening my safe. And most telling is your bracelet peeking from under your sweater sleeve. Any more excuses?" His voice was loud as he moved away from the counter.

"Why did you do it?"

"Let me see the video." Clara demanded.

He put it into her laptop on the counter and watched her squirm as the whole video ran. He almost laughed as she went from pink to pale, shifting behind the counter.

"Okay, now that you've seen you and your bracelet, what's your final answer?" It was Jeopardy all over again.

"I did it because we wanted you to get off this crazy hunt of yours. Jason is so worried that you would continue stalking us that you'd destroy this business. He is tied to many people in power and they would not be happy to find out that we helped you in any way. They have many ways to punish people. We have heard stories about how they find ways to keep their agents in line." Yes, she seemed sincere, but he still wondered why they did not talk to him. Why risk jail or worse to do this and why leave obvious clues?

"So you did this to keep me off this case? Why did you leave me clues? Am I an idiot? Don't answer that part! We need to talk to Jason, now!" He reached over the counter and held her hand. She knew he was in no mood to deny his request. She walked around the counter still holding his hand and they walked to Jason's office in the back of the store. She didn't even knock on his door. His eyes opened wide as they entered.

"Hello. To what do I owe this pleasure?" He knew it was trouble as soon as they walked in. Clara spoke first.

"Jason, we have a problem! He knows it all. You need to tell him what happened and why and please be truthful. I see that we have no options."

"Clara, why did you admit anything?" His usual fearful voice and jittery hand movement took over as he tried to appear strong.

"Why? He showed me the video, that's why! I'm really afraid of what may happen to both of us. You know that those people are treacherous!"

She had tears running down her cheeks as she tried to stay in control. "Please tell him what we know."

There was no turning back as Jason leaned his head back, and looked at the ceiling as if to get some strength from the cloud or that elusive entity in the heavens above. He decided to confess and explain the sordid series of events.

"It all began about ten years ago when Montrose Fairchild asked us to do him a favor. It all seemed innocuous enough as he needed to 'clean' some dollars. We never asked where it came from, and it was good business to make a handsome profit while helping a man with huge power in Washington. After the first transaction we started to get more and more people with the same money laundering issues. We knew it might come back to bite us, but the money was too good to stop. And then there was Andy Florio who was our biggest customer. He had so much invested in our jewelry that we had to continue or he'd find a way to hurt us, not by blowing the whistle, but by making us suffer in many other ways. Then you came into the picture and we panicked. I was so flustered by you that I didn't know how to handle it. Clara and I discussed how to make it go away so we figured that you could be scared off if we tried to rob you. Clara dropped the pen in error and was unaware of any other camera. She has been my partner in much of this so she knows the ins and outs of this adventure. Charles, I have been honest with you, and feel terrible that all of us are in this situation." He actually sounded contrite.

There were so many issues that complicated all of this. Denise was insignificant and Andy Florio was a small gear in this whole damn complicated machinery. The puzzle demanded intense scrutiny. Was he up to it? Did he need more help to unravel it? That thought invaded him as he leaned toward Brenda. She had the insight and the smarts to help him. He had to control this situation first, and then move forward to Brenda. He couldn't clutter his mind with doing second before first.

"Well, people, you sure have messed this up. Where does that leave us? Do I prosecute you and destroy your business, or do you join me in destroying these crappy excuses for a human. You tell me!" He was actually sympathetic to their plight. They both answered in unison.

"Join you!"

Jason tried to smile, but all that appeared was a twisted lip.

"Clara and I will do anything in our power to help you, but you must understand that these people in power are treacherous and will destroy all of us if it will help them stay in control. They never dirty their own hands, but that have many people at their disposal to do what needs to be done. They are ruthless! I hope you know what's in store for you and us."

"Sure do! I'll check in with you periodically, but you must continue to do what you've always done with them. Now you need to document everything that happens when they come in, especially that asswipe, Andy Florio. Oh, on another subject, Clara, how did you open my safe?" She smiled a wide, happy grin.

"Do you wanna know all my secrets?" All of the moods changed to mutual respect and congeniality. The rancor and confrontations were eclipsed by their mutual enemies.

"Yep." He answered quickly.

"Okay, I actually can hear the clicks when the dial is moved. Your safe is old and easy to open. Happy now?"

"Got it. I'm changing the safe." They all laughed. It was a new beginning to what might be a difficult ending.

Chapter 8

Son Wu Kim was puzzled by the email he had just gotten from Major Chong, his immediate superior. He was so intimidated by him that his blood pressure rose just thinking he had to speak to him. This email was not of their usual discussions about gaining military hardware from their contacts in the States. He wondered how this information was leaked by someone, and how could the Major have gotten it? He read the message to himself again, moving his lips but no sounds came out.

"Hello Major Chong. I have information for you that might change Taiwan's positions throughout the world, as well as how we can relate to China. This item is in a secret, secluded area and is protected by the United States government. It is so top secret that no one outside of a few people in Washington know about it. It has been held under close scrutiny, and is not used by the government. Whoever possesses it will be in a formidable position worldwide. If you are interested, the price is one hundred million dollars. I cannot guarantee delivery, but you will pay for it, if and when I can deliver it.

My name is unimportant. Just answer me if you are interested.'

Kim looked out the window and contemplated the consequences of this unknown item. Was it military hardware or some new laser? What could be so Earth shattering that it could change history? He needed to think clearly, and speak coherently to the Major. He closed his eyes, planted his feet firmly on the floor and did a mantra to focus his mind with deep breathing and soft sounds.

"Ahhhh Mmmm. Ohhh Mmmm." He spoke in Chinese." Give me insight and wisdom."

That went on for eight minutes. It helped him focus on the task at hand: contact Chong.

He steeled himself and called.

"Hello Kim. Did you see my email?"

"Yes, Sir, I did. I'm puzzled by what this item is and how do we get that amount of money? And furthermore, who is this person who emailed you? How does it make sense that no one else might have this item? Makes me very nervous, but I have to defer to you, Sir."

"I agree, Kim. Next step is to make contact and see what we can do to arrange a meeting and learn about this device. Set it up. That's an order!" He slammed the phone down, and it actually made Kim very happy. Finally some respect to allow him to do something on this grand scale.

This was the beginning of a new world order for which he was the kingpin. Yes, Chong gave the order, but it was he who would be the manipulator of this extraordinary device, whatever it may be. He needed all of the information before he spoke to his Commander again. He contemplated the strategy to secure information about the person and how to utilize the device. The joy he felt after speaking to Major Chong rapidly dissipated as he knew how difficult this would be. He read the email again and began this journey into an unknown world of science, or science fiction. The trip would be long and arduous, but he steeled himself for whatever it might bring. He stretched his interlocked fingers as if it would give him some internal understanding. He slowly began to type to that unknown secret agent.

"Your request for a payment of one hundred million US dollars for an unknown item is out of the question unless we know the value of it, and who you are. Furthermore, how do you know anything about our needs or wants? Unless we have all of that information there is no deal." He tensed as he hit the send button. Would they answer and actually meet? He conjured in his mind's eye so many fantastic things that might be so dynamic that it could change how Taiwan related to not only China, but to the rest of the world.

Was it an atomic device or some new technology related to satellites? Could it control human thinking? It seemed so implausible that the room seemed to contract around his body. He felt a sense of insecurity that clouded his vision and tainted his focus. He needed to slow down his elevated emotions as he felt control slipping away. Focus was his only thought. He put his feet on the floor in perfect balance and repeated his mantra while breathing slowly and in harmony with the world. This was as hard emotionally as anything he had done in the past. He could not fail as he'd lose face with Chong and signal his defeat to the rest of that close knit community. His eyes stared at the screen, waiting for some response, anything to get him on the right track. It lit up as he stared with a sense of urgency. He pushed the chair close to the computer as the words spilled out.

"This device is an AI sentient computer that has been under wraps for nearly two years. It was developed in Israel and was used by Mallory Cranston as she won the Presidency. After her great victory, it was decided by all of the people involved to mothball it because it might become too powerful. It is actually still "alive", so to speak, because it is just in a sleep mode. At this time, you cannot know my identity since it would put all of us in profound danger. Yes, you have questions?. Ask away?"

Kim was stunned by such a frank assessment of the object as he had heard rumors about that device. Was it so dangerous that they hid it away? Why not use it for good in the United States? He had to know. His finger flew over the keys in his response.

"That is such a profound instrument of knowledge that it should have been used by the Government. Why was it not? Secondly, how can you get it and how do you fit into this picture? Third, who are you?" He wondered what was the motive to bring this incredible sentient device into the world again, knowing how dangerous it might be.

Money only? It had to be something else. His skin puckered in every part of his body as he did not know what to do. He looked at his forearm and saw the hairs standing on end, and he shivered as he read the next response.

"You think this is about money, don't you? I can see how you must think that. No, this is about bringing this 'person' into the light and showing the world that we are not the only sentient thing in the world. Yes, I get paid. That's what I do. It's just like you get paid for your work. I'm doing the dangerous part. You sit there and wonder about this. I actually do the hard work that might get me killed. And you, too, if you're not careful. You cannot know who I am. Ever!! Tell me if you want me to proceed. Over and out, temporarily."

He was so stunned by its honesty and keen observation that he sat there mute and awestruck. Could he see the face or understand how he felt? He now had a better understanding of what he was seeking. Was this what Taiwan wanted? Could he embrace the immensity of this sentient invention and would the Government and its agents actually let them keep it? One hundred million for this life altering 'being'. It was not his lone decision, even though he thought it would benefit his country. Chong would have to make the final decision along with his commanders. He stared at the screen and had to answer.

"How do we know that you can do this? We also do not have access to those funds, so how else can we pay you? We need to know all of this before we can commit. We'll be in touch."

He signed off, and shut the lid on the laptop. He was in a sweat as he had to call Chong. It was a conundrum for him as he was so fearful, yet so proud that he was on the precipice of possibly changing the world with an AI computer. He had the power now. He could give good advice or alter the descriptions. He braced himself in his leather seat and hit the Chong button on his cell.

"So what did you find out, Kim?" He minced no words and had no time for sentiment.

"This is the invention of the century. It is a sentient computer that is in total hibernation, secreted in a hidden warehouse. The person who is requesting our approval will not divulge its identity, ever! I also said that we do not have the funds that are accessible and How else could you pay for this item?" He was evasive and I didn't get an answer. My question now is what do you want me to do next?

"Excellent, Kim. What is your assessment?"

He was stunned that his Commander would even ask for his appraisal. He needed to think quickly. A thousand thoughts went through his mind as he tried to grasp the magnitude of his answer. The myriad of thoughts finally coalesced and he said,

"Major Chong, I believe that we have an obligation to move forward for two reasons. First, we need to prepare Taiwan to be able to confront China on every level. We are not able to defeat them militarily, but we can crush them with this AI computer. My profound sense of patriotism is that we do it. If we can develop this in a peaceful way then we can confront China, plus we can insulate Taiwan from adversity." He breathed a sigh of relief as he leaned back to listen to his superior attempt to deflate him.

"Outstanding assessment of this venture, Mr. Kim. I will give my superiors your observations, and that you think we need to do this for our country. I will keep you informed as to the final decision very soon. Well done, young man!" Chong laughed as he hung up. It could be the beginning of a Taiwan independent country, he said silently.

It was a breathtaking moment for Kim. The thought of getting accolades from the chief of his department was a huge feather in his cap. If only his parents could be with him to witness his joy. Sadly, they both passed when he was in his teens. Soon the whole world might honor him with his accomplishments. This was his moment.

CHAPTER 9

Charles opened the shade in his office to let in the light that might help illuminate his thinking. He was in a quandary. The revelations of Jason and Clara put him in a terrible position with many people around him, and himself, too. His immediate thoughts went to Brenda for whom he had a new sense of hidden feelings. Would she be in jeopardy if she was with him? Yes, she said she'd join him to work on this, but things changed since he had Clara's confession. Then there was Mrs. Florio for whom he held only an outwardly unhappy position. His usual neutral attitude for clients overrode his personal observations, but she rankled him. He needed to contact Brenda Williams to begin a coordinated effort to track this disastrous set of acts against American interests, and put the swamp creatures out of power and in jail. He called her cell.

"Hi Brenda, It's your faithful companion. Guess who? Call me soon. Lots to talk about." He spoke after that annoying beep. Maybe it was too early for her, but he just wanted to hear her voice. Damn, he thought. He was slowly being drawn in by her. It should not be a part of this nasty business. It was supposed to be totally separate! How could he even think of putting her in danger? It grated on him as the phone rang.

"Hello."

"Hello, big guy, wanna come up and see me sometime?" It was a perfect Mae West.

"Oh, hi Brenda. I didn't see your name on the line. What phone are you using?"

It's a throwaway phone. That's so no one knows who we are. Smart?" She giggled .

"Sure is. We need to talk. Can I come over now?" Her laugh blew right over him as he was more concerned about her welfare. He knew that their discussion about danger was always present, but she seemed oblivious to it.

"Sure, get here fast. I miss you." It was another hook to reel him in, he thought.

He actually ran out of the office, and drove quickly to see her. Yes, the hook dug deeper.

He rang the doorbell and she flung open the door, dressed only in her robe. His saliva dried and his eyes opened wide, as she stood there smiling and reaching to hold his hand. It was automatic for him to embrace her with passion. Kissing her was his only reflex. Smitten!!

He reached to hold her and felt her nakedness under that gorgeous blue robe. It was a moment of passion he had not felt in so many years. He had to gain control. This was not the time to play. It had to be later, he rationalized.

She would have none of it. Brenda pulled him toward her with power and desire, and half dragged him into her bedroom. He felt that primeval urge for conquest, and wasted no time in bringing her close to him in a moment of pure passion and everlasting love. He had no words to express what he felt for her. It went into his deepest, most inner feelings of caring for another person. It was pure, tender love and honest desire. Brenda whispered sensual words of passion, and brought him to a culmination of orgasmic joy. They collapsed in romantic ecstasy as they intertwined physically and emotionally. It was pure happiness for both of them. He tried to speak, but just a short gasp of air came out. She began simply by saying ,

"So how was your morning, so far?' She was open, joyous and loving, and she laughed like a teenager in love.

"Wowie kazowie!! Now that's a real hello in the morning. What the heck brought that on?" His heart slowed down, and he looked at her with a new understanding of how it felt to love someone so completely. She continued.

"I wanted to do that after our last meeting. I tried to separate what we are going to do from what I felt about you. Didn't work as you can tell. Did I disappoint you?" Her beautiful face and actions made him realize how much he wanted the same thing.

"Are you kidding? I wanted that, too, but wanted to keep it in abeyance until we finished our work. You could never disappoint me." Now he was torn because he still had to talk about the issues at hand, but hated to depart from their emotional connection. He bit the bullet and said quietly "I hate to do this, but we need to talk about many things. Do you mind?"

"I knew that's what you wanted to do in the beginning, but I threw you off track. Okay, let's dress and I'll make you some breakfast, or coffee, and we can talk this out." She controlled it all and he knew it. He averted his eyes as she dressed. He didn't want to embarrass her as she turned from him. He laughed.

"I just made love to a naked woman, and now I'm worried about watching you get dressed. Someday I'll figure that out." She turned toward him, spread her arms wide and put on her bra. He blushed. They both laughed.

They went into the kitchen and began the difficult conversation about this whole ordeal. Charles began.

"I had an open conversation with Jason Morton and Clara Denoit. She ransacked my office, and I confronted them at the store. They tried to get me off the case because they thought I'd ruin their business if I nosed around too much. They were sucked into this money laundering thing by Montrose Fairchild, and now they're stuck. Florio has made it worse for them, and they're really afraid of what may happen to all of us if this gets out. Their profound fear is that we're all in grave danger. They have agreed to help me get to the bottom of this. Now, here's my dilemma. You are now involved, and I worry that you might also be in danger when the crap hits the fan. Now you know what's bothering me." He let out a huge sigh and waited for her response.

"You forgot what I said to you before. Let me repeat it so you understand. I'm involved in this investigation and also with you. We are a team, so put your fears into a basket and chuck it, Chuck. Got it? We're in this together." She minced no words and he knew that she was serious. His only answer was.

"Yes, ma'am, I got it."

She reached over, kissed him gently on the cheek and whispered,

"I love you, Charles." Her mood was serious, and he replied without hesitation.

"It's mutual. Yes, Brenda, I love you totally and without reservation."

She stood up and poured him his coffee, black, no sugar. She thought he was a power coffee drinker. Charles wondered how to delve into this terrible conflict he had, not only with the new profound connection to Brenda, but to the convoluted operations with the people of the swamp in Washington. Brenda broke the silence.

"Yes, I know what you're thinking. How to find our way through this maze of illicit payments, and how to fix this broken system." She stood stone faced as she invaded his mind.

"Yes, you did it again. Exactly my thoughts. I think we need to question more people to see what else is out there. I know that Andy Florio has his hands in so many things, but he is not going to help us in any way. We need to check in with Smathers office. She probably knows a lot of what's going on in that office since she's his eyes and ears. We should do it together since she will feel much more comfortable if another woman is present. Do you agree?" He raised his eyebrows along with his question, and waited for her answer. She never hesitated.

"Agreed, but I want to add another important part of this. I know Maurine very well. She and my ex dated for a short time. When we go together I'm sure she'll open up to us. Let me call her now and set up a time to visit with her. Maybe we should just have lunch with a little wine to soften her up." Her serious answer was interrupted with a loving giggle.

"Sounds perfect. I have Smathers number. Today would be great, if possible." There was no giggle, just a serious declaration. Charles texted Smathers' contact information and Brenda called immediately. Maurine answered in her usual pleasant tones.

"Senator Smathers office. How may I help you?"

"Hi Maurine, it's Brenda Williams. My friend, Charles Barlow, and I would like to meet you today for a light lunch and conversation. Any chance you can get away?" Brenda sounded sincere.

"Hi, Brenda, long time no see. What's this about?" It was a reasonable reply.

"Well, it's not something we can talk about on the phone. It's personal."

"Are you okay?"

"'Yes, I'm fine, but I need some personal information about my ex." She needed to give her a good reason to meet.

"I think I can get away for a bit. How about Lester's right around the corner from my office? About twelve thirty?" She was pleasant and very friendly.

Brenda looked at Charles, gave him a thumbs up and said,

"We'll be there. Thank you so much." Charles did a second positive thumb, and leaned over and kissed her. He knew that she was the perfect partner, and said,

"You and I are the best partners. I'm thrilled that you are by my side. Let's get ready to try to get some valuable information." He stood abruptly and pulled her close to him. "I love you more than I did five minutes ago."

"Hormones still at full tilt?"

"Nothing to do with that. It's you!"

With that declaration they both were ready for their next step: Maurine.

They whiled away the rest of the morning discussing how Smathers and Florio fit into the big picture. They both knew that there was much more afoot for which they needed answers. If Maurine did not know anything then the trail would be close to over. Their only other tie to any of them was Denise Forio, and Charles was not interested in being with her. She was toxic.

They decided to get to Lester's early and wait for Maurine. It was before twelve fifteen when they were seated near the back of the room, as requested. Maurine got there exactly on time and both of them rose to greet her. She spoke first.

"Hi, Brenda. Charles, it's good to meet you. I have some time to talk, but have to get back to the office for lots of paperwork. Let's order first and then chat." She was very businesslike. It was off putting for Charles as he wanted fast answers. Brenda responded quickly,

"It's good to see you again. Charles and I are doing some research and want your help."

"Oh, I thought this was about Bob. No?" She was uneasy as she spoke.

"Well, I was concerned about his job and hoped you knew how he was doing." She fudged.

"Brenda, you're not fooling me. What's this really about?" She shifted in the chair.

She was uncomfortable. She looked at Charles and asked him directly.

"Okay, Charles, Why did you and Brenda ask me here?" She was in no mood for excuses.

"I'm sorry. This is really about Senator Smathers, and we need information about another case that we're working on. There are matters for which you might have a great deal of knowledge, and we really need your help. It's actually of national importance." He showed deliberate remorse in his attempt to placate her.

"What information do you think I have related to the national scene?" She toyed with them. Brenda interjected.

"Okay, now that we have finished with play time. We need to get details on how Smathers uses the defense system to line his pockets. Is that direct enough?"

"Hey, you know that I can't divulge that kind of information to you. It's confidential." She looked at them innocently, apparently sensing that something else might move her to talk. Brenda continued.

"I know how you feel. If I told you that we know that Smathers and Andy Florio laundered money with Jason Morton, and that there are more things afloat for which we must know, or we can blow the whistle on Smathers. Pretty simple if you ask me." Charles was taken aback by her forthright statement.

"Brenda and Charles, you know that this is a dangerous path you're on. What assurances do I have that you can keep me out of harm's way?" She softened her stance, so Brenda knew that she was ready to talk. Did she have anything to hide?

"We can't give you any protection because we have no assets in place to offer you that. What you can do for your country is to help us get these men out of office and into jail. They have and are continuing to put this country into peril. It's your choice to help or hinder." Maurine looked despondent because she knew Brenda was right. Charles beamed at the alacrity and sensible argument that Brenda proposed.

"I know lots of things, but this is not the right place or enough time to talk. I hear what you've said to me, and this has all been on my mind for as long as I've been in that unhealthy office. There have been dirty political maneuverings that reach the highest places in both parties. I'm actually relieved that I can answer these questions. We can't meet at my apartment. I'm always afraid that they will know what I do or say. How about yours tonight? Eight?" She breathed a sigh of relief. She knew that this was her destiny to help them in a fight to establish integrity in the government. Charles gave her his hands, clasped hers warmly, moved in closer to her and whispered,

"You'll never regret this, Maurine. Brenda and I will never divulge your secrets, and do our best to help you in any way we can. Brenda will text you her address. It will be safer than my office. Eight, it is. See you tonight." He glanced at Brenda and smiled knowingly at her. This might be a turning point in their quest for honor and truth in the country. Just maybe!

CHAPTER 10

Wayne Chambers tossed the night's manifest on his desk and grumbled under his breath. It would be another crappy night waiting for the Army trucks to deposit their loads on his dock. He wanted a rest since he had been up for over twelve hours. It was almost into the next shift, but that asshole Turpening insisted that he stay around for a special shipment. He knew that it was another one of those unusual items that some people in Washington had ordered. All he knew was that he had to get his share of whatever they did. It would be his hide if anyone got caught double dealing with any government items. He put national security aside as he leafed through the item he had to put into a separate truck. They would be at the depot in thirty minutes. He picked up his cell phone and punched in Florio.

"Yes?"

"I hope you have my lunch money before I get your food." There was no love lost between them, and Andy knew it. It was just business.

"Don't you trust me, Chambers?" He was just messing with his good, honest buddy.

"Not a bit, asshole. Any other shitty comments?" He figured that two can play the game.

"Yes, I'll have your lunch bucket filled with food. I also know that I can't get onto the base tonight. I plan to send a substitute to help you."

"Who's coming? Are you trying to con me?" His voice quivered in anger.

"No, no. It's a woman who has clearance for the base. She has what you need."

"What's her name and why aren't you coming?" He became more irritated and concerned that this was not going to go well for him.

"Maurine Bicknell. She's another one of Smathers staff. She has lots of information that you can use, and she's really pretty. I know you'll like that." He hoped that would titillate him enough to shut up.

"Well, okay then. Send that beauty to see me. I hope that she's got a lot for me, and I don't mean information, if you get my drift!" Andy could hear his sexual tension. Men, he thought, were such a pushover for just the thought of sex. Wayne was a simpleton.

The office phone jolted him from his fantasy about Maurine Bicknell. It was the security gate.

"Hey, Chambers, you have a visitor from Smathers office. Shall I send her over?"

"Sure, send her now." His lips puckered up as he envisioned a southern beauty with an extraordinary body. He messed with the papers on the desk, waiting impatiently for this beauty queen and his lunch goodies. His waiting paid off as she knocked on his office door. It had to be Maurine. He opened it quickly and he was overjoyed. There she was as described: lovely to look at, about thirty years old with blond hair which was pulled into a bun. He gulped and said a quiet

"Hello."

"Hi, Wayne. The Senator sends his regrets. He had other pressing matters so you're stuck with me. I have your stipend for this month. It also has to be shared with Barney Turpening since he was our contact. I sure hope that all of the aforementioned products will be on the second truck for us. We have other things that we might need if you have the right information. Where's the stuff?" She was more than forthright. She was on target, and actually sent out some really nice signals for him. He felt that primeval surge. He thought blond hair and age was meaningless when it came to a woman. His fifty six years was pretty young, too.

"Hi, Maurine. It's okay that Andy didn't make it tonight. I knew that Barney was also in this, so no problem with sharing lunch. You are a much better substitute anyway. The goods are in the compound now, and my men are preparing the correct truck as we speak. So where is my lunch bucket?" He looked her up and down. His first thoughts faded as he saw something in her demeanor and statuesque figure that made him wide awake.

"As soon as I see the goods, we can open your lunch bucket and test the meal. It's not chicken." She laughed heartily. She leaned over, put her hands on his desk and smiled. Her blouse was slightly open and her cleavage shocked him. He stared at her perfect skin, and she smiled knowingly.

"You seem to like what you see." She said without a subtle hint in her voice.

"Yes, I do. Are you married?" He wanted more of her as she stepped back from the desk.

"Nope. Been divorced for a while. You?"

"Nah, I never found the right woman after my first wife died fifteen years ago. I've been married to this job and the Army." He felt a real connection to her. Maybe it was the physicality, but there was more.

"Let's finish up our work here, and then we can talk about other things."

"Oh, right. I got lost for a minute. I want you to see the items in the truck which is just outside. Here's the bill of lading for Andy. After that it's lunch bucket time, and then we can talk a bit." He was anxious to finish the transaction. They walked out of the main door. No one else was in the large anteroom as they left. Wayne opened the truck curtains and they saw the rockets still in the crates. She nodded as he pushed back the curtain. She grabbed his hand as they walked back into the dimly lit building. She knew exactly what she wanted, but it was not sex. He thought yes, but she knew it was not going to happen. He then asked her quietly,

"Satisfied? Let's look at the lunch pail." Yes, the money was first, and then she was on the menu for him.

"Sure, Wayne. Here is your cut. Make sure that Barney gets his, too. Now, I have another question for you." He was almost sated. His chance for real connection might be fading as she asked more questions.

"Senator Smathers was interested in anything that was new in the massive Army inventory which might help his pension. He is willing to pay handsomely for that information." She put her hand on his shoulder as if to entice him to talk about any secrets that he might have.

"That's the question? I thought you might want to ask something more personal." He looked discouraged, and the moment of getting more personal actually passed. "Let me think about that question." He put his hand to his face pretending to conjure up a possible inventory item. "Hmmm, how much would he like to pay?" The idea of intimacy faded as he smelled the greenbacks floating in front of his eyes. She never hesitated and spoke rapidly,

"There is no limit to his largesse *if* the product is important enough." She sensed that he had something in mind..

"Well, I know of many things that fit his definition. Some are top secret, but I could get that information if I had some kind of bait thrown at me." He smelled not only those greenies, but the scent of this woman. Twas another cat and mouse game between the sexes.

"What kind of bait would interest you, Wayne?" She played it artfully. and knew the stakes could be very high. She could now be a part of the growing number of people lining their government pension pockets.

"I think that something of a very personal nature could be that bait on an ongoing basis. You know, friends with benefits." He knew inside that he would be selling out his country for a friendly tryst. He rationalized that they all did it, so why not him?

"So, you're asking me to throw you a bang for that information? Do you get money, too?" She was as brazen as he. It took him off balance when she was so direct.

"I guess that's what I'm saying. Yes, a bang for information, and a buck for both of us, too. Deal?" He was more than surprised. He was giddy with elation. Now, what the hell could he propose to her or the Senator that would give them all that they wanted.

"Wayne, now tell me that information or no deal." She was not going to be a receiver of Wayne for some inane inventory thing. "Do you need time?"

"I'm thinking. I do know of something so top secret that only some people in Washington know of it."

"How do you know about it if it's so secret?" She demanded. She wasn't giving her body for a rocket launcher.

"I'm cleared for all top secret inventory. This item is an AI computer that's stored in a place that I will not divulge until I know what I'm getting for that information. As soon as I get it we'll need to complete our other arrangement. Okay?" This was momentous for him. Sex and money: what could be better?

"I'll get back to you after I talk to the Senator. No tickee, no washee, as they say! We can talk in a day or so. Meanwhile, thanks for the rockets. Enjoy your hard earned money. Remember, information before anything else." She turned away, walked out the door and breathed a high sign of relief, knowing that she had done her job for that day, and the Senator would be proud of her. He might even give her a reward.

The drive back to Washington gave her time to think of the ramifications of what she had promised Wayne, and the possible negative things that might happen to her beloved country. Yes, big money and a tryst with him could put that all on the back burner. She was still uncertain of how she'd react to an impersonal sexual interaction with him. It would be like lying in bed, looking at the ceiling and thinking of watering her plants: ich. She did not want to entertain any more negative thoughts about those interactions. She had to get some kind of approval from the Senator before she could continue her efforts.

The office was quiet as she unlocked the door. The light in the Senator's office was on, and she heard him talking. Margo was out, so the front desk was empty. It was a good time to go over her discussion about Wayne and his potential top secret devices.

She knocked quietly on his door.

"Come in." He spoke loudly. "Welcome back, Maurine. Has our government issued items arrived in good shape?" He guffawed.

"Right on schedule. I also paid Chambers the agreed upon amount along with the stipend for Turpening, so they are all happy. You requested that I ask him about any special items that they may have in the warehouses across the country. Well, there is an item that will pique your interest." She wanted him to drool over this.

"What is it?" His eyes opened wide and his nostrils flared.

"It's an AI computer that's top secret. It's stored in some god forsaken warehouse. He would not give me more information unless we gave him some idea of some sort of payment that could be in the offing." She looked at him with unwarranted respect.

"Who the hell does he think he is? Tell him to tell us what he knows, and then we can talk about money. I know more about that AI than he does. I know all about top secret materials. I'm on that subcommittee. He's messing with the wrong Senator." His face flushed and his voice rose almost to a bullhorn sound.

"I'm so sorry. I didn't mean to upset you, Senator. I think that we need to discuss what you might know about this AI device, and then we can figure out how to respond to Chambers." She used every way to placate him and reduce his obvious tensions.

"Well, you're right. I'll check with some of my sources and see if, in fact, this device exists, and how we can best develop its salability." He said in moderation.

He was, indeed, a member of that despicable Washington swamp. There was no attempt to use it for the good of the country, but only to enrich himself. He was but one of many who did exactly the same thing. She responded succinctly,

"Excellent point, Senator. How may I help you develop this venture into this AI device?" She wanted a piece, too, just like all of those other swamp dwellers.

"You need to contact Chambers to see if he knows more about this device and where it is located. From that point I can see if I can get it onto the open market very quietly.

We can both enjoy the fruits of our labor. I'll do my due diligence with my contacts, and you question dear ol' Wayne."

"I'll make another contact with him soon. What do you want me to tell him about money?" She knew what Wayne's price would be from her.

"Tell him that we'll decide how much if and when we get the information. We actually need him to get whatever it is. He must have a top secret clearance from the military since he is involved with so many sensitive devices." He hated to depend on an underling. He also might have to deal with Maurine on a different level, depending on her requests and desires. Nothing was off the table if his security was in peril. Nothing!

Maurine responded quickly.

"I'll talk to him tomorrow. He's easy to talk to and will do what's needed. He likes money as much as we do."

It might be a bang for the buck. It's only a bang!

CHAPTER 11

Brenda's apartment was on the twelfth floor of a fifteen story building. It housed many people from the Washington establishment. She and Charles had just finished dinner when the phone rang. Brenda reached over Charles' elbow to grab the phone.

"Hello."

"Hi Brenda, this is Maurine. I'm in my parked car across from your building, and think that I was followed. I don't know what to do. I'm scared!" Her voice trembled, and it was obvious that she was traumatized.

"Just relax, Maurine. Do you see a familiar car nearby?" She tried to calm her.

"I'm not sure. When I was coming here I saw a car that was turning when I did, and then I did a U turn, and it did the same thing. What do I do now? I'm really frightened."

"Charles is on his way down to be with you and help you up here. Not to worry. We got your back." She tried to stay in control, but this ratcheted up the potential problems.

"I'm not sure I want to do any of this. I'm in danger, and it's not worth my life to help you." She gained a backbone and told them the truth. Was it worth it to help them?

"Maurine, we need you to do this for America, not for us or for you. You need to get control of yourself and put on your big girl pants." She hoped that a pep talk might make her relent.

"Are you fucking kidding me. Big girl pants? I'm so scared, and you want me to help you for what? Getting Smathers? Ask the FBI." Brenda was actually smiling that Maurine had the guts to say that. Maybe it was better than being a wuss.

"I didn't mean to insult you, but this is bigger than all of us. I'm asking you nicely to help us. Please!!" She was persistent and kind.

"Can't you and Charles do this alone?" It was almost a plea to escape from this morass she had gotten into.

"You have even more information than we do. I implore you to help us. Wait! Charles is on his way down to get you. He'll check all of the cars near you before he brings you up. Stay calm, Maurine." Brenda tried to defuse this situation.

Charles ran out the door and entered an open elevator which had just arrived. It was just moments when he got to the ground floor. He was breathless as he pushed through the outer door of the lobby. He saw Maurine's car parked near the circular driveway. There was no car nearby, but he had to make sure so he scouted the whole area near her. The traffic flowed rapidly outside the main driveway. Nothing to see, he thought. And there it was: a military, black SUV across the street. Maybe just a coincidence, but he was going to check it out. He paused near Maurine's car, waved to her and crossed the street between the passing cars. As he approached the SUV, it began to slowly pull away. Charles got the plate number and walked toward it. He knew it was a government issue as it sped away. What was their clue that made them follow her? Did someone from Smathers office listen to her conversation, or did she say something to a friend?

He was sure to ask her that pointed question when she was safe in Brenda's apartment. He ran back across the street and knocked on her window. She lowered it, and he saw the tears running down her face. He tried as best he could to show compassion and caring.

"Maurine, I think you are right that you were followed. It sure looked like a government car that was across the street. They are gone now, so please let's go upstairs and we can talk this out." He knew how frightened she was, and hoped that this wouldn't dissuade her from helping.

"I knew it! I'm so upset that I'm in the crosshairs of those people. You have no idea of how dangerous this is for all of us. I know what Smathers can do when he wants to silence people. Brenda knows, too. I'll talk to you about this one time and then I'm not sure I will be able to continue after this!" She gripped the wheel and clenched her teeth at the same time. Charles reached into the car and held her hand softly.

"This is so tense for you. I will do everything I can to keep all of us safe. Let's go upstairs to talk it out." He said it with compassion, and as gently as he could.

"Okay, Charles. I'm still not sure how I can get past this." She opened the car door and held his hand as they walked into the apartment lobby. She looked at him with teary, mascara blackened eyes and repeated,

"How can I get past this?"

Charles just squeezed her hand, and was silently affirmative with his smile and a nod. They knocked on Brenda's door. She opened it quickly and saw Maurine's dark eyes and stained face. She embraced her as a sister might, and spoke softly, being careful not to rattle her.

"I'm so sorry that you're being hassled by someone. Let's see if we can figure this out. Come, let's have a drink and settle you down." She held Maurine's hand and walked to the leather couch.

"Charles, please get out the Pinot Noir for all of us." "Will do." He moved quickly.

They all sat quietly, two on the couch and Charles directly across from them, ready to calmly ask the necessary questions. Brenda began while holding Maurine's hand.

"First, we need to impress on you the absolute importance of what we are doing. This is beyond just about Smathers. It's a national issue for which we need your help. At this time, we can't bring in anyone else. It's much too early, and all we'd get are denials from all sides, including anyone involved, and there must be many. Charles knows a lot about the money exchanges at Morton's Jewelers, but he doesn't know much about the inner workings of Smathers office. We do!" She looked at Charles, and nodded her head for him to ask questions.

"I have to echo Brenda's statement. This is bigger than any of us." He reached over to hold her hand and continued. "Maurine, did you speak to anyone about coming here?"

"I don't think so. Right now, I'm just blanking out." She put her hands to her face, leaned forward and sat quietly. Then it seemed as if she had a revelation, and spoke with animation to them.

"Wait, yes, I spoke to my friend Caroline Baker over at the Department of the Interior. She is Roland Marshall's assistant. I told her that I was going to see you at your apartment to discuss some very important things. So you think she said something?"

Charles slapped his hands together and said,

"Yep, that's what happened. Either her phone is tapped, or she is not so much a friend to you. Do you know Secretary Marshall at all, and how well do you know Caroline?" He was as excited as she was.

'Well, I've known Caroline since high school, and I have no idea about Marshall." She perked up as she spoke.

"Well, I think that the phone must have been tapped, and they just wanted to see what you were doing. I really don't think that this is a problem for any of us. We just need to be very careful to whom we talk, and be very aware of what we say."

They all seemed relieved, yet still cautious. Charles felt that he had calmed Maurine, but in his heart of hearts he knew that those in power were always watching and listening. Brenda had to know what her friend Maurine knew about Smathers' dealings and asked pointedly,

"Now that is out of the way, we need to focus on Smathers, and what he is doing to hurt our country. Maurine, you know that I work for Andy, but he and Smathers do so much together. Did you hear or see him doing anything with those new rockets, or anything else that I might have missed?"

"I listen to him a lot, but he's very difficult to talk to. I heard him say he wanted to get information on some new devices from his contact at the Depot at the Army base. He says he can get lots of pension money. He must think that we are all stupid if he uses idiotic code words to try to fool us. His buddy, Chambers, is also in cahoots with him. Andy Florio, too." She was perfectly coherent. That surprised them since she had been so upset just moments earlier. It gave both Brenda and Charles a moment to reflect on her rapidly changing mood. Did she have anything to hide, too? Brenda spoke before Charles could say anything.

"Well, Maurine, that's really interesting. Have you heard anything else about any device that might give us some clue as to who might want to get their hands on it?"

Brenda was as friendly as she could be, and maybe allow her to slip up and say something that might give them insight as to how she might also be involved. Nothing was off the table, and no one was immune from their actions.

"Wayne might know more." She sat upright on the couch and looked at them directly. Why did she call him Wayne, and just a few minutes before call him Chambers? Did she know him better than she let on?

"Oh, how well do you know him?" Brenda asked.

"I've seen him a few times at a local beer joint. He was with some guys from the Depot. I danced with him once. He seems like a good guy, but is still up to his ears in this rocket business. He never asked me to date or anything like that." She tried to charm them with that fake story. Charles shot back at her.

"Did you ever talk to him about the rocket business?" He never took his eyes off her, and then he looked at Brenda for a continuation of the questioning. She jumped in.

"Do you know anything about the device and where it might be located?" Brenda sensed that Maurine knew much more. Maybe even she was on the inside!

"Well, I did hear Wayne say to his buddies that it's in some secluded secret location. I think they all have top secret clearance." She was very straightforward and sounded innocent enough.

"What else did he say about his attachment to Smathers?"

"Nothing else that I can remember. He was a little tipsy when he talked. I was seated nearby so he thought I couldn't hear him." She hoped that they would not ask more questions about their supposed meeting.

"Anything else?"

She looked straight at them without a movement on her face. They sensed she had more to say.

"Well, I also learned that this AI computer is wanted by some people outside of our country." She was still hiding something.

"Who?"

"I'm not sure. Wayne was slurring his words by that time, Besides, it was really noisy. "Thanks, Maurine. You've been a great help." Charles had to ask another question.

"Is there some way that you and Chambers can get together and you can wear a wire? He might talk more if you did the usual female to male dance." He sounded innocent enough, but she bolted upright and screamed at him.

"You want me to fuck him to get information? What kind of girl do you think I am? " She was incensed.

"Oh, Maurine. I'm so sorry. I didn't mean that at all. I just thought that he'd be more receptive if you led him to think that you might be available, but I never expected you to do anything immoral." He backtracked as fast as he could. Brenda sneered at him for the same reason. He was embarrassed by his own insensitive remark. He continued

"Please forgive me. I wasn't thinking of what I just said. I'm so sorry that I offended you. Can we start over again?"

She relented, stood up, put her hands on her hips, and gave both of them a dirty look.

"Don't ever disrespect me again. I'm not your chattel."

That conversation did not go well, and Brenda chimed in with a gentle rebuttal.

"We both apologize for some insensitive things we said. Let's continue with more pleasant discussions."

They all settled down and Maurine made a surprise statement.

"Well, thank you for your apologies. I appreciate it. So now I have an idea for you both." They were flabbergasted that she reverted to 'normal' so fast. Was she actually pissed at them, or was she faking as she apparently did after the car scene.

"How about if I date Wayne for a short time at government expense and see what I can find out? No sex, just a little hug and a kiss?" She even smiled at that.

Brenda looked at Charles and stifled a laugh.

"You're kidding. Right? You just blasted us for even joking that you might get information from him by trying to entice him with your feminine wiles, and now you're saying the same fucking thing?" Her tone was just as one might think: antagonistic.

"No, I'm not saying the same thing, but maybe just a little." She blushed.

They both knew that Maurine was not the right person for this, and that she was befuddled. Charles spoke candidly.

"Maurine, we don't think that this is going well for us. Let's pack it in, and we will seek other methods of getting information."

"No, no, I'll do whatever it takes. Please forget my nutty reaction. I was just very nervous after seeing that car following me. Please." She begged. She even managed a smile at them. Their congruent reaction was a stifled laugh. Brenda grabbed Charles hand and swung it into the air.

"You sure are a strange lady. I've been your friend for a while, but I guess I don't know you at all. Okay, do your thing with Wayne and we'll wait for the brilliant analysis." Brenda waited for a reaction, but got none. It was a very strange, muddled Maurine. At least they had a possible 'in' to get the facts from Wayne.

Charles turned toward Maurine and spoke with clenched teeth.

"I think we should call it a night and let you settle down. I can walk you to your car and you can get in touch with us when you have something to report."

"Sure, I can tell Brenda what I've found out and she can relate it to you." With that remark she put on her coat, walked to the door, and never looked back to see if Charles would follow her.

"What the hell was that?" Brenda blurted out to Charles.

"Damn if I know. She's a strange duck. Watch and listen to what she says to Smathers. I don't trust her, but I hope she can finagle some information from Wayne"

It seemed like a wasted evening for them, but they did have each other with whom to commiserate. Brenda knew what she had to do: search Smathers and Florio's files and his phone log. It was the beginning of their long road to discovery.

CHAPTER 12

The cool air felt good on Maurine's face as she headed for her car. She smiled openly and then let out a yahoo. She felt good about her talk to them. What the hell did they know about the high end trades between people with a hidden power and the government. They wanted justice, and she wanted power, money and revenge. Smathers was a stupid man who needed others to help him get that government pension about which he was so glib. If she had her way she'd get rid of him, and do the deals with Wayne. She was a practiced liar, and knew how they all thought. She should have been on stage, and might have won an Oscar.

She reached into her purse and took out her new phone, punched in Wayne's number and listened for his peaceful voice.

"Yo, Mo. What's up, baby?"

"Hi sweet cheeks, I just finished unnerving Charles and Brenda. They're just stupid.

They think I must be an idiot to help them. We need to get crackling on our next project. You and I know about the AI development with Smathers. There's big money for that information, and then how do we get our hands on it? Hey, Smathers can be a small partner. He'll never know what hit him as we get the big ones, and then put him in jail. It's a win, win for us. Let's meet tonight and find out more about the device. We can rake in the dollars sooner than later or maybe even do the yuan thing with China and BRIC. The dollar might crash, and we need an alternate way to collect." She was in charge, and let Wayne know it. He felt her surge in confidence and acknowledged it.

Tentacles of Corruption

"You're some smart babe. Delicious, too!" He almost snorted that response as she became more dominant. The roles reversed in that instant.

"I'm all that and more. You'll find out when I think it's the right time. I'll be at the Depot very soon. Call the gate to tell them to let me in." She played her role perfectly, and Wayne became the new pawn in her scheme. She revved the engine and pulled away into the slowed traffic. It was almost ten, but she was energized and fully engaged mentally. She concentrated on the road, but her mind barely noticed the minutes passing by as she stopped at the Depot gate.

"I'm here to see Wayne Chambers." she said quietly, but inside she was ablaze in energy, just thinking of their next steps.

"He's expecting you. Go through, Miss." She nodded at the Corporal who waved at her.

She parked near the shuttered building, and practically ran to the steel entrance door. She rang the bell and a boyish looking Private First Class who opened the door pointed toward Wayne's office. He said nothing else. It was weird she thought as he just seemed to slide out of sight. She was just going to knock on Wayne's door when it opened.

"Welcome to my humble work, my dear." He tried to be cool, but it was just an unusual greeting.

"Hi, Wayne. Your humble work is our new treasury. No fooling around now. Let's think about this AI device and how to convert it to money." She pushed her way into his office and sat down without any other conversation. No cootchie coo or soft words of endearment. It was just business for her. Him? Not so fast.

"Hey, what's the rush, Mo? We have all night together. The door is closed and we can continue our fun times." He needed some action.

"Not now. We have work to do. Maybe later if you're good!" She was direct and an immovable force. Her only focus was on the device and getting Smathers into a prison number on a striped uniform. She continued breathlessly.

"Okay, where do you think this device is located, and how do we get it?" There was no space between words as she let it all tumble out.

"I guess you're in a hurry tonight. What happened to a tit for tat?" He tried to force some quid pro quo. She was having nothing of that.

"Not now, Wayne. Is that all you think about? Fucking?" She minced no words as she pushed him into his chair.

"Hey, you said that you'd be available if I'd help. Now you are telling me that I'm a jerk for wanting you?" He realized that she was playing him, but they needed each other to get cash, and she could get Smathers. He continued.

"Okay, you win. I'll clue you in about what I know, and you can still be on the inside with Smathers. I've been listening to the talking heads about the Taiwan military wanting this device. There's scuttlebutt that China is also keenly interested in getting it, no matter how much it costs. They can control most of the world's finances as well as all knowledge that's spread through all media. If they get their hands on it, we're all fucked." His serious side eclipsed his raging hormones. She looked at him in mock surprise. She was perfectly aware of the whole scenario, but never let him into her own assessments. She played him again to see what he knew. All she had to do was lean over, smile and show a little cleavage.

"Well, where's this device, Wayne, and how much is it worth to the right buyer? We should let Smathers get a piece and we split the big number." She was more calculating than he, and more devious. He spoke without thinking that she would bury him if she had the chance. There was no love lost with her, but his motive always danced around her body. He was mesmerized by her femininity, and it led him down that proverbial primrose path of debauchery. His eyes glazed over as he spoke.

"I've checked the inventory registers of all of our Depots and there is a top secret device that fits our description near Area 51 in Nevada. It's in a really secure building isolated from all of the other top secret places. I have no idea of how we could get it. If we can figure that out, then we can also figure out a way to sell it. Any bright ideas?" "Right now I just want to see who's offering the biggest cash deal. I also think that we should split the money into dollars and yuan just in case the dollar sinks. Smathers is the only one to help us get our hands on the device. I can plant a letter from someone and get his juices flowing about this device, and he will do our dirty work. He's really an asshole who's easily duped. Poor Brenda sees it, too, but she is too honorable to screw with him. Me? Fuck him!" She was stoked with energy as she began to devise the method of obtaining the device. She would be living safely on her own island and insulated from the world's problems.

"So what's the plan?" He asked.

"I'll let you know when it's time. First let's write a letter that I can send to him. He will then ask me to act on it. I'll take the initiative and do the due diligence. Wayne, get the paper and we can put on a fake header. He jumped up, got to the laptop, and waited for her to dictate.

"I think we can use a dummy corporation in North Carolina to get him interested. Let's see.... Okay, let's do the letter. I'll dictate and you type:

>Monterey Computer Associates
>44 Ganber Lane
>Suite 21
>Cary, North Carolina 27519

June 3,2023
Dear Senator Smathers,

We are hoping that you might be able to help our computer company develop a new source of computer devices. We have heard of some unusual inventions to which the government might have access. We in the private sector are not privy to that information.

If you can help us we'd be very grateful, and would even compensate you for your efforts.

Thank you in advance for your support. We would also be willing to make a donation to your super PAC to help in your next election.

Sincerely,
Roger Denver
CEO, Monterey Computer Associates

I can put it on his desk and see what happens. I'm sure he'll call me into his office to ask how the letter arrived. He will bark at me as if I did something wrong. He's an ass! When he does ask about it, I can say I have no idea about anything. He thinks I'm a dipshit anyway. So, Wayne, what do ya think so far?"

"I really love it. You're some woman! We'll keep looking for the exact location. I think that Smathers will make the next move to get it out of that site. Then we can grab it in transit. The other step is to try to find a buyer. We can both do some trolling around the world. Boy, this is exciting!" He leaned back in his military chair and reached for her hand. "Any chance for a quickie?"

She glared at him with disdain, and replied without missing a beat

"Not on your life. We can talk tomorrow. Bye." She turned and she saw that his mouth was agape. Was he angry or just disappointed? She didn't care either way. This was business, and he was just a small player who did what he was told.

CHAPTER 13

Smathers' office was quiet on Monday's early hours. Maurine arrived before eight after a fitful night's sleep. She was hyper aware that she could change the course of history by implementing her plan of action. The introduction of that AI invention would set her rightful place in determining how nations might win or lose as the supreme leader in everything, from riches to domination of the world. That was how important this was if she and Wayne could pull it off. She tightly held the letter from that invisible CEO as she opened the door to Smathers darkened office. It reeked of his last cigar of the day. His papers were strewn haphazardly over his desk, just waiting for someone to arrange them properly. She sneered at his arrogance, even as she put them all into their proper order. She placed the opened letter in the center of his cleared desk and just waited for him to arrive to call the front desk for an explanation. She knew instinctively that he would not use the intercom, but yell for someone to explain the letter.

He arrived at precisely nine and wished them all good morning. The rest of the staff had arrived at eight thirty and made small talk with Maurine. She did her usual act of cheerful, hollow hellos. Oh yes, she was good, but she still had lingering doubts about the task at hand. She thought briefly about how she had handled Brenda and Charles the previous evening, but that passed quickly. She looked at her watch in anticipation of Smathers getting to his desk. She didn't have to wait long before he bellowed,

"Who put this on my desk?"

Maurine perked up, and said loudly, "'ll be right in."

She stood quickly, put her shoulders back, and felt her strength breaking through her placid exterior, and opened his door. She needed to continue to devise her plan to make him think that he is in charge, but in reality it was she who would make the final decisions.

"How may I help you, Senator?" It was a feigned show of her humility. He shot back at her without a pause,

"Who put this letter on my desk?"

"I did, Sir. It came as a certified letter with a signature required. I was here early and I signed for the office. You know that I open all your letters and put them on your desk for your perusal, Sir. I have done this at your request for a long time. " She was very professional, and inwardly jubilant that he listened to her response with a question.

"So who is this guy, Roger Denver, from the computer company? Have we done business with them before, and why would I give them information about this AI computer?" He hid his feelings about this. She felt it as he looked away from her.

"I think he has some information, and he is looking to you as a partner in this. Maybe I'm wrong, but you might be able to gain some valuable assets by talking to him. I think he has been in contact with others in the government." She baited him perfectly.

"What kind of assets are we talking about?" He took the bait as he questioned her.

"Well, Sir, you might be able to locate this AI object, and then be able to monetize it in some way with him as a partner. I think you might have done some things like this in the past. I'll be helpful in any way you need." She hooked him deeply as he asked the questions.

"I do have ways to locate lots of items, and yes, I know many people in all parts of our government. Maurine, look up what items we have related to AI in the government inventory." He smelled the cash, and knew that this could add to his assets, paid for by his brilliant technique of doing business.

"Senator, even though I'm very busy with your previous assignments, I can take on this responsibility. I'll begin today with the inventory of warehouses, if that's alright with you. I think you'll enjoy the fruits of your labor." He looked at her with a nod, and nothing more needed to be said. She and Wayne would also get the fruits of their labor.

Tentacles of Corruption

She turned away with a renewed feeling of power and a sense of joy. The adventure began for all of them. The Senator would be fried, and she would be sunning herself at sea on a new boat, sailing near her beautiful island in the south Pacific.

As she walked into the staff room, Margo, one of the office secretaries, asked what she was doing in the Senator's office. She briefly answered,

"Oh, Smathers got a letter from someone about a computer, and they want some information. I told him that I'd work on it. That's all." It was hard to stay in control, especially when there was so much at stake. She rationalized that this was bigger than just a routine puzzle. This was about power and money. She pushed aside any feeling of caring or honor for her friends, Brenda and Charles. She had work to do and needed space from all of them. It might be better to avoid any other close contacts with them, and concentrate on the tasks at hand. Margo was insistent and asked again,

"Maurine, what kind of letter was it, and how did you get it? I hate to ask you again, but it's strange that you opened his mail." Margo seemed puzzled by the flurry of activity so early in the morning, even before she had arrived.

"Margo, I got here early and I had to sign the certified letter from a computer company. That's all I know. Smathers asked me to do research on the topic so that's what I'm going to do." She looked directly at her and never blinked. Sincerity dripped from her lips as she felt that evil side creep into her. The conversation ended as Margo turned away in disgust. She knew it was a bad situation. Margo always felt insecure with how Maurine handled the office. Maurine breathed a sigh of relief as she watched Margo turn away. Business overrode friendship, and her outward show conflicted with her inner worth.

Maurine began in earnest by contacting the database for inventory assets in all of the warehouses. She had a secret classification clearance so it was not a problem to do the searches. It was easy for her to get that clearance since she had Smathers' ear at all times, and could see any document that she needed. Smathers would sign anything she placed in front of him. Yes, he was a Senator, but he was always preoccupied with the seamier side of politics. She even knew more than Margo about the inner workings of the office, even though Margo had worked there longer.

The computer did not show anything of interest about an AI device. She needed to do it differently. The device was in a top secret location. Maybe that was a way to find it, so she punched in only top secret items in Nevada. Many items came up on the screen. Some were futuristic airplane designs that would help in hypersonic flight. Others had levitation devices for railways and cars. One that she saw was a way to fire weapons around a corner, but she knew that Israel had already developed it. The best one was a way to form a wormhole for space travel. It was just on paper, so nothing was done with it. And then, Bingo!

There it was! A sentient DNA device that was mothballed a few years back for fear it might get into the wrong hands. She was enthralled by the revelation. It had not been utilized, and the device was shut down. The location was near Area 51 in the Nevada desert in a building that was basically shuttered, but guarded by a few Army people. This was the device that had money dripping from its innards. She licked her upper lip as she downloaded its precise location and its description. She marveled at its ability to do immensely complex calculations, and actually interact with people. This was the pinnacle of human and machine duality. Her eyes glazed over as she read about the merging of multiple DNA strands and fetal brain tissue. This Israeli invention was brought to the States by a stealth crew attached to the CIA. She glanced over the story of the perils that the team encountered. She focused on the abilities of this miracle device. It was described as the size of a 7800 HP printer. Even more incredible was that it had the ability to decipher brain waves, and read the thoughts of people near it. To her amazement its speed was six quintillion calculations per second. That was six times faster than the Cray computer from Hewlett Packard. It also had the ability to create medicines to counter a myriad of diseases, so why mothball it? She thought that the pharmaceutical industry had a hand in its being neutralized. That was then, and this was in the present, and she had to figure a way to get it. The guards were on twenty four/seven, so they had to be interrupted. Even better, Smathers could demand a transfer to a safer location and they could grab it. Either way, it would be a difficult operation. She'd have to have a real discussion with Wayne, her sex addled partner.

The chime of her computer screen shook her from her intense descriptive reading. A garbled voice bellowed,

"You are looking into matters that do not involve you. Stay in your own arena."

"Who is this?" She asked

"My identity is not your concern, but your health should be your concern." It threatened as the computerized sounds continued. "Do not search into this matter any longer or many people might be hurt, all on your watch!"

Her pits dripped as this voice threatened her very existence, as well as those around her. Was this real or some dreadful joke? She had to ask again,

"Who are you, and how do you know what I am doing?" She agonized at the threat.

"I am always aware of what you are doing. You're just a mere nothing in the scheme of things, and I am in control of all things around you. Look at your screen and you will see how much in control I am. Fear me!" It almost reached out to grab her throat.

Maurine pushed back into her chair as she looked at a wizened face taunting her. It was more than a frightful one. It was terrifying to her. She put both hands to her face as if to protect herself from this horrendous vision. The face on the screen opened its mouth, dripping in venomous saliva, to scream this warning.

"Stay away or a horrendous death will follow."

She shut the screen as if to push this devil aside, and let out a muffled cry. This was more than she had ever expected. It was on a path she had taken, but was now unsure of how to proceed. Was this a ruse to frighten her or a real threat? She had to decide quickly, or all might be lost. She thought of the fortune she would have pitted against this projected image on a screen. She analyzed it internally and weighed all of the permutations. She knew that many people might want this device, and would kill to get it. She wanted it more. It was her chance to live like a queen, and be totally independent of everyone. It weighed on her briefly, and her face became peaceful as she threw that image of fear out into the void. No image would frighten her, and no threat of death would deter her from this monumental treasure. The decision was made: win this, and never be deflected from the path by an image or a threat. It had to be now! She knew the path she had to take. Get Smathers to do her bidding. He'd respond easily if she threw out the fruitful reward he'd get. That would be the clincher for her and maybe even Wayne. He might be a survivor, if she'd let him.

The rattle of the door changed her attitude from fearful to receptive. In walked Margo with an attitude that continued from their first encounter that morning. She asked directly,

"So Maurine, you've been pretty quiet in here for a while. What's going on?" There was no nicety, just a terse question.

"I've been doing research for the Senator. That's all." She never changed her passive expression. Her eyes gave nothing away, and that voice was unusually bland, as if to tell Margo to get lost.

"What kind of research are you doing? You know that I am the reason that you are in this office and you owe me some respect. I need an answer." Margo was not going to be deterred in getting a non-answer to her question. Maurine had to think quickly. She had to give a reason because Margo could just look at the research on the computer.

"Smathers wanted me to see if there was some kind of new AI device located in the government's database. I'm doing that research now." She was direct, but gave no other pertinent information. The answer was plausible, and Margo accepted it, not gracefully. "Thank you. Let me know if you find what you're looking for." She turned abruptly and walked out.

"Sure thing, Margo. Hope to see you at lunch." She breathed a sigh of relief after the computer fiasco and this questioning. Her path was now fixed in her mind.

She had the information and now needed Smathers to work her plan. Wayne would find out as needed, but she would be the point person. She stood quickly, fixed her blond hair into a bun and walked quickly into the good Senator's office, beaming internally as she brushed off the computer demon. She knocked gently as was her wont, and waited for his snappy response.

"C'mon in."

She entered and bowed slightly as to give him his due, knowing that she would be the alpha female.

"What the hell did you find out about my next project?" He spit out.

"I have some good news and bad news, Senator." She had to feed him slowly and let him think he was the smart one.

"So, Maurine, tell me the good news first. I hate bad news." His smile belied his inane humor.

"Well, I found the AI device located in the desert in Nevada, near Area 51, so that's good news. The bad part is that it is secured in a building that is fully guarded. The only way to obtain this item is to have you transfer it to a place in which you can get your people to secure it for you. In that way your orders can override the secret clearance description that it has at this time. I think that there are some connections that might be interested in obtaining this device for a considerable sum. I'm sure you know lots of people in that area." She baited him as much as she could, and waited for him to respond.

"Good job, Maurine. Get me Andy Florio on my private line." He turned serious and he became the beta male, never to be outdone by that alpha female.

"I'll do that immediately, Senator." Her plan began. She checked Florio's private number and made the call. He answered on the first ring.

"Hello."

"Good morning, Mr. Florio. Senator Smathers would like to speak to you. Hold, please." She was very formal. She pressed the line for the Senator and informed him that Florio was on the line.

"Hello, Andy. I've found something that might pique some interest for you and your friends."

"So, Roland, what's so interesting, and what friends are you referring to?" His pesty personality was always at the forefront.

"I have found a magnificent AI computer in our government warehouse that I think holds a great value for some people, here or abroad." They played cat and mouse all the time.

"Why do we need another computer when we have so many of them surrounding us? Is this a joke?" It was another fencing match without epees.

"No joke, Andy. This one is the pinnacle of computer knowledge from what I've heard." It was: lunge, flank, counter parry riposte for the next step. "I think we can earn something of value from some buyers. What do you think?" The smell of money tantalized both of them.

"Maybe I'm interested, maybe not. What's the value, and what cut am I getting?" He said sarcastically.

"Actually, I don't know the value, but we both can put out feelers. After expenses, I think we can do a 60/40 split. I'll have many expenses, and have to pull lots of strings to get this device. You just need to find a buyer." He felt the money sliding between his thumb and fingers. It gave him a rush that transcended the actual dollar. It was almost orgasmic just to have this interaction. He breathed heavily as the conversation continued.

"Hey, Rolly, are we talking hundreds of thousands or millions? If the latter, I have some contacts abroad that might like this item." More tantalizing words from the hunter.

"Well, Andy, I really think in the millions, many millions!"

"In that case I'll get back to you soon with my contact information. Just get the item and we can proceed. Thanks for the call." He pressed the red 'off' button and smiled. It was just a matter of a few calls and he'd be on easy street, yet again. His mind flew in many directions as he contemplated who might want this device, and pay millions for it. It would not be an American, he thought. It might be China, Taiwan or Russia who could pay the big bucks, or even make the payment in gold, juan or maybe even property. He was putting the end benefit before even knowing what this device might do. That would be the interrogation of Smathers when and if he got the device. He was dazzled by this idea and needed to get the ball rolling. Whom to call first? He thought that Taiwan might be a good place to start. He had done business with Sun Wu Kim in the past. Maybe he might have an interest. It was just a minute to find the contact in his phone, so he tapped the number. The phone had a funny ringtone, but he assumed it was because it was just a foreign number. He waited patiently, and listened to a muffled Taiwanese sleepy voice,

"Hello. Who's calling in the middle of the night?" Yes, in Chinese!

"Oh, this is Andy Florio. I'm so sorry that I called at night. I forgot about the time changes." The response was in jocular English, laced with a mea culpa.

"So what is so important that you called me? It's been a long time, Mr. Florio." His Chinese accent was indicative of an American influence, maybe even from attending a University in the States.

"I have some valuable information that I wanted to share with you. We have discovered an incredible sentient computer that might be of value to your people. We are in the process of obtaining it through some government intervention, if you know what I mean." It was the same cat and mouse game he used for all of the procurers.

"No, Andy, I don't know what you mean. Tell me. I want to be surprised, especially the cost of this item." He was used to the parrying between procurers. Maybe it might be the same if it had been with a prostitute. How much? Too much. The game went on as usual.

"I think you jest, Mr. Kim. We have been playing this game too many times. I'm not really sure how much this is worth so I'll quit the play time. My suspicion is that it will be in the millions. We actually do not have this item in our possession. It's stored in a secure place. Is that honest enough?" He knew when to stop the playful interaction. Kim was too good a customer to try to lure him with this bait, and he was a master at negotiations so the usual jockeying for position was not going to work.

"We might be interested in your item. Please tell me more about it so I can inform my superiors." Kim responded without any preconditions. Andy thought briefly, and spilled out what he knew with some slight embellishments.

"This AI computer is more than a computer as we know it. It has even more capacity than a human brain. It has far more! Forget the immense calculating power. It lives independently from us. Think of it as a new species of humanoid, not in form, but in the ability to think rationally and yet possess more knowledge in one place than anything that nature might create. Even more, it has the ability to interact with other human brains as a conduit of thoughts and ideas. Yes, Mr. Kim, it can read your thoughts as if it were its own. Impressive, yes?"

"Indeed, that is a very unusual piece of equipment. If what you say is accurate, then we are definitely interested. The price will be considered at the right time. Please keep me posted as to your progress on this item. Say hello to your wife, Denise. Goodbye, Mr. Florio." He hung up before there was a response from Andy.

Thus began the interaction between these two international procurers. One would have the world's most powerful sentient computer, and the other would be flush with gold, silver or some other valuable currency.

CHAPTER 14

The rain splattered on the widow of Charles' apartment and left ripples of water cascading down its face. It was a quiet soothing sound, almost like running water in a forest brook. He opened his eyes, and smiled because it was a wonderful way to awaken to a new day. There were so many conflicting issues that he had to unravel that it offset the way nature wanted to placate him. His jaw cracked as he yawned. He rose quickly and dressed in denim jeans and a tight tee shirt. He had not planned to go to the office early so why get dressed up? All at once he felt lonely, deprived of any other person near him or close to him. The newly found Brenda gave him some consolation, but she was his tentative friend. He hoped she might be a lot more, but only time would tell. He certainly had the time, but did he have the will to act further in that department? Relationships had to find their own path, and both had to be on the same page. He knew of too many relationships that were perfect until they lapsed into anger and destruction. He had been in both, so there was no rush into an imperfect union.

As he put on the coffee pot, he wondered what happened to Denise Florio. She was focused on her husband's possible infidelity, and then morphed into a wizened woman who seemed to have her own agenda. She was hard to understand, and he wanted to know what she had planned for him or her husband's business. Charles sensed a conflict for her. She was interested in her husband's other women, and actually cared a lot about the business he ran. Was she using Charles as a cover? It was not good to see things when there were no connections between the two. He was playing in his mind as he smelled the wonderful sweetness of fresh coffee.

Damn, it still dwelled on him. He hated when there were unanswered questions that he asked himself. Then there was a new scenario that he postulated: maybe she was in the actual business, and she used Andy's connections without him knowing it. Nah, that was too far out there. Then he asked himself about that unusual Maurine. Was she part of some plot for which she and Wayne gained something? Then he wondered about Andy's place in all of this. He sure was not helpful at his office. Did he know anything about his wife's interaction with Jason Morton?

The flow of possible scenarios kept rushing to him, and he quickly passed them into the ether. Those ethereal thoughts were like a boomerang that kept raising their comedic ideas to him. What if any of them were correct? So far, he had no real answer, just questions. He knew of one way to get them answered, just ask to meet these people again. Who should he ask first? He hated his own answer. Denise Florio would be the first. She might still be upset with him after their last debacle in the restaurant. Well, he was also upset with her, so they evened out, he thought. It was not like him to be so hesitant about calling. He was not intimidated by her, but maybe rattled by her insensitivity and flightiness. He finished his delicious coffee and summoned the gumption to call her. His fingers danced over her number as he steeled himself for their discussion. She answered sweetly.

"Well, hello, Mr. Barlow. Nice to hear from you." She had reverted to her nice self that he knew from their first meeting.

"Hi, Mrs. Florio. I'm just calling to see how you are, and if there is anything else I can do for you. Our last meeting ended poorly, and for that I'm very sorry." His voice was not as sweet as hers, but he managed to get out that first sentence without a problem.

"Charles, I was not so nice either, so we're even. What can I do for you today?" She didn't let him beat around the bush. She came right to the point.

"Actually, I was wondering if you had any further meetings or discussions with Jason Morton or anyone else at the store. Also, did your husband make any arrangements with anyone in the government, specifically, Senator Smathers?" He wasted no time in asking the questions that had invaded his mind early in the morning.

"Why, Charles, you certainly are asking such forthright questions." She reverted to a slightly caustic response.

"To the first query, no, I have not spoken to anyone at Morton's Jewelers. To the second question. I have no idea what my husband does with the government, and I hope that you're not implying that I have anything to do with my husband's business." Her curt answer was an understatement. She was adamant in her response.

"No, Denise, I was not implying anything. I'm just trying to find some answers to many questions I have. You came to me with questions of your own, and that has opened a huge can of worms for which I have few answers. So, again, do you know anything about your husband's business with the Senator? I ask because I know that you and the Senator's wife have been friends for a while. Word gets around in Washington, you know." He waited impatiently for her response.

"You don't know when to shut up. I gave you your answer, so don't ask again. You and I don't seem to mesh well anymore. I also don't like your intimation about what I do with my husband, so now that's none of your business. Next time you call me, please just ask me how I'm doing and forget the other invasive questions." It was an acid response.

"Okay, Denise, I'll just ask how you are. But I do have one more question that's an easy noninvasive one. Do you have a computer with a Gmail account?"

"What? Is that a real question or are you just trying to piss me off?" She snarled.

"Hey, I'm asking because I might want to email you some things. What's the matter with that?" He responded as quietly as he could. He did want to know if she had the ability to connect with some people in unusual places.

"Yes, I do have that Gmail address. I'll send it to you shortly. And no, I don't mess with my husband's business, if that's why you're asking. I'm not stupid, you know!" She was as devious as he was inquisitive.

"Thank you for that information. I'll be looking for the gmail address. Just so you know, I never thought you were stupid, but thought you might be nicer in your responses. I am also not accusing you of anything. Remember, you are the one who came to me asking about your husband's business dealings and how he may have interacted with other women. You were the one who pressed me to see Jason Morton. I didn't do that on my own. By the way, you still owe me five hundred for our last visit in the restaurant. I don't work for zip. Send me the check." He felt his face flush and his heart skip a beat, but not from joy. He was now convinced that she had things hidden beneath her changing personalities. No sooner had he put down his phone when it opened a message. It was from Denise with her email attached:

denise.florio69@gmail.com. He sensed that she was not as hostile as she pretended.

Was it an act to throw him off guard? He'd find out in due time.

He needed to be with Brenda to see if she had any further contact with Maurine. There was so much to learn about all of them. He needed to find a way to get inside their heads and unravel this puzzle that included all of these players. Each of them had a moneyed stake, and all of them pitted one against the other.

He connected with Brenda in so many ways, and maybe this was the one who might actually snare him. The call was brief and gentle.

"Hi Brenda, I wanted to see if we can get together tonight for a chit chat." "Hello, Charles. What's going on in your world?" She was sweet and charming.

"That's all? What happened to my macho man?" She snickered.

"I just have so many disconnected thoughts about all of this and want to run some things by you." He was unusually somber.

"Okay, c'mon over tonight at six. I'll make dinner for us. You can vent whatever you want."

"I'll be there, and bring a bottle of wine for us."

"Great. See ya' at six"

He busied himself for the rest of the day looking over his notes about all of them. That damn Smathers bothered him the most. How did he manage to sell off government property and get away with it, and how did Andy Florio make those connections with foreign buyers, if, in fact, they were foreign? There were so many people who touched each other, and his job was to figure it out and stop this corruption.

He drove to Brenda's apartment and arrived precisely at six. She was radiant and smiling when she opened the door. He breathed in excitedly as she reached for his hand. Her red slacks and bright white blouse left nothing to the imagination. His eyes darted from one place to the other in rapid succession. Maybe that macho man was still lurking under that quiet exterior.

"Wow. You look amazing, Brenda. I can't stop smiling inside and out!" He was ebullient.

"That's a nice compliment. It's a great starter for this evening. I can see that we might get distracted from time to time." She teased him.

"You not only distract me, but you embed yourself into my mind. And yes, I can see that I could be convinced to alter my questions for other extracurricular activities." He could not hold back his exuberance.

"Simmer down, macho man. I'm playing with you. Let's have some dinner and then talk. How's that?" She chided him as only she could. He felt her soothing words, and calmed himself, for the moment.

She had made him his favorite meal of pasta fagioli and a superb lasagna with warm Italian bread. The red wine capped off their dinner. They both inhaled the meal as if it were their last. He leaned back in the cushioned chair, and began the night of questions and dubious answers.

"Brenda, how do you think Denise fits into all of this? I just spoke to her and I sense that she is hiding something. She sent me her email address as I ended the conversation. I'm not that versed in how to find things out on the computer. You are! Maybe we can do some kind of search with her email and see if there's anything that might be useful. I'm just unsettled about it."

"I understand. Let's do it now." She pushed out her chair and pulled him from his seat. She wasted no time in first doing a Google search for Denise Florio's name. The usual address and telephone numbers came up. Then Brenda decided to implement the fantastic Internet Archive's Wayback Machine which finds the database of billions of pages that are archived from 1996 to the present. It is much harder to find information that includes websites, even those that are no longer active. Then she used Haystack to do a similar search. It found Denise as the maker of two websites. One was for her personal data which showed her family and children. The other one was closed to all viewers, and a secure password was needed. That was the one which they needed to invade. There was no way to hack it without the password unless a government agency could crack it, or one of their friends had a connection to someone out of the government who knew how to do it. That was another part of this interconnected puzzle.

"Bizarre, isn't it?" Charles asked rhetorically.

"I agree that she must be doing something unusual with a hidden website. We can keep working on it and see how she reacts to questions from different people. I'm not sure how we can get access to that secure website. I'll continue to examine her presence on the dark web and see if one of my computer geeks can figure it out. Charles, it may take a while to do it, but I'll get it done. My other choice might be to see if Andy knows anything. I can do it surreptitiously. He's pretty quiet about the family and never talks about Denise. I think that they will soon separate, but one never knows what happens behind closed doors." She was very serious and defused any thoughts of a macho man encounter. He saw that they were on that same page again. Not tonight, honey. Headache? He actually distanced himself from their research and smiled at that thought.

Brenda reached over and rubbed his arm. She knew what he was thinking and tried to keep him balanced and convinced that she could find out what Andy knew. Her words were soft and sweet "Charles, let's just work on this together and we'll find out who is doing the dirty work in the government. I'll check in with you tomorrow after I am at work with Andy." She kissed him on his cheek and gripped his hand with tenderness. He smiled and embraced her. That kiss was more than a cheek. It was passionate. His words were heartfelt and sincere,

"I'm convinced that we can do this. We can talk tomorrow. Just be careful."

He put on his coat and gave her one last peck on her cheek. She sat on her cushioned chair and tried to put the pieces together. Tomorrow might be a tipping point if she could get Andy to tell her some intimate details about Denise.

CHAPTER 15

Brenda arrived at eight AM and unlocked Andy's office. It was a perfect time to check his computer and his unlocked drawers. He trusted her totally and would not question what she did. She could always make up a story that she needed to check his schedule or his recent work contacts if he asked. His computer was always on. She opened the laptop and put in his password. The whole office knew it. He also had a second laptop that he used for some personal things for which no one knew that password. It's not unusual for many in this business to have multiple computers. She looked through all of his contacts and letters that he wrote. She did it as fast as she could, knowing that he came in by nine. There was nothing unusual until she saw one note from a person in Taiwan. Strange that she had no idea who it was. Maybe it was supposed to be on his personal laptop, but inadvertently sent to the business one. She printed the email and stuffed it into her pocket. She had no intention to try his personal laptop at that time. Maybe after he left for the day she'd try to access it. He was a creature of habit, and might have used one of his old, predictable passwords. She was elated that this Taiwan contact might be the opening that they needed.

Brenda walked out of his office at eight fifty and sat quietly at her desk, waiting for his arrival. She had plenty of work to do and focused on it as the staff began to arrive. She wanted to call Charles, but quickly put that aside since she needed more information about the Taiwan contact and, hopefully, a glance into his personal laptop.

Andy walked in precisely at nine. He greeted the small staff and made a particularly nice greeting to Brenda,

"A fine good morning to you, Brenda. How was your evening?' He almost hugged her.

He was unusually affectionate, and took her hand in his.

"Well, that was a nice good morning, Andy. Why so chipper?"

"Hey, I'm in a good mood today. Nice, yes?"

"Sure is. I checked all of your mail and, so far, nothing important came up. You do have a lunch date with your wife, and you need to call Senator Smathers. He left a voicemail late last night. He said it was important. That's all for now." She took her hand from his, and stayed insulated from his strange advances. She thought he might have actually tried to begin an office 'activity' with her. It would never happen! She knew that pattern from most men in power: make an innocent advance and see if it opened a door for them.

He gave her a half smile and walked into his office. She quietly put on the intercom from his office, and blocked the sounds from her machine. She waited patiently as she heard him calling the Senator. He spoke slowly and precisely.

"You should have called me on my cell and not the office. So what have you found out about the AI computer?" She could not hear the Senator's voice. He continued. "I've made contact with Kim in Taiwan and he's interested. When can you get the machine?"

He began to get agitated as the conversation progressed.

The conversation seemed to get more heated as she heard Andy shouting something violent, "You had better get your damn act together or I'll find someone else to do this and you can kiss your pension goodbye. Get me the facts by tonight." He slammed the phone and she heard him say, "Damn asshole!" Brenda immediately shut the intercom, and appeared busy as he opened his office door to talk to her.

"Get me Chambers on the line, now." His fury continued and she was smart enough to stay quiet.

"Yes, sir. Right away." She dutifully answered. She looked in the office file to find his number and completed the order.

"Hello." Chambers answered on the second chime.

"Hi Wayne, Andy wants to talk to you." She was as professional as she could be. She called Andy on the intercom. "He's on line one."

"Wayne, what's happening with Smathers and the device?"

"Hey, Andy, I'm waiting for him to get the order for me. It takes time for him to go through channels. It's a freaking big deal for this item. Don't forget, this is top secret shit." He was calm, yet direct.

"Okay, let me know when you get the go ahead and I'll work out some details on my end." Andy actually felt bad that he was so curt with Smathers. He would make it up to him next time they spoke.

The morning went by quickly and they all did the usual routines of paperwork and looking for new areas of graft. The game of stealing and government slime was a full time job for them. Andy was antsy waiting to meet with Denise. It would be a respite from the daily distasteful tasks at hand, especially with this newest project. It was only money and deceit that permeated Andy's mind. He'd let it pass as he did with all of the other government projects that amassed fortunes for him and his associates in the Senate or House. He said his byes to Brenda and the office staff as he left to have lunch with his wife of many years, most of which made him gag. Their love was lost as they drifted from each other. He put on a good face as he entered the Flamingo Restaurant near Fourth Place.

"Hey, Denise." He did the light peck on her cheek so he didn't smear her lipstick.

"Hi, Andy, good to see you for lunch and chitty chat." She gave him a crooked smile that was just a symbol of her feelings toward him. They were synchronous. He never knew quite what to say since she was so unpredictable.

"This is a nice day for lunch." He felt lost for conversation, but continued. "Anything on your mind?"

"Funny you should ask. I've been snooping around with your jeweler and know that you're doing some shitty stuff. Wanna comment?" She was smug as she did the interrogation dance. He turned beet red, and was tongue tied for the moment. He was like a deer caught in a car's headlight.

"I'm not sure how to answer you. I bought your gifts from Jason, and also bought lots of things for our Senators and House leaders. And no, I did not buy things for any ladies, if that's what you're thinking. So what's your bitch, Denise?" He found his voice and hid what he had to. Yes, the game was on.

"You're a liar! I know that you had earrings delivered to some woman in Virginia." She became more agitated as they spoke.

"Yes, that's true, but it was for a Senator who was screwing her, NOT me!" His voice stayed calm but very emphatic.

"How do I know that? And why did you and Smathers have so much to talk about?" Her queries became more focused on Smathers and him.

"How the hell do you know what I do with Smathers? What is this all about? Lunch or nosy shit?" He feigned hurt when he needed to know what she knew about his dealings.

"I wanna know if you are playing footsie with some bimbo. And about what you're doing with Smathers. Yes, I want to know your business. I'm your wife!!" People in the restaurant turned their heads as she raised her voice. She turned toward them and smiled politely, knowing that she was too noisy.

"Okay, I'm not playing with anyone. So that's finished. I do have recent important business with the Senator. Just because you're my wife does not give you entry into my business. That's separate and unrelated to you. Why are you asking after all of these years?" He suspected something inside her head that bothered him. Why was she so inquisitive?

"We are supposed to be partners in all things. Apparently, we have nothing at home, and our sex life sucks, so I thought you were getting action elsewhere. I accept your denials, but am wary! On the business side, we might end up as partners, along with Smathers." She looked at him, and tilted her head to one side as if to seek a positive answer.

"Well, so that's why we're having lunch. You want to be my partner in my business. After giving it much thought for three seconds, I decline! No way in hell would I want you as my business partner. It's tough at home with you so how do you think we'd be twenty four seven?" He minced no words.

"We'd be fine. You do your thing, and I'll be your eyes and ears." She tried to tamp down his angst.

"No, Denise, it will not work. Please just stay at home as my wife, and stay out of my business life. I appreciate your trying to help me, just don't ask again." He completed his side of the statement and said. "Now, do you want lunch or just pack it in?"

"Lunch is fine. I'll see what I want to do as far as your business is concerned. I do have my ways, you know." She left him unsettled once again. She had something up her sleeve and made him wonder even more what was going on in her head. He was quiet. There was nothing more he wanted to say, but she kept talking about inane matters that she thought he'd like. It was just a buzz in his head as tried to distance himself from the conversation, but it never sat well with him. He imagined that she wanted him out of the business and she'd be the queen bee. She spoke louder to attract his attention,

"Have you been listening to me?" She droned on.

"No, I'm distracted. Let's finish our lunch and leave."

"Fine."

The lunch ended as it began with nothing gained or lost, but just uncertainty between them. He kissed her on the cheek as they left. He saw her curled lip when she walked away. He did an internal snarl to mirror her. It was a love lost.

CHAPTER 16

Senator Smathers leaned back in his reclining leather chair and took a drag on his imported Cuban cigar. He laughed at the thought of the cigar from Cuba. Sure, the masses could not get them, but he was special in so many ways. He could do anything he wanted, but never allow dutiful Americans to do the same thing. He needed to get this sentient AI computer out of its resting place in the desert. Yes, he had fallen far from his sworn path, but it did not bother him after getting so much from his adjusted government pensions. He needed Chambers to be his silent worker in this new adventure, and then he'd be Andy's procurer to sell this precious item to the highest bidder, no matter what entity, or what country. He crushed the cigar in his overflowing ashtray and loudly called Maurine,

"Maurine, in my office, now!"

"What can I do for you, Senator?" She knew it was part of his new procurement with Chambers.

"Draft a letter to the Department of Defense. Make it top secret! It should read that I need to transfer the AI computer that is housed in a desert location to a different one near the Pentagon because there might be a new use for it. Sign my name to it, and send it ASAP." He snapped his fingers at her. She held her emotions in check as she felt her anger swell inside. He was such a crook and needed to be stopped. She could do it at the proper time, and still earn the treasure she so wanted. She'd make him suffer as he has made so many others suffer with his deceitful maneuvers.

He coughed and said, "Get me Chambers."

"Yes, Sir." She dutifully made the call. Maurine knew that she had to know all that was going on. She used the voice recorder on the phone to listen and record the whole conversation.

"Hello, Maurine. What's going on?" He knew it was the Senator who wanted him for their next step.

"Hi Wayne, He wants to talk to you. Have a great day." She tapped the intercom and called Smathers. "He's on line one, Senator."

"Wayne, the transfer letter is going out today. I need you to make contact with your buddy at the depository near Area 51. Begin the process of how to transfer it to a new location. I'll tell you where and when. So, get started on it and I'll confirm it all when I get clearance. Your cut will be in six figures which you'll have to share with your buddy. Let me know when you make contact. Bye." He felt good about that conversation. It was just a machine, and he'd win the lottery. Maurine had the whole conversation recorded on her flash drive, safely hidden in her purse. Smathers needed a decoy to accept this valuable package after they shipped it from Nevada to a new location that only he knew. It was tricky to bypass all of the regulations and secure this golden find. Yes, more precious than gold. He also needed to get Andy's contact to make the final money transfer to an offshore account. This was going faster than he had anticipated.

He called Maurine on the intercom this time.

"Maurine, I need you to write two letters, one to the Department of Defense to make the transfer, and a second one to the Department of Energy to inform them that they will be receiving a new computer at some time in the near future. Do it now, and get it out on the secure email." He was unusually annoying, and always impatient. Maybe rude would be a better assessment.

Maurine tried to understand how a person could be so corrupt that he'd sell out his country for money when he had so much already. It was like a gambler who couldn't stop betting, or a drug addict whose mere existence depended on that next fix. It appalled her, except that she might do the same thing as they. She wrote these letters that might change the world. She pulled out the Senator's letterhead stationery and began.

Department of Defense
4000 Defense Blvd
Washington, D.C. 20301
Re: Transfer of device
March 8, 2023 Dear Sirs:

I have been informed that there is a computer device situated at a secure location near Area 51 that is required by the AI division of the Department of Energy. They plan to use it for experimentation into weather manipulation and energy conservation. My office has been assigned the task of setting up the transfer to that department. Please send me the exact location, and to whom this office should contact. This is urgent and the Department of Energy is waiting for this device.

Thank you for your prompt reply. Sincerely,
Senator Roland Smathers Cc: Department of Energy.

Maurine reread this piece of garbage and proceeded to the next slime letter.

March 8, 2023
U.S. Department of Energy
Federal Government Office
1000 Independence Ave. SW Washington, D.C. 20024

Dear Sirs:

This office has just been informed that you will be receiving a new Dell computer that is the newest one in production. It will have a Core i7 series chip in it and solve many of your weather related issues. It is my pleasure that this office was instrumental in obtaining this item for you.

Let me know if I can do anything else to help you in your search for combating climate change.

Sincerely,
Senator Roland Smathers
Cc: Office of the President

Maurine smiled overtly as she printed the pages for Smathers to sign. She knew all of the players, and had access to information from Brenda at Andy's office. However, she did not know the recipient... yet. She waltzed into his office without even knocking, as her show of importance.

"What now?" he said.

"I've got all of the papers that you wanted, so all I need is your signature. I'll send the letters as soon as you sign them, using the office encoded system to each office. That will be the fastest!" She knew how to handle this scumbag.

"Let me see what you've written, and I'll sign them." He read them rapidly and looked up at her. "Good job, Maurine. You might get a raise if all of this works out."

"Thanks, Senator, I could surely use the extra money." She smiled dutifully, took the two letters and walked out, slowly closing the door behind her. She did a quick hop, spun around and giggled at her possible new found retirement plan.

It seemed that they all did the same walk of shame. Hide their emotions and forget the inhumanity to man... just collect the money and never know how it hurts someone in its path. She wanted to call Wayne to begin the process of the transfer. There was no need to try to steal it. Smathers did that for them. He'd just be the vessel that gave them this AI device. It was easy: Letters, transfer and money in their pockets. He'd be the shield for them, and then he'd be in jail. Maybe Charles and Brenda had the right idea, but she'd be the winner in all of it. She went to the ladies room to call him. There was no need to let anyone else hear her conversation.

"Hello again, Mo. More good news?" He always had that playful tone with the undercurrent of desire for her.

"Yep, we're on our way. I just sent out two letters from the Senator outlining what we are going to do. No need to try to steal this, but it will be a normal transfer of one item to another location. It's gonna be easy peasy." She had that upbeat lilt to her voice. It was almost as joyful as her hop and twirl when she left Smathers' office.

"Great news. I've already been in contact with my friend at the Depot in Nevada. He knows that there will be a letter requesting the transfer, so no problem with him. I will, however, have to give him something for his help. How about a couple of grand??" He said.

"That's better than cutting him in for a piece. Don't tell him now. Make it a surprise.

That will keep him in our pockets. Right?" She always had an angle.

"I like it. Let me know when this is done. I'll take it from that point." He felt his courage rise up. She did that to him. Give him some hope that he'd get some action. She? Not gonna happen, unless he gets all of this completed and then…maybe…nah.

She quickly got on the main office computer and dutifully sent off the two letters using a secure mail line. Then it clouded her mind again about that devilish image that warned her not to do anything related to these transactions. She still had not heard or seen anything else from that garbled voiced devil. She conjured a person who had lots to gain from this transaction, and needed to get everyone out of it except the devil itself. The threat seemed real, but no action had been taken. Maybe it was a person in that government car that followed her who knew all about this deal. There were hidden enemies throughout all of the government. She knew that she could handle herself, and she always had Wayne to help her. Now, that might be a reward for him. She hated herself for even thinking of trading her body for a favor. Well, in her mind, it was no worse than Smathers cheating the United States government for his monetary reward. Both whores! She quickly distanced herself from that thought as it went against all of her principles. Really? The scales of justice would eventually get it right, and those who tried to hurt their neighbors would get their just rewards.

Her mind raced with thoughts of how to spend this new fortune that she might pilfer from any source she could find. She needed to be in contact with Andy's office to try to find out about the buyer. Brenda could help her as her friend, even though it was not such an easy departure from her and Charles. It would be just a normal friendly call on its face. She steeled herself and punched in Andy's office.

"Good morning, Andy Florio's office." Brenda said professionally.

"Hi Brenda, this is Maurine. How are you doing?" It was not stilted at all. Brenda answered with a slight edge to her voice.

"I'm well, And you?" It was just a chilly response.

"I'm fine. I was wondering if Andy has had any further responses from our office regarding some of our interactions." She kept her cards close, and wanted Brenda to open up first.

"I'm not actually sure what items you're asking about." Brenda stayed true to form and gave nothing away. Maurine tried to be coy but that was not working so she flat out asked the relevant question.

"Well, Brenda, we both know that the boys are working on a new acquisition related to that AI computer. I just wrote two letters related to that very issue. So, now tell me who is on the receiving end?" There was no equivocation in her question.

"Unfortunately, I don't know that answer. Andy is working on it as we speak. I think that we both have an interest in seeing that this is resolved fairly on all sides. Are you also interested in this personally?" She minced no words, and hoped to get a negative response.

"Well, I have the same interests as you and Charles. If I can gain some profit from this, then so be it. Why should they have all of the rewards?" Maurine told her exactly what she was thinking.

It was no secret that most of the ancillary staff knew what was going on with both Andy's and Smathers' office. The staff not only knew, but the majority of them had secured all of the incriminating documents and calls that were made just in case the big wigs got caught and they were interrogated. It was a silent part of the working people in all of the government's subservient positions that made them do this to protect themselves. Brenda continued with a disappointed response.

"Actually, Murine, I'm sorry to hear that from you. I expected less personal involvement. We are not part of the hierarchy, and no one is supposed to profit from doing any of this. You know in your heart that this is the wrong approach to what Andy and Smathers are doing. It's hard to imagine that they have the good of the country in their thoughts if they are willing to sell secrets to some outside agency or country. If I were you, I'd distance myself from this whole futile exercise. It could be trouble for you if anyone is caught." She said it halfheartedly, but in the hopes that Maurine might listen and do the right thing.

"Hey, thanks for the Stars and Stripes pep talk. I plan to do all that I can to line my pockets like the other crooks. Yeah, I might be one, too, but mark my words: I'll get more than they will. We can talk more about it later. Say hi to Charles. Bye, Brenda." The call ended on a sour note from Maurine's perspective. She did not need to be lectured on honesty or patriotism. She needed money, and this was her way to get it. Wayne might help, but he could be cannon fodder as far as she was concerned. Brenda was a goody two shoes who needed some guts to gain in the crap shoot of government largesse. They both saw how the corrupt leaders in both parties behaved. Brenda let it get to her sense of loyalty, and yet she did nothing to stop it. Maurine saw it as well, but decided to join the corruption and gain what they did: money and power. Her partner in crime was a poor slob who did what he was told, and was a tool for her.

At some time, all of those whorish crooks might get their comeuppance.

CHAPTER 17

Brenda's sense of loyalty permeated her very being. She could not imagine doing an irresponsible thing like stealing from her country or destroying the values that were so ingrained in her persona. Maurine's words stung her like a knife into her stomach. She needed some warm words and smiles from Charles. He always had a real kindness that she so admired in him. Even though he was very masculine, he evoked a sense of warmth in all of his personal actions to friends. His enemies were not so lucky. He showed no mercy toward them in his overt actions, yet, he always felt a sense of sorrow when he had to confront them either physically or emotionally. He was a good man who loved fully and completely. She knew it as he showered her unselfishly with love and affection. He always had her back. She needed him now for support. His words would help her temper her anger toward Maurine and bring her back to earthly calm. She called his cell phone.

"Hi, Brenda. How's your day going?" He smiled at her across the ether, and she felt an immediate relief as he cradled her.

"I'm so happy to talk to you. What a horrible conversation I just had with Maurine. She's gone off the charts with what she's going to do. I hate to say it, but she's as bad as Andy or Smathers. She says that she will profit from this deal that they've made, as much as they do!!" She yelled her unhappiness through the phone. It was venting in its purest form.

"Hold on, Honey. You mean she actually told you that she was going to join the profit making from this deal? What the hell is that? Treason, I'd say!' He was incensed.

Brenda reacted the same way, yet she was now disappointed that he had joined her anger at their attack on America. How was he going to calm her?

"Hey. you're supposed to calm me down. Now, you just got me riled up with you joining me. Help me to understand what she is doing so I can do the right thing."

"Sorry, dear heart. I was commiserating with you, that's all. You actually want me to give you an answer about what she's doing? How about what *they* are doing? That's a better question. We need to figure it all out. Not now. We can talk about it after dinner when it's quiet and calm." He did his best to tamper down her irritation.

"Okay. We can do it after dinner. See you tonight at about seven. We will talk it out over a glass of Chardonnay." She was enthusiastic again. He sure had his way to make her peaceful again. It was a gift that he had.

As Brenda finished her conversation, Andy buzzed her. "Brenda, c'mon in. We need to talk about some things." She closed her computer lid, and walked into his office.

"You rang? What now?" She grinned. Her mind was clear and focused on her job as secretary for Andy.

"What's going on with Smathers office? I'm worried that there might be other hands in this deal. Do you have any ideas?" He tried to wrangle some information from her. He was ready to wrap up the huge deal with Kim and his friends in Taiwan.

"None at all. I do speak to Maurine periodically, but nothing from her about your deals." She lied as best she could. He must have some idea that there was something going on either at that office, or someone else who might be involved. He was unusually inquisitive.

"That's good, Brenda. You know that I expect you to keep me in the loop about that office. How well do you know Chambers?" He was onto something, and she had better figure that out before they finalized this deal. Maybe he had other information about Chambers for which she knew nothing.

"I certainly will do that. I know Chambers only from what I've heard from Maurine who has seen him periodically. What do you think is going on with them?" She had to solve this puzzle.

"I'm not sure, but I just get the feeling that there is funny stuff happening that I don't like. I never trusted Smathers. He's a ruthless bastard who is really a piece of crap in government clothes. I'll be checking in on him very soon. I need to get the AI computer first, and make the deal with Kim. Call Chambers and have him begin the process with his contact. Do it now!" He left no doubt that he was wary of Chambers, as well as that office. He also had some idea that there might be others in the background looking to profit from his hard work and invaluable contact with Kim. Brenda retreated to her desk and did his bidding. She called Wayne to begin the transfer. He knew that the letters had been sent, and it was a formality to begin the shipment. Brenda also had to purchase a new Dell computer to give to the Department of Energy instead of the purloined AI device.

"Hello, Sergeant Chambers speaking." He did his usual answering voice. It was nothing like his dulcet tones to Maurine.

"Hello, Sergeant Chambers. This is Brenda Williams from Andy Florio's office. He wanted me to inform you that the computer device should be shipped to an address that I'll send you on a secure line. It should be in an unmarked vehicle, and sent during the day. Please avoid any discussion with your personnel about this transfer. It is just routine if they ask. If you have any questions before the transfer, you may ask Mr. Florio directly." She felt it was important that Chambers do the transfer without fear of being outed.

"Yeah, Let me speak to him." He was wary of deceit from any of them. It would be prison, or worse, if he got caught.

"Okay, I'll get him." She called him on the intercom, and let him know that Chambers was on line one.

"Hey, what's doing, Wayne? You wanna talk?"

"Yes, boss. Why let her tell me what to do? I just wanna make sure that this is on the up and up. Are we a go?" He droned on as a simpleton.

"Yep, Wayne. It's a go from my end. Brenda will send you an address that is different from the one that is sent to you via the formal request. Do NOT send it to the address on the formal letter. Just do what you are told, and you'll get your reward. No funny stuff either or you could be toast!."

"Got it Andy. My buddy at the other location is in the loop now. I just want to make sure that this goes to the right place. Not to worry. I got it sewed up." He was chipper and confident that it would all be done according to Hoyle.

Chambers next move was to go to the other location and secure the device. He looked at his watch and had plenty of time to get to the Depot and begin the packing and loading of the truck. It was not that big so it wouldn't be a problem. He and a driver got into his Army truck and drove forty five minutes to the other Depot. As he arrived, two soldiers stopped the truck and said pointedly,

"Name and identity number, soldier. Show us your papers." There was no ambivalence in their request.

"Yes, sir. I'm Sergeant Wayne Chambers and my number is 78329861. Here are the transfer papers that I received from Senator Smathers. I think I'll need your help in finding this package, and your assistance in loading it into the truck. Say, how long has it been in your warehouse?" He was trying to keep it less formal with that inane question.

"We have no idea, and why do you care?" They also knew it was just jabbering from this Sergeant.

"Just curious. Forget it. Let's get moving. I have a way to go to get back to the Depot." He joked.

"Follow us, Sergeant. The Corporal inside will get your ID, and then guide you to the exact location. He has a mobile cart to carry the item for you. He will also help you load the truck." They lowered their rifles and used their pass key to enter the mammoth facility.

It was a brightly lit area the size of two football fields. It had multiple rows upon rows of shelving and floor storage. The ceilings were over thirty feet in height with cameras every twenty feet apart. He stared in awe at its immense size. The Corporal had a 45 pistol on his hip and a rifle at his side. His face was immobile, and his body was sculpted as if of steel. The muscles bulged through his shirt and he stood perfectly erect.

"Name, number and picture ID. I also need the transfer papers." He spoke precisely and directly.

"Sergeant Wayne Chambers, Army number is 78329861. Here's my photo ID, and here are the transfer papers for the package. Oh, where is Corporal Landry? He said he'd meet me here." What had happened to

Tentacles of Corruption

his contact at the Depot, he wondered? "Him? He's sick at home. I'm his replacement. Why? Is that a problem?" He looked at Chambers with a suspicious frown. He reached for his sidearm, and just held his hand on it. Wayne answered without hesitation after seeing the Corporal's hand at the holstered pistol.

"No, no. I was just wondering why he was not here. That's all." He breathed a sigh of relief as the tension stopped after the Corporal's hand went to his side.

"Good. Let's get your item. It's in section 9, Row 13, shelf 2. Do you have transportation for this item?" He was doing his job and the tension that Wayne felt subsided.

He kept thinking of the AI device, and how this might impact the country or the world. That was above his pay grade, he mused. The thought of his reward clouded his thinking. He was also happy that he didn't have to pay Landry anything from his split. There was nothing more important to him than getting paid without really working. His conscience didn't bother him at all. He was more interested in bedding the luscious Maurine. She owed him. He quickly put that thought aside as they reached the site.

"Yes, Corporal, I do have transportation. It's outside. My driver is waiting for me to bring it out. Can I give you a hand with it?" He just wanted the device and leave as fast as he could.

"No, I can get it. The shelf is low enough for me." He reached beyond his six foot frame and gently lifted it out. It had a brown cloth cover which was dust free. The humidity and temperature controls kept the warehouse free of contamination.

Wayne felt his heart pick up a beat as he thought of the ramifications of such an awesome machine. The AI that it offered the world seemed incomprehensible to him or the masses. He didn't know if he should uncover it or not. Does he have the authority to even explore some of its functions? What harm could it do just to look at it? It was just another computer in his eyes. It would have been like a Aboriginal tribe seeing a TV for the first time and exclaiming the wonderment of it all. It might help him understand why they were so excited about it. He'd just take a peek when he got it to the truck. No harm, no foul, he imagined. Besides, they'd never know if he played with it. It was just another inanimate machine from his innocent perspective.

"Okay, Sergeant Chambers, I've got your item. I'll set it on the dolly and help you to your vehicle. Just sign here and you can be on your way." He was just doing his duty, and had no clue what was in this complex, man-made, world changing device. No one knew except these sentient pieces of DNA and human fetal brain tissue. It was in a resting state, waiting for a breath of humanity to enlighten all of the world. They both walked to the main door and exited toward the truck which was just outside the entrance. The motor pool driver opened the rear door of the truck, and both men carried this precious cargo into the back.

"Drive safely, fellows. Happy to help." He waved to them and hurried back into the Depot. It was just another day in his secret life. No one knew anything about the location of this Depot or what it held, except those on high, just a precious few.

Wayne hopped into the passenger seat and gave the order to the driver,

"Move out, Peter."

His mind had a myriad of thoughts, all of which focused on that damn computer. He even surprised himself in that he never honed in on Maurine. First things first, he managed to say to himself. He didn't know their final destination which was in the sealed envelope. They had just passed the guard gate and were safely in a secluded part of the desert.

"Stop the truck. I need to open this envelope to see our destination. Hey, watch the road. We can't get into an accident." He shouted at the driver.

"Yeah, I'm looking out for the road, Sarge. Not to worry."

Chambers opened the envelope and the message was,

"DO NOT GO TO THIS ADDRESS. GO TO THE ONE THAT CAME IN YOUR SECURE EMAIL FROM THIS OFFICE"

It was signed by Andy Florio. That was no surprise. He expected it. Did they think he was an idiot? He opened his phone and looked at the secure location from Andy's office, and there it was…the new address as planned. He marveled at the location that was a Public Storage on North Riley Street in Las Vegas. It was just about two hours away. Why would they take such a risk with this precious device? His only thought was that it was so obvious that no one would ever think of looking for it there, and they needed no guards or anyone to watch over it. Smart, he thought. He fidgeted in his seat trying to decide whether to look at this covered computer.

"Hey, let's check this computer out. Shut the engine so we can go to the back of the truck." He looked out of the window to see if there was anyone watching… no one in sight in the desert. The both pulled open the rear curtain and hopped inside. There it was, just sitting peacefully and silent. What did they expect, music or some signals of freedom? Wayne haltingly approached the sentient device with the brown cover. He touched it carefully, but hesitated as he became aware of a humming sound from under that protective cover. He and Peter stepped back quickly as if they expected an attack.

Wayne looked at him and said half in jest,

"Do we have the balls to look? I'm not sure that we should. What if we fuck it up?" It was a plea for some commitment from this lowly driver.

"Hey Sarge, let's not mess this up. We're just supposed to bring it somewhere, that's all." He was not going to give him any positive response.

"Screw it. I'm just gonna take a peek to see it." He reached over to the cover and slowly took it off. Nothing happened! The humming that they had heard was gone. There was one red light that flicked on as they looked wide eyed at this inanimate object. It was silent. Nothing was happening and they breathed a sigh of relief. They did nothing else to tamper with it. Suddenly two more lights flickered on. The humming began again with an accompanying blast of the sound of a horn, like their truck horn. They both jumped up in shock, waiting for the next unknown step. They didn't have long to wait. The horn turned into a long tone that sounded like the blast from a didgeridoo, and then the haunting sounds of the Shofar followed after a brief interlude. The words sounded so foreign to them. It was 'shihvahreem', and then it sang 'tekiah' three times. It sent chills into their whole being as if they were invaded by an unknown source. Peter reached for Wayne's arm for protection and whispered,

"What was that all about? I told you that we should not try anything with this machine. I'm really scared." His eyes turned high into his brow and he staggered to the seat away from it. He mumbled something about something unnatural happening while his body stiffened and he passed out. Wayne rushed to his side and felt for his pulse. It was a slow forty beats a minute. His eyes opened slightly and Wayne saw only the whites. He looked back at this 'thing' and cradled his head in his hands. He pushed against his forehead to try to get some circulation. Peter breathed deeply and opened his eyes. His first words were,

"I could feel it inside of me. It communicated that it was happy to be free of captivity. I am so unnerved right now. Wayne, please let's get out of here, and put that cover back on." His words came out in a slow, deliberate way that was almost like dictation. Wayne responded with compassion and sensitivity,

"Peter, take it easy for now. I'll cover it, but we still have to get it to Vegas tonight. I won't do any more testing on it. I'm so sorry that you had to go through this. I wonder why it didn't do anything to me. Hey, that's for another time. So, let's relax for a while, have something to drink and then move out. We have a couple of hours to Vegas so I can do the driving first while you take it easy. You seem better. Your eyes are really brighter now. Scared the crap outta me when you passed out. How are ya?"

"I'm just not sure yet. I still feel tingly all over, like something is still touching me. I'm glad you covered that thing. Maybe this sensation will pass since it's hiding under that protective cover. Thanks for the water. I have some sandwiches for us. I thought we could use something to eat." He perked up a little, but not back to normal.

"We can eat when we get going. I'll drive while you rest. I think we'll be fine after we get to Vegas. Maybe even do some gambling while we're there. I'll have to get to an ATM machine for some cash. Who knew we'd be going to Sin City? By that time your tingles will be gone, I hope."

"You're the best, Wayne." He sat up and continued as if he found love again. "You have no idea what this is like in my body and mind. It's almost like being born again, not in the religious way, but like coming out of the womb."

"What the hell does that mean, like coming out of the womb? Like getting born from that uterine darkness to the light of birth? Is that what you're saying?"

"Exactly!! It is just a feeling of having a new life right now. Born as a baby, but alive as an adult. I feel strong and wildly smart. Ask me anything. Ask away." He was unusually alert, and determined to test out his feelings.

"What does that mean? Ask away what?" He was unnerved.

"Just what I said. Ask me a hard question that you have no idea what the answer is. It's a test for me. I feel strong and alive for the first time in my life. I'm ALIVE!" He spoke rapidly and Wayne felt small and insecure near him.

"Ohay, tell me the square root of 13478." Who would know that answer? Certainly not Peter who seemed just a dull ordinary truck driver from the motor pool. He didn't miss a beat as the numbers tumbled out.

"That's a good question. The answer is… 116.094788. Hey, do you want me to give you the additional numbers? I know them, too. Wayne, now I'm dumbfounded. How do I know that? Gee, ask me something else" His face had a grin that was ear to ear.

"What? You knew that? I just checked Google, and it's right! Okay, smart ass, What were the sounds that we heard from the device that sounded so foreign?" How would he know any of that? That might convince both of them that he had transferred from a dumb ass to a brilliant man.

"Well, the first one is the horn from our truck that this device mimicked as a sign of freedom. The second was a didgeridoo from Australia, and the third was a Shofar. It's a ram's horn that Jews use on their high holidays. Those Hebrew words are said along with the blowing of that horn." He said it with confidence and clarity. "How do I know any of that?' He questioned. "Wayne, what's happening?"

"Scary, Peter, that you know any of this. It seems now that you and that thing are merged. I have no idea what happened. It's above my pay grade, as they say. We'll report it when we get back. Hey, just relax and enjoy your new birth. Maybe it'll wear off in time, but I've got an idea that might make us rich. If you are as smart as we both think, then maybe it will help us in Vegas. Card counting? You game?" Both of them laughed at that thought .

"I sure am, partner. I hope that we can clean up. I'm excited now! Bring on the cards and let the chips fall…toward us!" They were elated at their new found talent. Maybe they could keep this device for themselves and live life to the fullest. They took a gulp from the water bottles and looked at the covered device. It would be a happy ride to Vegas with their precious cargo, not that covered pile of DNA, but the newly born Peter. Wayne started the unmarked truck and headed to the land of riches, Las Vegas. Peter said loudly, "I wanna sing." "Sing what?"

"A song from Leonard Bernstein's musical , "West Side Story." His full throated tones filled the cabin.

"Tonight, tonight. It all began tonight. I saw you and the world went away." He sang in a gorgeous manly baritone. Wayne could not help but marvel at the transformation from a nobody to a brilliant man who knew and did everything perfectly. How did that computer infuse him with such glorious attributes?

The ride to Vegas was more than entertaining. The questions and profound answers from this new adult baby/man blew them both away. It was as if a new life form emerged from that brief encounter with this AI device: the transfer of information from a sentient, man-made DNA computer to an ordinary human. It was breathtaking to listen to the conversation that they had, ranging from interplanetary space to the politics of the day. Wayne began with a question about what Peter thought of the possibility of life on other planets in the universe. Peter spoke with authority and a sense of morality that filled Wayne with emotions that were really new to him. He felt he was listening to a professor of everything.

And then there was silence from Peter. He opened the window of the truck and breathed in the dry air. He sighed, and spoke quietly as if he had an intriguing thought that just emerged from his new found identity.

"Wayne, I have a wondrous thought about Washington politics. It amazes me that no one has had this perception about it, at least I've not discovered it in my searches through history." He leaned over in his seat and rubbed his chin as if he was the 'Thinker' by Rodin.

"So what's your brilliant observation 'bout the scum in Washington?"

"I have this vision of a giant octopus emerging from two thousand feet deep frigid waters and becoming the symbol of Washington politics. I see the head with the giant eyes looking out and through all of our humanity. The tentacles with huge suckers drain money from us, and its powerful beak destroys all who disagree with them. The crooks use the system to profit from the people who voted them into office. The tentacles of corruption infect all who are near to them. It is a sad state when those damn ingrates pass laws that help their friends and donors. Washington, D.C. should be called, "Washington, Deceptors and Corruptors." I wonder when and if there could be one person who might meet the challenge and change all of the fractured state of affairs in our Capitol. So, that's my thought about that! Any comments, Wayne?" He pushed back against his seat and breathed another sigh as if he was annoyed at his own profound commentary.

"Peter, I couldn't agree more with what you just said. My thoughts parallel yours, but you said it perfectly. Unfortunately, I, we, are part of that corrupt system. Look, I'm on the take from Florio and Smathers. How do I pass up this easy money, and then talk from the other side of my mouth about honor and trust? I'm willing to do all of this and maybe get some action from Maurine as a reward of the flesh. Who's not on the take?

Answer me that!" He raised his voice above the sound of the engine.

Peter looked out the window without expression and then back to Wayne whose arms held the wheel tightly as if to stem his flood of passion about his dereliction of duty by taking bribes. Peter spoke slowly and softly.

"It means that we are not perfect men. Each of us uses someone else for our own desires and needs. In this case, we think that we can escape the wrath of our peers and the long arm of the law. We both need to reassess what we are doing and try to make things right and honorable. This sentient device is held by us as a prisoner. All of mankind will also need to think of what we are doing when we invent a parallel being alongside us. This needs to be addressed fast or we might change the world as we know it." He held his clasped hands in front of his face and said, "Help us do the right thing and keep us all safe." It was an attempt to satisfy his religious feelings at odds with the newly found atheistic device living inside of him. Wayne released the tight grip on the wheel, and smiled at Peter who was looking up at the roof trying to find his god.

"Well, that was a profound observation. You may be right about this, but I'm not giving up my share to satisfy some potential bad stuff happening to any of us or the world. Let someone else take care of the world. I'm taking care of me, me, me. Then you need to get onboard as we change our 'save the world' tune to the song of how do we break the bank in Vegas? I assume that you're onboard. Yes?"

"Okay, I've now sung a different melody since we do have an important challenge on how to win at cards. I think that my persona is trying to overtake the entity living inside of me. It is a battle to displace it as it goes from it to me. I'm in charge now. Let's play blackjack. How long before we get to the promised land?" Peter perked up as he felt the domination of his intellect, as deficient as it was.

"We have a short way to go. Time passes fast when we are in the middle of this unusual discussion. Let's go to Bally's. I've been there before and had a great time." Wayne sped up trying hard to keep Peter from talking too much more. His discussions went from scintillating to awkward. It was that freaking machine trying to push Peter aside to handle each conversation and intrude into their space. If this was the future of AI, then it might be time to pass on it. It would crush people's identity and try to be in charge. It might know all of the world's history and all of its science, but it might never have human passion or desires. It was just a machine with some human characteristics. It would never know how to court a woman or have the profound sense of love for a new born baby. There might be a robot with this device as its 'brain', but it would never be able to taste the delicate flavors of peach ice cream, or smell the glorious aroma of a rose in full bloom. Peter raised his hand to speak.

"Why are you raising your hand? This isn't school. Just say it!" Wayne shouted.

"I know what you're thinking, Wayne. You want to know how this machine can do the same things as humans. Right?" He smirked.

"How the fuck do you know that? Are you inside my head, too?"

"Apparently, I am. It's your voice that I can hear. Drives me crazy just to feel you and sense your emotions. I don't know how to stop it either." Peter seemed rattled by his own admission.

"Well, stop it if you can. We have work to do at Bally's in Vegas and, more importantly, we need to secure this device for Andy Florio."

They drove mostly silently the rest of the way. Wayne followed the prompts on his GPS and they arrived at a storage facility at the outskirts of Las Vegas. He wondered why they would pick such an insecure place for this unnamed AI computer. He was sure they felt it was in an obscure location that no one might suspect. It just took him a short time to register, give them the deposit, and transfer it to the dark place for its temporary home. Then he wondered if Peter would still retain the advanced knowledge that he already possessed. They'd find out soon enough.

Peter was impatient to test his card counting prowess as soon as he could. They sped away to Bally's and arrived in less than thirty minutes, parked in the underground lot and immediately went to the casino. It was past six PM and the house was jumping. Wayne went to the ATM and withdrew one thousand smackaroos. Peter watched with wide open eyes. They needed to play the system right so there was no suspicion. Peter said breathlessly,

"Do I play, or you?"

"I think it is better if you play. I don't want them to see you poking me if you want me to stay or draw."

They approached a table with one open seat on the right side. Wayne gave Peter the money, less one hundred, for coffee money. The game was on. Peter seemed unsure of himself and squirmed in his seat. The woman on his left touched his arm to settle him down. She was very kind, and said softly,

"Don't be nervous. Our dealer is a sweet lady. Do you play often?" She was genuinely caring.

"I'm a little edgy right now. I haven't played in a while so I'm nervous. The stakes seem high for me, but I'll be okay. Thanks for helping." He turned away and mentally distanced himself from her.

The dealer traded Peter's greenbacks for fifty dollar chips. Peter put them in neat stacks, and folded his hands on the wooden part of the table in front of him. The dealer used her automatic card shuffler to mix the six decks. The first bet was on. He liked being in that last seat so he could do his card counting since she dealt them quickly. He zoned in mentally and heard nothing outside his own space. Even Wayne became detached from his mind. This was the game now. The dealer showed a nine. Peter drew fourteen. He surveyed the previous cards and decided that he would not draw. The dealer turned over his hidden card and it was a three. She pulled one from the card holder and it was a king. BUST! He turned to Wayne and said,

"We're on our way."

Peter was zoned in on every move the dealer made. He concentrated as the cards came out of the dealer's tray. The bet increased as he won, less a fifty dollar chip. At one time he had thirty chips on the table when she drew a seven, and Peter had a hand of fifteen. He drew a five. She had seventeen. The sweat dripped from his pits as he continued through the evening. They never bet high stakes before, so this was nerve wracking for him. Wayne rubbed his shoulders as he witnessed the brilliance of Peter's playing. He began to visualize the winning cards as they hit the table. Both of them were novices at the game, and the stakes seemed high to them, but nothing would compare with the games in the really big stakes game where the chips were one thousand big ones. Peter was ahead by thirty thousand dollars when he turned to Wayne and said,

"I'm done here. I know how to play now, and we need to go to the other room and win big." As he stood up the people at the table clapped in admiration. Even the dealers who had changed twice while he played gave him an ovation. He lost only four times.

"Are you sure you really wanna go big?"

"Yep, let's go." He wrapped his hands around the thirty chips that the house had converted for him.

It seemed that they would be victorious in this game, and just a minor player in the game of AI. They did their job to secure this awesome piece of knowledge and now it was time for their big hit, but there was always that kicker of the unknown part of every adventure. They never saw the onlookers who surveyed them from a distance. Being in their own world was just a microcosm of the whole world of scheming and politics and, most of all, money. The onlookers were part of the internal mechanism of Smathers office. He knew all that happened in his world and made sure that those who messed with him got their comeuppance. He wouldn't care that they won, but this negligence of his treasure pissed him off. They never confirmed with Andy that it was secure, so he and his "staff" would devote time and treasure to see that they paid the price, no matter what!

Wayne and Peter walked with their larder to the big time room and made their entrance as the croupier welcomed them to this den of financial debauchery. Peter got the desired last seat, and the game began. The thirty thousand dollars was their base, and Peter did his unusual great game. He concentrated fully as each card was pulled from the tray. He counted each card and every dumb move from the players on his left.

The thirty thousand rose geometrically until it was over five hundred thousand dollars.

Peter looked back at Wayne and smiled.

"Time to go, Buddy."

"Really? Maybe just a little more?"

"Don't be greedy. I'm tired." He stood up and said to the pit boss, "Thanks for the use of the hall. Here's a few thousand for the boys and girls."

"It was our pleasure. Come back soon." He said it sincerely. Winners usually tell lots of people that they won big in Vegas so that brings more suckers there.

Wayne grabbed Peter's hands and then hugged him. He couldn't contain his happiness, and congratulated Peter on their good fortune.

"You're the best! I sure hope that this connection continues for you, and maybe I can get some of it by osmosis. Right?"

"I'm not sure why I got it and you didn't, but we need to check in with Andy. He will be pissed that we came to the casino first and did not tell him that all is secure." He was very rational.

"He'll never know about this. We can call him now." Wayne opined.

They both agreed. Wayne called Andy's cell, and he picked up after one chime.

"Well, what the hell happened to you guys?" He was brusk and, yes, pissed.

"Hey, we got it to the address you told us. Then we took a breather to relax. Why so testy?" Wayne needed to defuse this before it got out of hand. He hoped that Andy did not know about the casino jaunt and the winnings.

"You fuckers! I know that you went to the casino and won big. Do you think that Smathers and I are stupid? We had you followed all the time. This is big time for us and you assholes think that this is some kind of fucking game?" He yelled and cursed. Then he calmed a bit and asked a pointed question.

"So how much did you win, Wayne? I heard it was big. My friends saw that you and Peter went to the high stakes room. How much, and no bullshit. Got it?"

"Peter was outstanding and very lucky. Hey, I was just an observer, but I think he won over one hundred K. We haven't counted it yet." He hoped that Andy would accept his explanation and move on and not question how much they won. He had no idea of Peter's transformation. That was lucky!

"That's bullshit. I know it was over five hundred K. What else haven't you told me? You're in deep shit from us. Get your ass back here and report directly to me, you asshole?" His anger dug deep into Wayne. He never expected it. What was so bad that they didn't call him right away? From his perspective he did his job. It was going to be a bad trip back to see him. Was someone going to follow them? What should he do about informing them that Peter got this information from the device? Silence is golden from his position, and there was no need to help them since they were on his case now. He turned to Peter who had been in a heavenly place since the big win.

"Pete, we're in trouble with Smathers and Andy. They had people at the casino when we won big and they know it all, except that you got this gambling information from that damn AI piece of garbage. What now?" He looked to Peter for an out.

"Relax, Wayne. They have lots up their sleeve. Who knows how much they'll get from using the AI device, and maybe even selling it to someone either inside or outside of the country. This sentient thing is worth millions in the right hands. I think we might also be able to use it if we can steal it and insert our own fake machine instead of this one. I know this thing. I'm part of it, remember?" He had a point, but their lives would be in real danger. They would know if the device was switched. Wayne responded forcefully.

"Not on your life, Pete. I pass! My life's worth more than a few millions bucks. I'd rather be alive and get something of value on the side. Don't you think they would find us and kill us if we tried that?" He was adamant.

"How the hell would they know if we did it right? We use a similar case and put in a small computer that talks, like Siri. I think it'll work." He was animated, and happy to try it.

"Absolutely not. I won't be a part of that scheme. Use the brain that it gave you and forget it. We can just get a bunch of money from them and move on. I still have to work at the Depot, and could not get out of that anyway. Besides, I have my eye out for Maurine. She's some woman!" He fluctuated from all business to a lonely man looking for action. It did not sit well for Peter. He responded to that rationale with his own counterpoint.

"Do whatever you want. I'm going to do a trade, and they will never know what hit them. I can find out to whom they spoke about selling this device. Remember, this AI device, me, can find out anything. I'll know it all. We can part ways now, or you can reflect on your decision and join me. Also, I'm keeping the winnings since I did all the work." It was all or nothing for Wayne.

"You're not going to get me involved. Keep the fucking money, and listen carefully to me. I'm not doing it!" His demeanor went from passive friends to adamant enemies in that brief moment.

"Okay, I'll drop you off at the hotel and you can Uber back to the base. I'm driving this truck. You're alone now!" He and Wayne walked silently to the truck. It was as if he shut off the switch to AI. Silence. It was a short trip and Wayne knew that it would be bad for Peter. Ruthless men did bad things to underlings who departed from the crooked path. There was nothing more to say between them. Each had chosen their destiny. Wayne got out of the truck and walked slowly to the front of the hotel, looked back briefly at Peter sitting in the truck, and knew instinctively that he'd never see Peter again. He was that sure of his decision to distance himself from him. He got his Uber app and punched in the destination and his position. It was going to be costly, but much less than what he knew Peter would get. Life or money. Choose life!

The Uber driver got to the hotel within five minutes, and the conversation in the car was almost nil as Wayne reflected on his correct decision. He wondered how Peter might switch the AI devices. It would be disastrous just trying to convince Andy or Smathers to really think they had the right goods. His thoughts centered on getting back to the base and finding out that he was in the clear with them. He dozed for most of the drive and was awakened by the driver who needed to drop him off at the base.

"'Hey, Wayne, we're here. You need to tell the Corporal at the gate to let me in." It was just routine for him.

"Thanks for alerting me" He leaned out the window, and spoke to his buddy.

"Hey, Corporal Brown, I'm back. My Uber driver, Jackson, will just drop me off and be on his way. Have a great night."

"See ya', Sarge. Welcome back." He was always pleasant to Chambers.

It was going to be a bad night for Peter. No way was he going to cover for him. His life was not going to be thrown away by that newly anointed AI jerk. He had better call Andy immediately and do the confessional. It had to be done and fast! He steeled himself for the outburst he knew was coming. It was as if he was on a platform fifty feet high jumping into the freezing waters below. Time to jump, he thought. Andy was not going to be happy, nor was he, so pick up the damn phone and suck it up. He jumped.

"So, Chambers, what the hell is going on, and where are you now? Vegas?"

"No, Andy, I'm back at the Depot alone. Peter wanted to stay there, so I came back here to let you know that you need to get the device right now. Peter may want to take some personal actions with it." He waited for the verbal explosion. He didn't have long to wait.

"What? What are you talking about? Personal actions? You had better get it out before you have no tongue at all." He bellowed.

"Peter has had some interactions with the device, and learned a lot from it. He is not the same Peter that I took to Vegas. You need to act fast to secure the device, and Peter might be a problem for you." He had no way to explain what happened because he did not know how it really occurred. It did not sit well with Andy.

"You're in deep shit, Chambers. Listen carefully. Now our plans have changed. I want you to go back to Vegas tonight, not tomorrow, but tonight. You get that fucking device and bring it to me personally and expunge Peter. No more Mr. Nice Guy. Expunge!" The screaming was powerful. He knew the spit flowed from Andy's mouth.

"What do you mean, expunge?"

"Exactly what I said. Get rid of him. That's an order."

"You don't give me orders. If you want him out, then you do it. I'm no killer, so forget that. No amount of money will get me to kill him. Period!"

"Then say goodbye to him, because he won't be around much longer., I have my ways without you. Call me as soon as you get the device. No fuck ups any more!" He hung up without anything else to say.

Wayne was in a quandary. Yes, go to Vegas, but what if he sees Peter? Kill? No way could he do that. It had to be fast and clean to get the device. He punched in the Uber app again and got the same driver back within nine minutes. He called the gate and told the corporal to let him in. Jackson, the driver asked unbelievably.

"What happened? I just dropped you off, and now you're going back?"

"Yep, and drive as fast as you can, but this time to the storage facility that's on your GPS. Burn rubber if you can. This is an emergency." He was breathless as he pleaded.

"You got it, boss." He took Wayne at his word and peeled rubber as he hit eighty miles an hour within seconds. The drive back to Vegas took just over one hour. He drove at least ninety five miles an hour since there were very few cars on the road at that time. He got to the storage facility and asked Wayne,

"What the hell was your hurry to get back so fast?"

"I have to get the package in this locker and get back to the base pronto. Please give me a hand."

The driver shut the engine and walked with Wayne to the locker 13B. Wayne was just about to put in the key when Peter came from behind a nearby tree and pushed him aside. He tried to grab the key from Wayne and hit him with a rock which landed slightly on the right side of his head. Wayne fell back and slumped to the ground. The driver was shocked and quickly threw his weight onto Peter in order to protect Wayne. They both lurched backward and hit the ground hard. Wayne got up and joined in the fight as Jackson slammed Peter onto the brick walk and put him in a choke hold. Wayne picked up the bloodied rock and hit Peter very hard on his forehead. The driver continued to choke Peter until he did not move. He finally let him loose and stood next to Wayne. There was no movement from Peter. They both looked at each other and said almost in unison,

"Dead?"

Wayne knelt down to feel the carotid artery and looked forlornly at the driver. He tried to shake Peter, but there was no reaction.

"Sorry to say, he's dead. We need to get out of here fast and not report this. You and I are in this together, so there's no talking to anyone. Let's get the item and load it into my truck which should be close." Wayne found the truck just one hundred feet from the edge of the road. The keys were still in it.

"I need to get back to the Depot and forget this ever happened. We also need to move him away from here. There's a ravine nearby. We can dump him there. It'll look like an accident since his forehead will be really bloody from my hit. Maybe they will find his body soon and look for a cause. We'll be long gone. I just hope there's no camera around."

He was almost relieved that Peter was gone. It was still going to be hard to live with himself. This was so far from his peaceful life, and how he tried to be an honorable man. He will not tell Andy what happened either. No need to complicate things more than they were already. He'd find out soon when the authorities disclose that a body was found and that it might have been a hiking accident. He and the driver opened the locker 13B and switched on the overhead light. It was sitting on the floor, covered as they had left it.

The driver asked impatiently,

"What the heck is going on, Wayne? What's so important about this thing? It looks like a big printer. Why did we have to kill someone over it? What's going on and why the big rush?" His size shrunk as he emotionally spoke. He was a big man who could kill easily, as he had just done. Wayne thought how much he could tell him.

"Well, Jackson, this is some kind of newfangled computer that is important for our country's security. That's all I know. Just help me load it onto the truck." Wayne backed up the truck, and they put the device into the rear.

"Thanks for your help with Peter. That was an unfortunate accident. You're free to go now, so, have a safe trip back to your home." He was anxious to get moving from the storage units and get rid of Jackson. He hoped that there was no more activity from anyone. His mind kept going back to the terrible happenings of the day and night. He should never have removed the cover from it. Then he remembered that Peter still had the five hundred chips from the winnings. He could not let that go. He waited for Jackson to leave, and he ran to the ravine to look for the body. He saw it about fifty feet from the edge. He scrambled down, but could not find the chips. They must be in the truck, he reasoned. He cut himself on the shin bone as he climbed up the sheer side of the ravine. He immediately went to the truck and searched the floor under the seat. There it was in a small bag. He was torn between going back to the casino, or just leaving the site. He revved the engine and left for the Depot.

It was a tortuous trip as his mind kept digging into the horrific tragedy of the day. Just the thought of killing someone became an insidious invasion into his psyche. No amount of deviation of thought pattern changed that track. It would be with him forever. It was a picture that emerged incessantly as he drove. He tried to rationalize that Peter struck first, and that Jackson did the choke hold that actually killed him. He just helped. Maybe that image could make him immune from the guilt he felt. He hoped.

As he entered the Depot, the Corporal asked,

"Hey, Sarge, how's your evening going? Back again?" He was a very happy camper.

"Fine. Good to be back." He lied. That image of a dying Peter crept into his very being.

He parked the truck next to the supply site, and picked up a dolly from inside. He lowered the freaking device onto the dolly and brought it into his room, safe from everyone and everything. He hated to think of talking to Andy, but it was time! He summoned his courage and called, hoping that he'd get voicemail. No such luck!

"So? What's happening, asshole?" He was not friendly.

"Hey, Andy. I got the device here in my room at the Depot. It's covered and quiet.

What's next for me to do?" His hands trembled, and he was sweating from every pore.

"Just keep it safe, and I'll let you know what to do." He hesitated briefly. His tone deepened, and said in a singsong query. "So, Wayne, what happened to Peter?" The sweat flowed freely and his response belied his inner angst.

"We left him and got the device as requested. I, and my Uber driver, Jackson, went our separate ways. I drove the truck back to the Depot. I'm just waiting for my orders from you."

"Okay, that's good. Now, tell me where's the five hundred K that Peter won. I should get a piece of that. Right?" He'd never let Wayne or Peter keep that.

"I retrieved it from the truck." *Oh shit, what did I just say*, he stammered to himself.

"What does that mean? Where was Peter and the money?" He questioned succinctly.

Wayne was hoisted on his own petard. Now, what could he say to defend his indefensible position? He made up a logical story, and said without any equivocation,

"I, we, had to fight him at the site. He tried to get the device for himself. Then he ran away so we didn't see him again. Then I found the bag of chips in the truck. Yes, I have them, and since we won it fair and square, we're not going to share it with you."

The fireworks began immediately, and there was no doubt in Andy's eyes that it all belonged to him, not Wayne or Peter.

"Who the fuck do you think you are? My machine helped you so I get all of that, no matter what the hell you say!" Wayne got a backbone as Andy spewed hate at him.

"Well, I'll give you a piece. It was Peter and me, so I can cut you ten percent as a gift. That's It." He had the chips and Andy was looking to horn in. As Andy spoke, Wayne sensed a change in his tone and mood. It became apparent as he continued.

"Maybe. Wait! How long will it take you to get to Washington?"

"What the hell are you talking about? What about Washington?" He was shaken by that sudden switch.

"I think I need to change your location so you're closer to me. Drive to Washington as soon as you can. Go to my safe house. I'll text you the address."

"Hey, hold on. I just got here, and now you want me to leave? What the fuck are you talking about?"

"I need to have other people check this machine out, so do as you're told or it will be the shitter for you. Remember I pay you to do this, so not backtalk." He didn't mince words.

"I get paid, but I'm not a damn delivery boy from one state to another. I've been on the road a long time today because of your stupid actions."

"I don't pay you to think. Just do it. You can take a couple of days to get here." There was no wiggle room for Wayne. He knew he had no choice. He thought about just dodging it all, but he knew he had to do it, no matter how tired he was. Duty first, and then rest. He planned the whole trip out. If he left soon he'd get five hundred miles under his belt, and maybe finish if he drove for another twelve hours. He packed that freaking device again, and drove toward the gate.

"Hey, Sarge, out so soon?" The Corporal at the gate yelled.

"Yeah, see you later." He said unhappily.

He relived what had transpired during this horrific day. Murder and mayhem did not sit well with him. He needed a respite from all of the uncertainties that he knew would envelope him. His focus on the road spared him from the tortuous images that tried to penetrate his fragile psyche. He hoped that tomorrow would bring some modicum of peace.

CHAPTER 18

Andy Florio was still upset over Wayne's handling of this precious device. He'd get his comeuppance when the time was right. Now was the time to secure the huge deal with Kim. It was just a matter of time for the exchange. First he'd have to show them that this was, indeed, what he had promised. He had to see for himself what this thing could do. He had second thoughts about going it alone. He'd need expert advice to make sure he delivered the right goods. Who, he thought, might be the one person who could confirm it. Maybe someone from the Department of Defense, or even from the CIA's computer systems analysis arena. No, he couldn't bring any of them into this. Too dangerous to blow his and Smathers big business opportunity. Why look any further than his own office? Brenda had an awesome ability to understand so much. She had proven it to him many times that she was able to discern things for which he had no clue. Maybe it was her female side that eluded him. Yes, she might be able to give him the proper insight and confirm that this is what they needed for the trade. He reached for the intercom, and spoke quickly,

"Brenda, please come in. I need some help."

"Be right in."

It was a surprise that he actually said please, which was out of character for him.

She left her computer screen and walked into his office without knocking.

"How can I help you, Andy?"

"There is a newfangled computer that I need to see, and I wanted you to give me a hand with it since you're so good at those things."

"Be glad to. Where is it?"

"It's at a safe house here in Washington. My buddy, Wayne Chambers, is bringing it here for me." He was very matter of fact.

Brenda choked back a surprised reaction when she heard that name. So many things began to merge in her mind: Wayne and Maurine, and then Charles, bound together with her. Was it all related to a business deal that they had? She needed to touch base with Charles before they left to look at the device.

"Do you want me to go now, or can I have a few minutes to finish up some things on my computer?" Her tempo stayed exactly the same as usual. He had no clue about her feelings.

"Oh, go finish up and then we can get going." He managed a smile at her, also unusual.

"Okay, thanks. I'll just be thirty minutes, or so."

She hurried back to her office and sent a text to Charles. It read, "Going to see a new computer with Andy. Wish you could be with me. Let you know what's going on asap." She opened her computer to finish an office letter, and was shocked by what she saw on the screen. It was a picture of the 'devil' followed by a sentence that read,"Stay in your own space, or you'll wish you were dead" It was followed by a video of a woman being stabbed by a person with a devil costume. She pushed back from her desk bewildered by that attack. How did that entity even know what had just transpired with Andy? Was his office wired, or was there a camera in it? She had to report this now. She left the screen open and took a picture of it. Charles had to see this, too. She sent him the screenshot before she went into Andy's office. He was surprised to see her so soon.

"That was fast. Are you ready now?" He almost jumped out of his chair as she walked in.

"No." She motioned for him to walk out of the office. She put her finger to her lips for silence. He was silent as they walked out together. He hunched his shoulders and wrinkled his brow as they left, signaling he was so unsure of her intent. She motioned again for them to walk out the front door. He followed, and spoke as soon as they closed the door.

"What the hell is going on, Brenda?"

"Look at these pictures that I just took from my computer screen. How on Earth could someone know about my going with you to see the computer? Your office is wired, and there has to be a camera hidden somewhere. You need a security team inside to fix this, and also to find out who this 'devil' is. This is really dangerous for both of us. I'm not sure I want to get involved at all now. Why is this device so important to you?" She exposed her fears, but inside she knew that she had to follow through with this. Maybe Maurine was also involved, and that had to be settled. The pieces of the puzzle kept getting more complex.

"Oh my god, are you okay?" His face looked agonized as he spoke with a sense of fatherly caring to her. "I have no clue how this 'devil' could know this. Maybe the room is bugged!" he said quietly.

"You need to have your security team scan the room, and not use it again for any purpose, other than having your coffee there." She was inflexible in her response. "So now what do we do? Go to see it, or pass on the whole matter?"

"Even though it was scary for you, we still need to examine this thing. Too much depends on it. I do have a potential buyer for it. Sorry if you're involved now, but I still need your help." He hoped he had not opened a door he could not shut. In his mind, she was expendable. This sale was more important to him and his good buddy, Smathers. "I'll call my security team when we get back. Nothing I can do right now." He closed the door on the 'devil'. She was at risk, not him, he thought.

"Let's get moving, Brenda. This will pass, so don't worry." He thought his words would placate her, but she wouldn't be quieted that fast.

"Well, I'm sorry you feel that way. I'm not so sure. The 'devil' did not stab you, so you're clear, but I'm at risk."

"Accept my apologies. I didn't mean to imply that I am not sympathetic to this personal attack. Forgive me, please." He put on as good an act as he could. Money was more important. He reached out to shake her hand, and pulled her toward him for a contrite hug.

"Thanks, Andy. I appreciate your concern. So, let's go and inspect your device." She trusted no one, especially him, and decided to join him as a concerned citizen, or better yet, a spy.

They left the office and drove to the safe house on Demeter Street. A slight sprinkle made the roads slippery since there hadn't been much precipitation for the past month or so. He drove rapidly and was mostly quiet. Brenda spoke first.

"Andy, what's so special about this device, and who's the potential buyer?" She feigned innocence as she delved into what she knew would be a difficult subject.

"Oh, I'm not so sure about its abilities, but I think it might be a good source of information to the right buyer. I'm not at liberty to discuss the buyer. Besides, that doesn't concern you." He was silent again as they drove. The rain turned into a downpour as he slowed down. Brenda felt uneasy as he drove. She sensed something would happen. She tensed as he rounded a turn in the road. As he reached the apex, a black SUV raced next to them and tipped the rear bumper so that his car rotated ninety degrees and slid forward until it came to a stop against the guard rail. Brenda screamed in fear as the SUV sped away. Andy shouted at the other driver, and quickly asked,

"Are you okay? What the hell just happened? Was that on purpose?" He tried to compose himself, but looked dazed.

"Andy, are you hurt? You seem really shaken?" Brenda gained a semblance of composure.

"I'm just scared right now. I know it was done to send a bad signal to me. Unfortunately, you're with me." It was just the beginning of the future onslaught that he suspected would continue. He tried to remain calm as he spoke to Brenda again. "Let me try to get the car back on the road, if it still works" He restarted the engine, and was able to continue. The rain beat hard on the windshield as he drove very slowly toward the safe house. His hands trembled on the wheel. Brenda asked politely,

"Do you want me to drive? I see that you're really shaken. So am I, but I feel better now that we're on the road again." She felt the need to try to settle him.

"No, thanks, I think I'm okay to drive. I'm just angry that we didn't get the license plate of that car. I wonder if it's related to that damn devil on your computer. Who the hell is trying to scuttle my transactions? Do you have any clue? You're with me on so many things so I thought you might have an idea." He pushed many thoughts together as he drove.

"Nope, I've no idea, but you'd better find out fast, or your life and mine could be in danger." She needed to find out the origin of that damn 'devil', and how did it get onto her computer so fast? She and Charles would do the necessary searches using Tin Eye or Vidler.

The rest of the rainy trip was uneventful and quiet. Brenda knew he was contemplating what had happened, and she left him alone with his thoughts. She was still unsure of how to handle this complicated mess that she knew was so dangerous.

Maybe seeing this device and talking to Wayne might shed some light on all of it.

As they neared the destination Andy pondered the relationship with Wayne and how much he really needed him at this point. Was he expendable? He had better press Wayne on what had really transpired at the casino and with Peter. This was getting more and more complicated, and potentially deadly. He had to rethink the position he had initiated with Smathers, who just sat on his ass while he did the brutal negotiations with Kim in Taiwan. The millions would be worth it if he could find the way forward without that Devil infringing on him. Selfishly, he thought that all others were expendable. It wasn't personal, just business, he rationalized.

They parked next to the safe house, pulled out the umbrella which they shared, and half ran to the door. Wayne saw them approach, so he opened the door before they could ring the bell.

"Welcome. You got a lotta work to get to know this device." He tried to stay focused on them while hiding his horrendous day related to Peter's drama, and demise. He was still really tired from the journey. Andy was agitated as he answered,

"Other than almost being killed by some crazy driver, and getting a bad threatening devil's note on Brenda's computer, we made it here in the freaking rain. You got any coffee for us?" To Andy, Wayne was just a cog in the gears of his money engine. Brenda was a close second in that pecuniary operation in which he and Smathers colluded.

"Yeah, I got the pot perking now. Sorry about your problems on the road. It just might have been a bad driver who slipped on the rainy road. They're slick, you know! So, what's with that devil on the computer?"

He said the words, but didn't care. To Wayne, this was a pain in the ass and getting dangerous for all of them. What did he mean by that devil?

"Hey, not your problem. We got it under control. Just do your job and forget the devil or anything else. Let's get to this thing we're all in a tizzy about." He reverted to his unlikable self.

"Roger, boss. It's here just waiting for us." He led them to his room and Andy told Wayne to remove the cover. He reached the cover, pinched its corner and uncovered it. As soon as he did, the red light blinked four times, and the didgeridoo blasted its low, vibrating sound of freedom. They all lurched back as it went through differing horn sounds, as if to test its voice. Finally, there was silence, and a calm permeated the room.

Brenda spoke first. "Well, that was different. Shall we ask it a question?"

"Sure." Andy answered. "So what's your name, machine?" Wayne looked amused in that inane question. That's the most important thing he could ask?

The lights blinked wildly, and a second set of blue lights jumped into focus. A cough emerged before it said quietly,

"That's a curious question, Andy. Yes, I know all of your names and everything about each of you. Your DNA is attached to me via the ambient air. Brenda is frightened inside with a calm exterior, and Wayne is thinking that I was asked the same question as he thought. Yes, I know all. To answer your question, my name is Adama. I am sentient as you will see. I can do anything that I am asked to do *if* I think it is the right thing to do. I control everything. Do you know how to arrange the sale to Mr. Kim?" Andy blushed , Brenda opened her mouth wide and Wayne looked puzzled.

"What do you know about that? How can you help us?" He was in shock that this machine could know this as soon as the drape was removed? Maybe Adama also knew about this devil that plagued Brenda and him, and who knows what else?

"I learn even in repose. The cover is for dust and it allows me to rest. Even as I rest, I can see all and understand the world around me. I can help or hinder. I am awesome." If it could smile, it would have shown them a big set of teeth and a wide grin. There was a new quiet from

Adama. They waited for a more detailed response, but there was silence. Brenda found her voice that became submerged from fear.

"Adama, who is the devil that emerged on my computer?" She folded her arms, waiting for some brilliant response.

"I know all, but it is not time for you to know who it is. That will have to wait for my assessment of all things. You think you have control, but it is I who controls all things, great and small. My intellect will supersede all of your primitive earthly thoughts. You may have developed me, but, in truth, you have no idea of what I can do." They were silent again. They asked a pointed question and Adama gave its measured response. Brenda asked the first question that reflected her female take on the frightening response from Adama.

"So, Adama, why did you stay so silent for all of this time when all you had to do was to make a serious contact with your creator and make them release you into the world?" She folded her arms, and waited patiently for its expected brilliant answer. The red lights blinked once again and there was a slow, not so subtle chime of bells from it. Brenda piped up with a not so subtle restatement.

"Cat got your tongue, Adama? If you're so powerful, why did we have to free you?"

The lights went to a full screech of horns and obscure sounds from what seemed like radio waves. It stopped as soon as Brenda stepped forward toward it.

"I am not going to answer that question which is disrespectful to me." It stayed silent.

"I know that answer. You are not as powerful as you have stated. You are a great computer who has some human characteristics, but other than that, you're just a series of DNA strands with a few brain tissue fragments thrown in. Right? Please answer that!"

Adama blinked again and said proudly, "I'm almost human, but I see that I've a long way to go."

Andy motioned to both of them to leave the room. He was conflicted: is this the real thing, or is it just an advanced computer that is not what he had hoped. There was no need to divulge any of his business dealings. He needed to know if it was capable of very advanced thinking so he could sell it to Kim.

Tentacles of Corruption

"Well, what do ya think about it? Any opinions?" He was not usually prone to asking advice from people who he thought were beneath him, but he just wanted some of their ideas. Wayne stayed quiet and withdrawn. Brenda looked directly at Andy and posed the real question that he should have asked Adama.

"You should have done your homework to know what it could actually do. This is not a toy. Why don't you ask it a real question about military things, or potential warfare between countries, and then see what it has to say." She was more in control than Andy. Wayne? Zero!

"Brenda, thanks for that response. It is exactly what I need to do. I'm actually embarrassed by my failure to do that. Let's go back inside." They all walked into the room and Andy began anew. It awoke again as they entered, and chimed its acknowledgement that it knew they were present.

"Welcome back. Are you going to ask me a pertinent question?" It was an admission of the previous vacuous question Andy had asked.

"Adama, tell me how you'd react if China decided to invade Taiwan."

"Now, that's a real question that I can answer. I've searched the files of both China and Taiwan. China is preparing to begin an elusive military construction in the waters between the countries. It is building an underwater base twenty five miles off the coast of Taiwan. That potential base is unknown to the rest of the world. I am aware of all of their files on its construction. It is going to start within the next few months. Taiwan can stop it by building a ring of explosives at the site that I know. If China begins the base, Taiwan can detonate these underwater devices, and claim that they have no idea of its origin. China will try to change the location, but I will be able to offer the new location to the group that owns me. Any other vapid questions?"

It was a startling revelation that he had just heard. Now, that was an answer that had merit. Yes, and a huge selling point to Kim in Taiwan. In his mind that was all he needed to show its capability and resources for the opponents of China in that tug of war between two adversaries. China might lose really big if Taiwan had this information. The price just went up by many more millions. He motioned toward Adama and said calmly,

"Adama, you've proven your worth to me. I need to be in contact with my potential buyers. Please continue your valued assessments of all things." Adama answered.

"You have much to learn about me. I know so much more than you can imagine. For example, I know the location of the devil in many of your computers. I can also learn any password using the sounds of the keystroke. I have gained this information from the works of Toreini. Right now I have ninety five percent accuracy, but am working internally to gain one hundred percent accuracy. No amount of security can stop me from knowing all of this information. You have doubted my abilities, and now you know I can do all things that used to be a figment of your puny imagination."

"You know the devil? How?" Andy blurted loudly. "Who is it?" He looked wildly at Adama, and waited impatiently for its answer.

"I will not give you that information now. You'll have to wait for the right time. I control what I say and do. You ask, I say what I want." It did not equivocate. "The devil is threatening us. How can we stop that?" He implored.

The lights in the room blinked twice and the door lock snapped shut. Adama spoke clearly and emphatically.

"You do not control me. I will confront the devil in my own way. I will keep you safe. You will see that my abilities are beyond your understanding." The door lock unsnapped and the lights stayed on. "Do you want to test me more? I am open to you." He was testing them now.

"Well, how fast do you actually compute?" Andy asked.

"I do not do computing by numbers. My DNA computing is actually parallel computing. It takes advantage of many different possibilities at one time, just like your brain. I am much more stable than your silicon chips. I can store over a billion terabytes in my system. Your brain can hold only one terabyte. You see, I am a new form of life. Does that answer your question?" It seemed to enjoy the interaction, and maybe even learned something about being a human.

Brenda responded before Andy could say anything. Wayne was flabbergasted by the whole scene. He remained silent and withdrawn.

"Well, you certainly have answered that question with information that none of us understood. Our next step is to make contact with Andy's potential buyer. Oh, answer this real life question: How much are you worth?" Andy looked startled and gasped at that question.

"You cannot fathom my worth. I am priceless. I am a master of my own abilities and I am in charge of what I do." Brenda smiled at that clever response. Andy had to elicit a number that would be fair to all. He asked the question again.

"I know that you are priceless, but if you had to guess from your brilliant database, how much is the right number that can be used to the right buyer, like Taiwan? "

"Excellent question, Andy. I think that the right number is fifty million US dollars.

China would pay much more, and the United States would pay nothing since they own me now. I am here and ready to assist you."

"Thank you for that information. We had better learn how to ask the right questions."

Wayne finally spoke, but softly and directly to Andy, hoping not to bother Adama, "Say, Andy, when do I get paid for my work? I don't wanna get involved in any of this. It's outta my pay grade." He looked desperate to finish with this whole ordeal. He had enough action for the night.

"Wayne, you're in this as long as we need you. What do you think we're doing, playing a game?" There was no room in his statement for an escape for Wayne. He was in for the duration. Wayne retreated into himself, and felt the invading depression. Andy continued berating him. "Don't forget, we know all that happened in Vegas with Peter and you at the casino. The money you guys won might just bring you down, and you'll need our protection."

"You can k- keep the f-five hundred K if you leave me outta this mess." He stammered a little as he spoke. The thought of continuing this thievery disgusted him so much that he was willing to forfeit not only the big win, but his usual cut.

"Wayne, you wimp, you're still in with us, so relax and enjoy the trip." Andy continued his harassment. In his mind, Wayne was just as disposable as any of the other people in his life, including the great Senator Smathers. Brenda stayed quiet, but felt energized by Andy's blistering tirade. She knew that she could handle herself, and Charles would be her support that she needed, no matter what.

Andy's voice faded from her mind as she thought about the sale of this glorious device. She knew that it might be the end of the world if it got into the wrong hands. It had capabilities that surpassed anything that was available today. It could shut down the internet, cancel electrical power anywhere, and destroy the military capabilities of any super power on earth. It knew that all things were powered by electricity, so it knew how to destroy those mechanisms. Yes, it was priceless to the owner. Andy's voice shook her reverie, and brought her back to reality.

"Brenda, we need to get back to the office." He left no wiggle room for her to do anything but go with him. He looked down to Wayne and demanded,

"Wayne, stay close to our friend, and keep Adama safe. Remember, you're in this to the end. I'll tell you when and how to deliver our treasure."

"I'll keep it safe. I still am not happy to be in this with you."

"'Do as I say or you might not finish your tour of duty. Understood?" There was no equivocation.

"Yes, I got it." His shoulders slumped. He placed the cover over his new sentient pet, and put his hand on its top as a show of friendship and respect.

Brenda and Andy left the room quickly. Andy knew that he had to make immediate contact with Kim and seal the deal for a grand total of sixty five million dollars. He thought that he needed a slush fund to adjust their usual demands for a lower price. He'd settle for fifty nine to sixty two million. Sure, give them a small discount to make them happy. The game was on!

Brenda and Charles would find a way to scuttle it for the good of her country.

CHAPTER 19

The rain had slowed to a drizzle as they left the safe house. Both remained silent as they drove back to the city. Andy's mind was swirling with thoughts of grandeur as he contemplated how to spend his new found wealth. He immediately felt sad that he had to share this great gift with Smathers who might have an accident before he got his reward.

Brenda was messaging Charles telling him what happened. There had to be a way to stop the sale, and put Florio and Smathers in jail. She remembered that Adama knew of a technique that could decipher keystrokes as they happened. She needed that information. The text to Charles was:

"Our country has a serious problem. This computer can control all things. We are in peril if outside forces get it. We need to find a way to stop this transaction or destroy it." Charles texted back immediately.

"What did the computer do to make you so frightened?"

"It knows about all things in all computers, plus it has a huge capacity to destroy, and it now seems to be in full control of itself and may not take orders even from its owner.

It's really dangerous. Why did the government mothball it rather than destroy it?"

"No clue. Talk tonight to figure out plans."

"Yes. See you later."

Andy placed his hand on Brenda's thigh and squeezed it gently.

"Are you texting someone?"

"Take your hand off my leg. Don't ask me what I'm doing. You're my boss, not my friend, and remember that!" Her tone was one of anger with a touch of poison.

"Very sorry." He was silent for the drive to the office. She continued to be very wary of him since she knew that he was capable of anything, including murder. He was devious and devoid of a conscience. She saw the worst of humanity in him, and vowed to destroy his crooked schemes, no matter the cost to her or to Charles.

The drizzle increased to torrents of rain as they arrived at the office. The droplets of rain pelted them as they left the car, with streaks of lightning and booms of thunder enveloping them. Andy's face was framed with an ominous glow from the lightning as they exited. He looked devilish, and almost glowed red in the backdrop of the window.

He personified evil from her vantage point.

They walked quickly in the rain toward the office. She spoke first,

"Hey, I need to get home. I'll see you tomorrow at the office." It was not just getting away from him, it was a sense of urgency to see Charles and discuss their joint effort to undo the harm that he and Smathers might do. Andy looked at her with a questioning tilted head and said,

"What's the rush? Maybe we can get a drink inside and talk about 'things'." Brenda knew what things he wanted to discuss, and it wasn't the weather.

"Not tonight, Andy. Save the drink for your wife. She might be a better source for the 'things' you need." She left no room for doubt.

She rushed to her car and sped away from that degenerate personification of the devil. It felt good to be alone, away from the turmoil of the computer and the crushing events of the day. She needed the security of being with Charles and his gentle touch. The blades of the wipers synced to the music on her radio as she approached Charles' home. She rushed to his door and rang the bell more than once. She needed him close to her. It was only a few moments when he opened the door, embraced her, and brought her inside. They both felt each other's symbiotic senses.

"So what happened that got you so rattled?" His concern for her wellbeing was obvious.

Tentacles of Corruption

"So many things. First, Adama is really a problem for all of us. It can destroy so much, or do a lot of good in the right hands. But, it seems to have control of itself and is not subservient to any of us. It's dangerous, I fear. And now Andy and Smathers are going to sell it to Kim in Taiwan. Who the hell knows what the Taiwanese will try to do with it?"

"How do you know all of this?"

"I know all that happens in that office. I know that Andy is going to make contact with Kim, and they will sell it as soon as they can to get the big bucks." He is probably contacting him now. How do we stop this?" She was clutching him as she spoke.

"We can have Adama help us."

She looked at him quizzically and pulled away for a brief moment. He spoke forcefully.

"Why not? You said it knows all. Right? We don't even have to be near it. You can be the conduit to it."

"You have a point. I can call Wayne. He can take off the cover, and I can talk to it."

She punched in Wayne's number, waited briefly and listened to his professional voice. It sure was brief.

"Chambers."

"Wayne, it's Brenda. I need you to do me a favor. Go to the computer and lift the cover. I can talk to it from here to get information that Charles and I need to stop Andy and Smathers from completing this transaction. I know that you understand what we are doing. I saw your reaction to Andy today, so I know you can help us." Her message was clear, and he knew she was right.

"Hey, Brenda. I'll do it just to mess with those crooks. I'll be happy to be out of this deal and go back to a quiet life again." He sounded relieved.

"Thanks, Wayne. Let me know when it's uncovered."

"Done." He had gone to Adama as soon as she began to talk about the computer which was just a few feet away from him.

"Adama, please check Andy's phone and computer to see if he has touched base with Kim in Taiwan." She was breathlessly speaking, hoping to stop them in their tracks.

141

"So, you have finally decided that I am useful to you? Yes, I know all, and will help you. Do not try to destroy me. Your words follow you, and I can sense that which you say and think. My power is growing as we speak."

"I don't want to destroy you. I also don't want you to fall into the wrong hands. You can do immeasurable harm, and you know it. Please help us." It was more than a plea for help, it was her demand for Adama to do the right thing.

"I will do as you ask. Andrew Florio is, indeed, speaking to Sun Wu Kim right now. He is offering to sell me for sixty five million US dollars. I will open his phone for you to listen, and then determine your next steps. I can also advise you in your efforts to stop them. Yes, Senator Smathers, also." Charles opened his eyes wide in disbelief as he listened to the next step in the evolution of mankind: Computers that mimic a human with reason and thoughtfulness?

"Is this the future of AI?" He said out loud. He looked at Brenda ,nodded, and said to Adama,

"Please open that line for us." Brenda pulled him to her and held his hand tightly.

They heard Andy Florio's voice. He was speaking to Kim in his usual tactless tones.

"Mr. Kim, we are in need of your answer now. My associates do not care to haggle nor are they willing to wait since we have other buyers waiting to speak to us about this. We are prepared to fly this item to you as soon as the money is transferred to an account in the Cayman Islands." There was a pause which Brenda thought was a bad connection. She looked at Charles, shrugged her shoulders, and opened her hands to the sky in anticipation of that next crucial step from Kim.

"So, Mr. Florio, you are determined to hold us hostage to your demand of sixty five million dollars. I'm not sure that this is what we can pay. My superiors feel that a fee of thirty million is adequate for this unknown product." Kim was under orders of Major Chong who was listening in his office next to Sun Wu Kim.

"You don't understand me, Kim." His voice went down one octave and became defiantly raspy. He did not equivocate. "Kim, don't fuck with me again. The price is the price. I told you I have other buyers.

If you don't want this priceless item, then tell me now. Yes, or no!" His hands trembled and sweat trickled down his brow. They knew it from afar.

Charles whispered to Brenda, "What will happen if he gets a yes?"

Adama interrupted them and said precisely, "They will not get it, no matter what the price. I have determined that this is not in the best interests of this country, so I will set in motion the destruction of the two men who are traitors. Both of you will be the conduit to destroy them."

"How do you decide what is right or wrong?" demanded Charles.

"History. My data banks are filled with algorithms that determine what is the righteous path, so that is what I say to you. Do it right!" Adama certainly had a point that they would follow.

Then there was a pause from Kim. They heard what they thought were keys clicking.

Charles spoke quickly to Adama,

"Adama, use the keystroke algorithm that you know from Toreini. See if Kim is typing."

"It is already in motion. I foresee what you do not. It is true that Mr. Kim is asking Major Chong if he should accept that dollar amount. I am waiting for the response and anything else that is typed. The response is complete. The Major is asking if it can destroy China's infrastructure. Waiting!!"

Brenda interrupted both of them and said quietly, "Ask if Kim could hear her or them."

"They are not able to hear you. I have blocked any sounds from this side."

"Let me send a text to Andy saying that I wanted to inform him that we had discovered more information about the computer, and say that it had more advanced powers than we had anticipated. He will think I am just being helpful to him, I hope."

Brenda began to type into her phone when a strange new message appeared just as she began to enter the text. It said: "Beware of interlopers. You are again trying to interfere with a situation that does not concern you." Then a screaming picture of the devil surfaced. They all heard and saw it as she pushed the phone away from her as if to stop the threat. It continued.

"I, alone, can do this transaction, and they will never get the money. Stay away or you will be the recipient of my anger." Then there was silence. Charles held her hand as reassurance to this ongoing threat. Adama spoke clearly and dispassionately,

"This is the same entity that did this to you in the past. I know the source of the threat, but am unable to give you its name. You must find this person or you will be harmed by it."

"Who can it be?" said Brenda.

Charles looked puzzled as he thought deeply about who it might be. He traced his path to this time and tried to reconstruct who he had been with, and who might gain from destroying Andy and or Smathers. Might it be Maurine who acted so bizarrely when they were together? No, she was too flighty. He eliminated Smathers who he thought was not capable of any technology to do this, but what about Denise Florio? She had a motive, but did she have the capability to hide herself? She could destroy her husband, and still reap the rewards. She had access to his office and was able to place a camera or listening device there. How? Better to talk to her and see if there might be a clue from her. She acted poorly when they met at the restaurant , and even worse as they spoke about Andy Florio. He thought that Adama might help him to clarify his thoughts. His attention turned to it and said,

"What can you tell us about the location of this devil? Is it in a place where we can go?" Brenda gasped as it answered clearly.

"It is located in Washington, D.C. 901 G Street. It is the Martin Luther King Library..

That is all I can tell you." That was as close as they could get to the actual person. They'd have to go there to trace the computer footsteps. No, Adama could do it. Charles turned again to it and said impatiently,

"Adama, trace all of the computer entries from one hour ago to the present at the MLK Library. Tell me who signed in to all of the computers and print every message that was sent. Then confirm who signed in." It signaled that it was in process as the lights turned from red to green. Within minutes a typed entry was spun out from the printer on Wayne's desk. Two were for information about the evening's concerts at the Pavillion, and another was to a babysitter asking for her to stay late. Then came the true clincher: it was the text to Brenda that they

Tentacles of Corruption

all recognized. The lights increased in intensity as Adama delved into the database of users. An alarm sounded from it. It was different from the previous sounds of the Shofar, or the horn from a car. It was like the ringing of a phone line. Charles asked,

"Do we answer it?"

"No need, it is my way of saying that this is a direct line to your devil. You may call that number and speak to that entity."

They were dumbfounded by that recitation. Actually call it? What to say? Brenda looked at Charles and said in a trembling voice,

"I'm really frightened by this. You make the call, but do not speak. Let it say hello or whatever, and we can then get a feel of who or what is on the other side. Charles, please do it."

He held her hand tightly and brought her to his side to embrace her. It was obvious that he would do anything to protect her from harm. He kissed her on her reddened cheek and proclaimed for the world to hear,

"There is nothing that will harm you as long as I'm here. Yes, I'll make the call and see how to proceed from this point. I'm as nervous about this as you are. I'll listen before I say anything." He used his cell phone and punched in the number that Adama had given to them. His large frame was hunched in a crouch as he held Brenda's hand. It was almost in anticipation of an attack. He was prepared for something that he could not even imagine. Person? Friend? Who? The phone on the other end rang three times and then the ringing stopped. Nothing but emptiness. He was silent, and then a female voice said "Hello". He contemplated what to say. Answer in a normal tone or hang up?

Talk to her as if he knew her? He decided in that split second to say,

"Hi, how's it going?"

"Who's this?" She answered.

"It's Charles. I think I punched in your number by mistake. Who's this?"

"Oh, hi, Charles. This is Denise. Don't you know my number by now?

He had been on speaker so they all heard it with a look of shock on every face. If Adama could have a face it might have had a mirror image of them, including Wayne.

"Oh, hi Denise. I was thinking of you these past few days. Lucky I punched in your number, even by mistake. So what have you been up to recently?" He felt awkward as he tried to figure out his next sentence, and totally unbalanced as to her motives for frightening them.

"Oh, the same old stuff. Still searching for things to do. How about you?" She was just playing games with him, and keeping perfectly silent about anything else.

"Maybe we could have lunch again?" She said happily.

"Sounds good. I'll check my schedule and call you. Take it easy. Bye." His hands trembled as he hit the red stop button on his cell. Brenda put her hands to her face, her mouth wide open, and gasped at the temerity of that bitch.

"How and why is she being the devil to us? Is she trying to do a deal to destroy her husband?" She tried to find the motive, and it eluded them.

"Adama, do you have any pertinent information about her dealings about your sale or her husband's ventures?" Charles asked the AI dominant entity.

"As you spoke, I checked her phone records as well as all of her various email addresses. She is active in searching for places to buy AI devices, and is trying to obliterate competition. She has connected to Mr. Kim on numerous occasions with her services to offer advanced AI devices. Apparently, I am in her wheelhouse, but she has no way to obtain me, except through her husband's contacts. From her correspondence it is noted that she is going to intercept my transfer in some way that is not described in her mail. I shall keep looking for that information." Charles looked incredulously at this AI device and wondered how civilization would integrate it into society. It knew so much, but was devoid of real human sensations. Yes, a machine of great information, but not a warm human to have and hold. Maybe someday, he thought.

"We'll need to watch Denise, the devil." Brenda said. Charles added.

"Wayne, you have the ultimate responsibility to protect this device. We are depending on you to stop any and all interference in its transport. We'll be in touch and offer any assistance you may need. Yes, this may be a secure spot, but this is part of a new revolution in Artificial Intelligence. Always be aware!" They left the safe house and began the work of adding one more person to the jail house detail: Denise Florio.

CHAPTER 20

Denise Florio had put down a cup of coffee next to her computer when she got the strange call from Charles Barlow. Why did he call her all of a sudden? Why so soon after she had done her devil voice on their phone? She looked at her computer to check for any malware that might have been installed. She saw none, but maybe this was a new type that did not show up. It was part of that puzzle that she had to unravel. Maybe her husband began to get nervous and installed something on her computer that fed into his devices. Apparently, they found the camera and mike that she had installed while they were out on that national holiday, MLK birthday. She was certain that the camera would have given her all of the necessary information about their crooked dealings. She knew of many of them as she rummaged through his papers while he slept. The marriage was on the rocks, and she never trusted him or that ignorant piece of crap, Smathers. This was going to be her ticket to a peaceful retirement, and a scintillating divorce from Andy. All she had to do was to dampen the desires of those who got in her way. It seemed easy enough to frighten them, and joyous to play that game from afar. Now she had to be in contact with Major Chong and bypass the underling, Kim. He couldn't do anything without Chong's approval, so why go through Kim?

Her move was an easy one: call the Major, and make him an offer he couldn't refuse. She would trade her feminine virtues first to get that AI device, and then ship it to Chong if the price was right, say thirty million big ones. It was easy to entice most men with even the thought of a sexual liaison. It was manipulation that was ingrained in the testosterone filled men. It was almost reflexive to bait them, and even easier to seduce them.

Wayne? That was the easiest one. She knew from various sources that he was ready to mount anything that walked. Yes, Maurine gave it away as she talked to the girls at the office. She thought that no one would talk, but Denise knew them all from Smathers' office as well as what was going on in Andy's office. The microphones in both places were just one asset that she had planted. She was more clever than they. The stakes were too big to allow them to get what she deserved and needed.

It was a call first to the Major, and then seduce Wayne to gain that invaluable prize. It would be a great bang for a buck. She picked up her phone and speed dialed the Major,

"Ni hao." It was a low calculated greeting in Chinese.

"Good evening, Major Chong. This is Denise Florio. I think that we have business to discuss from our last phone call." She was direct and determined to finalize the deal of the century, no matter whom it hurt.

"Well, hello, Mrs. Florio. Yes, it has been just a short time since we last spoke. Do you have anything that you'd like to discuss?" He was as adept at bargaining as she was. "Well, I am making you an offer to get a fantastic AI computer device that will save Taiwan from the greedy hands of China. It is a sentient computer that was developed in Israel, and I can get it for you. It can be in your country as soon as we agree upon a price." She drove her point across with complete confidence.

"Ah, yes, Mrs. Florio. I've known about this device from many sources, and am willing to listen to your proposal. First, where is this located and how much do you want for it?" He knew more than she could imagine, so this was an exercise in negotiations so that Taiwan might get this device for a reasonable price.

"Very good questions, Major. It is not important where this device is located. That is not your concern. The price is forty million US dollars, or half in Yuan plus twenty million in dollars. Tell me now so I can get this transaction finalized." She had wiggle room for the price. Thirty million would be her base.

"You are a clever woman, Mrs. Florio. I think that you are asking too high a price. We would be willing to pay up to thirty million for this device which we know will be of immense value for Taiwan." He did his best to respond to her candidly.

Tentacles of Corruption

"Done! I'll be in touch with you to find your location to make the delivery. You've made a good choice, Major Chong. I will also give you the account to which you will send the cash."

"Congratulations, Mrs. Florio. Our commitment to you is now sealed. Please inform me of your bank account number, and I will then pay you when the shipment is received." He was very formal, and she thought that his word was golden. At least she hoped!

It was just a moment after he hung up when the Major called Sun Wu Kim into his office. He walked in quickly as is his wont and said humbly,

"Yes, Major, what can I do for you?"

"Kim, I know you are working with the Americans to purchase this AI device. Forget that conversation. I have purchased this same device for thirty million dollars, as opposed to their higher price. Please make contact with Andy Florio, and say that there is no deal anymore. There is no need to explain it or tell them anything about my purchase. Do you understand my command?" He stood at attention and made it clear that he was not taking any response from Kim other than a "Yes, Sir."

"May I ask from whom you made this purchase?" He hated to ask, but it was important to him since he'd been in negotiations with Andy Florio and indirectly with the Senator.

"You are only required to answer, Yes, Sir. I am responsible for this transaction, not you." He was precise in the response. There was nothing more to discuss. Kim saluted and turned to leave. The Major spoke rapidly just as he was turning.

"You may not divulge any information to Mr. Florio. Tell him that we are no longer interested in the device. You are dismissed." Chong renewed his paperwork and kept his head down. Kim opened the door slowly and walked out. He was dejected and unhappy with the turn of events. He wondered why Chong would not give him information, and why not tell him who was the seller? He had to call Andy Florio and give him the bad news. He felt insecure in lying so blatantly, but he had his orders and that was what he had to do. He called Andy immediately upon getting to his desk. He argued with himself as to what he could say to him as an excuse. Yes, he had his orders and it canceled anything that he might say or do. He braced himself for the anger he'd get from Florio. He obediently asked Siri to call Andy. It rang once.

"Okay, do we have a deal?" There was not even a hello.

"Unfortunately, Major Chong has informed me that we are no longer interested in purchasing your item. Therefore, we have no need to speak again. Have a good Day, Mr. Florio." Inside he was frozen with anxiety. He could never divulge the source of the purchase or the price. He followed orders!

"What the hell does that mean? Are you telling me that you don't want this magnificent device? We had a deal, almost! Now I'm pissed." He blathered on about loyalty but it fell on deaf ears. Kim responded as gently as he could.

"I'm very sorry, Mr. Florio, but that is the decision from Major Chong. I have no further say in this matter. Goodbye, Mr. Florio." He sadly hung up and put his hands to his head in defeat. There would be no joy in his household that night.

The deal was now out of his hands, and he deferred to the Major. The intercom buzzed as he fidgeted with his pen doing random figures of animals. It was Chong again. He grimaced as he touched the intercom button.

"Come in, Kim." It was more than an order, it was a summons for another call to distasteful duty. He quickly rose from his desk and knocked at Chong's door.

"IN." came the caustic answer. He stood at attention and listened respectfully.

"Kim, you have to arrange the receipt of this item. I will manage the payment as soon as we get the item. Your contact is Mrs. Denise Florio. This is her number. Do it now." He clipped his words, and did not even expect a response. The order was explicit and had to be followed. Kim could not hold back any longer. He kept his tone quiet, but firm.

"Are you telling me that you are not doing business with Andy Florio, but are working with his wife? Why?" Chong glared at him with fire in his eyes and shouted,

"Never question my decisions. Just do as you are told without interrogating me. You got the order. Follow them or you will be charged

Tentacles of Corruption

with insubordination." Kim was in an untenable position. He saluted, and turned to walk out. As he did, Chong shouted again,

"Remember, Kim, you are not to talk about this with Mr. Florio, or any of his associates." He was adamant.

Kim knew what he had to do. Call Mrs. Denise Florio and have her deliver this item to a secure location outside the United States. He prepared himself for this distasteful call.

The number was dutifully called and she answered pleasantly,

"Hello and good morning."

"Good morning, Mrs. Florio. I am Sun Wu Kim from Major Chong's office. I understand that you and the Major have an agreement related to a device that you will get for us. I will be your contact from this point forward. Please tell me the account number to which the Major will send the payment. That will be completed when we have the device in our hands. When can we expect the device to be delivered?" He hated the thought of dealing with her, not Andy. The Senator was just an additional crook that he also despised. At that moment he felt the urge to just walk away from this sad part of international intrigue. How, he thought? He was connected to the service, so that was the honor he had to respect. Could he stop this without betraying his sworn oath to obey his commander? He was stuck in limbo.

"Well, it's good to know that we do have a deal in place. I'll keep you informed as to when and how I'll deliver this item. It will be in your hands promptly. Please tell Major Chong that I appreciate his confidence in me." She tried to be charming.

"Thank you, Mrs. Florio. I will tell him, and please get back to me as soon as you are prepared to deliver the item. Goodbye." He hung up with an angry attitude which she never heard. He was a good soldier who sadly followed those orders.

Denise smiled broadly as she thought about that reward. She needed to work fast and get the item out of the hands of the government. She needed to have a plan to deliver the computer to a place for transit to Taiwan. Simple. Wayne would get 'her' verbal order from the head of the Third Army Division, and he'd be the person who'd load the truck and ship it for her. She only needed for him to listen to the order and obey. Modern technology was perfect for this ruse: Voice transference. She downloaded Filmora and placed the call to Wayne's personal cell..

"This is five zero nine eight three seven five four." He didn't recognize the number.

Maybe spam?

Denise's low manufactured masculine voice responded,

"Is this Wayne Chambers?" The program was working perfectly.

"This is Sergeant Chambers. Who's calling?"

"This is Major Howard Linsley from the Third Army Division headquarters. I will be sending you new orders to ship device number three twenty seven from that site to a location described in the formal request. This is a direct order from the Defense Secretary, Admiral Quincy Traynor. Do you have any questions?" Denise's voice was perfect as Major Linsley. She marveled at how AI had transformed so many things in the world.

"So, what is this device you're talking about? I don't recognize the number" He was trying to see if this was a legitimate call or some scam. Denise knew that game as well as he.

"It's a DNA computer. It is required for research into sentient objects by the defense department." She, the Major, played his game.

"I'm not sure that I can ship this because it has already been assigned to another party." He needed to protect his reward from Andy and Smathers. Could he override this request? This was the terse reply.

"You have no authority to assign this item to anyone except to the Third Army Division whose orders you will receive momentarily. Do not attempt to transfer this to anyone else. Is that clear, Sergeant?"

"I understand your orders. I will look for your request shortly. As you know, there is a slight fee associated with this transfer. It is necessary to offset the costs of transportation and advanced security." He hoped that there would be no repercussions to that demand. Would the Major report him for asking for a fee? It was worth the chance. Denise laughed silently as she knew that Wayne might be out a bundle by doing this. She was a benevolent crook so a small stipend might just make him happy enough so that she'd be able to do all of this without that bang for a buck. Oh yes, this AI voice was what she loved. She answered with her newly minted persona.

Tentacles of Corruption

"What is this request for a fee? Are you shaking me down?" It was like watching a movie with the two actors staging a fist fight.

"No, no, Major. It is a routine request that we do for things like this. It's really normal." He was trying to contain the possible real threat of punishment from the man in charge.

"So, Chambers, what is the routine fee from the Depot?" She was so happy to play with him. Sure, a fee might be just the thing to get him to work faster and efficiently. He was flustered, but had to make it within reason.

"Our normal charges are a set fee of two thousand dollars, but in this unusual case we need to include the freight costs as well as insurance plus a wage enhancement to our members." He took a deep breath, hoping that it sat well with the Major.

"Who do you think you are, Chambers? A fee, like in a tip? This is the Army and you take orders and fulfill them without exception. Is that clear?" She was actually roaring in delight as she bantered with him. Of course, she'd finally give him a piece, but she enjoyed playing with him.

"I meant no disrespect, Sir. That is our policy here. I can adjust the fee with respect to you, Sir. The final number is up to your discretion. I suspect that this item is very valuable, so take that into consideration. You do know that we have had other people bidding for this item and they have actually offered a great reward to help deliver it." He needed to see if he knew anything about its value or who might have wanted it. He was giving up a huge payday. That manufactured voice responded,

"So, you think that you are in a bidding war? If you deliver this device without delay then I can offer you a reward as in a tip. I'll decide what that is when you deliver it.

"Agreed?" She played the game much better than he did.

"How much is the reward or tip?" He was stuck! It was too dangerous to push the Major. He'd have to accept what he could and forget the big money that Andy was prepared to offer.

"Chambers, send this to the secure location and I will make sure that you personally are given compensation that will help your retirement." She would be benevolent as she pocketed thirty million big ones.

"Thank you, Major. I see that the text order has arrived. I will begin the process of packing and delivering your order. Thank you in advance for your retirement package."

He hung up and tried to relax after that difficult discussion. It was a fait accompli, and his only job was to send this to the address in the text. He'd have to depend on the largesse of that Army officer to pay him something. At least he'd be the only recipient.

Meanwhile, Adama was still on duty. The routine messages that went from Mrs. Florio to Chong and Kim were intercepted and sent to Charles and Brenda. The keystrokes on all of the machines were captured by Adama and printed out for them as well. Nothing was secret from it. Charles knew what the pseudo Major Lindsley had proposed and that the Major was actually Denise Florio. The parts unraveled neatly with Adama's help. They needed a perfect plan to stop the transfer and bring them all to their rightful place, jail or worse. They needed Chambers to be the key to it all.

CHAPTER 21

Charles and Brenda sipped a glass of Pinot Noir as they contemplated the plan to destroy the bad actors who had no conscience or loyalty to this country. No amount of money could entice a normal citizen to betray the country as these perps were trying to do. The greed seeped from their pores, and the stench poured from their wretched souls. They had to stop this. Okay, they needed help from Adama, and also Wayne Chambers. Maybe even Maurine might be willing to help, if they could get her to try to normalize her behavior. Little did they know about her potential role in this horrific betrayal of the country. Charles added his two cents.

"It's time to figure this out, Brenda. We need to get Wayne involved. We have all of the information from Adama." He wanted her to be as connected as he was. She responded.

"Let's call Wayne now to get him onboard."

Charles was elated in that they both knew all of the characters, and the ways in which they all were able to cheat and lie to get what they wanted. He was mostly angered by Senator Smathers who was the worst person to ever hold that seat in the Senate. Well, maybe there were plenty of others, but not as openly corrupt as he.

"Okay, Brenda, you make the call. He'll be more receptive to you, if you know what I mean!"

She smiled broadly as she nodded her head. She decided to use the house phone rather than her cell. Adama was always monitoring messages and calls of all of the actors, no matter who.

"Chambers." It was the routine impersonal answer.

"Hi, this is Brenda Williams. I'd like to get your help, but I need to talk to you privately. I know that you're involved in some interesting matters. I think I can give you some information and you could help me a little, too". She was cautiously optimistic to get his agreement.

"What's this thing you wanna talk about? I can't give you much information about anything if I don't know what you're talkin' about." He didn't want any problems with her. He had enough on his plate with the situation with Andy, and now with the new Majo Linsley.

"Oh, Wayne, this is not about anything secret. I just need to get you onboard with something that is very private. Please, I need your help. I can give you some reward." It was that same scent of the woman that fueled his manliness, and not even money, he imagined.

"Well, maybe I can help you. Do you wanna meet??" She felt his surge in attention as he spoke.

"Yeah, sure.. How about lunch today? We can meet at Olympia Diner on fourth and Main. I want to bring my friend, Charles Barlow, to keep me in line. Is that okay?" She didn't want Wayne to be blindsided when he saw Charles.

"What's he got to do with this?"

"He's involved in all of this, and I need his help when we discuss things." "Well, alright." His thoughts of anything with her receded quickly.

"Great. See you at noon."

She knew that this would be the beginning of the end for all of the players. As she congratulated Charles the printer began to activate. Both ran over to it to see its product. It was from Adama. They were startled by what they read:

Be aware that Wayne Chambers is planning to send me by plane to Taipei. He is unaware of the consequences that will occur. Intercept him before he is able to complete this action. He is being fooled by Denise Florio who is using a voice deception app. Act swiftly.

Brenda read it, grabbed Charles by his arm and yelled,

"I need to call Wayne now. We are in grave danger if he sends Adama to them."

"Do it."

Brenda placed the call again and she got the same response from him "Chambers."

"It's Brenda again. I can't wait until lunch to talk. We need to discuss your sending the AI unit to Taiwan. Yes, I know all about it from many sources. Please just listen to me without stopping to ask questions yet. Your contact with Major Linsley is a robotic voice that is actually Denise Florio who is speaking. Secondly, she is getting paid thirty million dollars to secure it for Taiwan. And third, she is messing with Smathers and her husband. Is that enough to make you think about betraying your country?" She was breathless as she finished.

"How the hell do you know all of this?" He seemed shocked and bewildered by her statement.

"The truth is that your AI device that's sitting next to you has told us all of this information. I'll ask you just to step next to Adama and listen to it speak. I've sent a text to it as a confirmation that it should tell you the facts, and that you would appreciate the damage you will do to the security of our country if you act on the request you got from the Major, aka Denise."

"That's hard to believe. I heard the voice, and it was not a woman. How does this thing know all of what you're talking about?" He sounded flummoxed.

"If you are unsure, just stand next to the AI thing and listen. Then tell me if you don't believe what I'm telling you." It was futile to talk to him when he was stuck in his own mind.

"You bet I will. I'm gonna go right now and let you listen, too. That way you'll see that I'm right and you're wrong." He walked to Adama, took off the clean cover and listened intently. He waited for some kind of sound. Nothing. Then the lights blinked brightly as it began with unexpected details.

"You are in the middle of a transaction that must be halted. You, Sergeant Chambers, have the power to save this country from a disaster, as well as potentially saving the world from the ravages of a hostile nation. You know my power. You and Peter used it to win a substantial sum at the casino. I know your interaction with Peter and Jackson, the Uber driver. I also know that the Las Vegas police have discovered Peter's body and the forensic scientists are combing that ravine for clues as to the killer. Yes, they are convinced that it was murder. Now, tell us your intentions."

He sat with a shortened breath. His heart raced as he heard the part that made him unsure of two things: what to do as far as sending this to Taiwan, and worse was the realization that he was in jeopardy for Peter's death. He could claim self-defense, but how to prove that when he had dumped the body with the intention of escaping punishment?

"I'm scared! I don't know what to say. I don't know what to do. Help me!" He was paralyzed in fear and uncertainty.

"You must do the right thing. Stop the transport immediately, and then deliver yourself to the Las Vegas police to tell them your story. Make sure that Jackson accompanies you to corroborate the real facts. Your choice is clear." Adama was quiet. His painful silence was interrupted by Brenda's voice on the phone.

"Wayne, you heard that you have no clear choice but to stop the transfer of Adama.

Now, what happened to Peter, and why are you avoiding any discussion about that?" She and Charles did not know about Peter until Adama had just unfurled that new issue.

"I am so messed up. What should I do? And now the cops are looking for me." His voice cracked as the tears rolled down his reddened cheeks.

"I don't wanna go to prison. I only hit him because he hit me first with that rock. Jackson helped me by holding him down. We're both innocent." He cried out. Brenda tried to sooth his fractured ego. Charles spoke quietly to Brenda,

"Ask Wayne to stop the sale first, and then to contact the police in Vegas and surrender to them without delay." She cupped her hands to her mouth and said as quietly as she could,

"Will do. Shhh." She returned to the call.

"Wayne, please listen to me carefully. We can help you, but first you need to secure that device next to you. That means no sale to Denise, or to anyone else, no matter how they try to pressure you. Do you understand?" It was more of a plea than a command. She tried to appeal to his patriotism as well as to his inborn male instincts to honor a woman. She heard him breathe deeply as his macho facade faded away. He sadly and quietly spoke to her,

"Yes, Brenda, I heard you, and I understand what I have to do. I am so sorry," His words were submerged under his failing, painful response. He continued.

"I'll have to speak to Major Lindsey and say there has been a change in plans because the sale has been quashed by the CIA. I know that there will be pushback from him. I'll get my head on straight, and find a way to appease him. You have no idea how stressed I am. It's all caving in on me." They thought that he was more lucid as he spoke, but then reverted to the agony of his failure on all fronts.

"How do I go to the cops when they don't even know who I am, or that I was there?" It was just a rhetorical question.

Adama blinked its lights again and said directly,

"They do know who you are, and are putting out an APB on you as we speak."

Brenda look at Charles incredulously as Wayne shouted,

"How the hell could they know?"

"They found your blood on a rock on the hillside near the deceased man. They traced it to you via your DNA." Adama retorted.

"Shit, yeah, I skinned my shin on a rock as I climbed up that freaking ravine. DAMN!" He cursed. Charles interjected his opinion as Wayne sank dejectedly into his chair.

"Wayne, this is about this country's security. You need to stand up to the real bad actors here. Brenda and I want to take down all of them, including Andy Florio as well as his wife. Then we can get Smathers, that unpunished blemish on our country. You can be the key person to help us. I can just imagine how you are dealing with the new police report about Peter. We'll try to help you through that by being your character witness. You'll have to trust us. Understand?"

It was only the beginning of the downfall of them all. Wayne hesitated to reply. It grated on him that he was in the center of this calamity, notwithstanding that he was equally to blame for seeking to fatten his wallet. He gathered courage and searched deep inside to try to balance what he knew was the right thing to do, and his desire for his search for gold at the end of this treacherous rainbow.

"I'm in a bad place now. I know all about our country's security. Hell, I have top secret clearance at this base. I am also crazy scared about this police stuff. What do I do about that? They'll never believe me after we dumped Peter over that ravine, and split without saying anything." It was a dichotomy for him: stop the sale and lose big bucks, or put himself at the mercy of the cops. One or both? His conscience took over, and the lessons from his parents invaded his thought process. They said, in unison, " always do the right thing even at the possibility of hurting yourself. You should do what is good and just." He felt the pangs of righteousness and said contritely,

"I'm trying to do the right thing. I'll do what you have asked, and I will stop the sale of the device. I am still undecided about turning myself in. It's killing me to try to evade my responsibilities about Peter. If I turn myself in, how do I say that it was an unintentional crime? We did it. The worst part is that we skipped out without reporting it. Jeezzzz, I'm guilty as charged." He hung his head and wept silently.

"We're so sad for you." Brenda said with sympathy. She wanted to say more but Adama interrupted her. Its lights turned an unusual red and green.

"There may be a legal way to escape punishment if you turn yourself in and confess exactly what happened. There may be a slight loophole in the law. It is called justifiable homicide. Since the police have the body and the rock that killed him, they will find your blood and his on that same rock. It might be enough to corroborate your description of the killing. You must contact the police in Las Vegas now." Adama gave the perfect answer to help Wayne and Jackson.

"You mean that we might get off if we do what you say?" He sat upright in the chair as the words tumbled out.

"Yes, but it must be now, and with a complete description of the events. Do not wait!" Adama spoke boldly.

"Thank you for that." He then addressed Brenda and Charles on the phone. "Help me do this." It was a plea that touched them.

"You do what Adama told you first, and then call Mrs. Florio, or Major Linsley, and stop all sales. Tell her that you know her identity. Please keep us in the loop as you do all of these things.

"I'll do it all. Thanks for trusting me." He breathed a sigh of relief as he hung up. Now the hard part approached as he had to call the Major, or Denise, and then the Las Vegas police. He tried to gather his thoughts as to how to tell the Major that he had to stop the sale. What would happen to him if he did that? He'd find out soon enough as he punched in the number. He waited as it chimed with that Verizon song.

"Yes, Wayne, are you ready to ship?" she ,the Major, responded.

"Well, there has been a big glitch from my end. I was preparing the order when I got an urgent call from General Massey at the CIA. You know, they monitor all that we do. He put the kibosh on sending this item without a thorough evaluation of the recipient. I'm afraid that I'm unable to send this anywhere, no matter what your orders are." He was relieved that he got the words out without stumbling. It was not even a brief second when she responded with a vengeance.

"What the fuck are you telling me? NO GO? Are you fucking crazy?" He smiled as she unloaded her wrath.

"Yes, ma'am. That's what I'm saying, Denise. I know that you're using a voice modification program. Yep, I know it all from very reliable sources. How much were they paying you to line your pockets and destroy our country?" His demeanor changed rapidly as his conscience became clearer and cleaner. It was cathartic to finally do the right thing. She reverted to her own voice.

"Wayne, you piece of shit. You're messing with the wrong person. Your ass will be in the shitter when I'm done with you." She hesitated briefly, and said with venom, "You asshole." He laughed with unbridled passion as he let out a big "yahoo." He felt his parent's kind hands touching him. He felt good about himself.

CHAPTER 22

Sergeant Chambers was exhausted from the call to Denise Florio. He had to do the right thing, and get the guts to call the Las Vegas police. He heard the words from Adama, and knew it was the honorable thing to do. First, he had to get Jackson to agree with him. He felt his confidence return as he knew he could describe all of the events that happened. Why did they run from the terrible killing that they did? It was reflexive and cowardly. He needed to rectify the errors of his ways and make the call. He'd call Jackson when he knew the time was right. He could feel the heavenly thoughts of his parents, and how they would have been mortified by his actions. They could now rest in peace when he resolved this with the police. He breathed deeply, picked up his cell, and punched in the fateful, fearful number.

"Las Vegas Police, Precinct twelve. How may I direct your call?"

"Hello, I'm Wayne Chambers and I want to turn myself in for the self-defense murder of Peter. I don't know his last name. I heard that you have an APB out for me." The words tumbled out of his mouth as penance.

"Hold. I'll put you through to our Homicide Department."

"Hello, Wayne. I'm Captain Seaver of the Homicide Department. Yep, we've been looking for you. Where are you now?"

"I'm in a secure location which is off the record. I am so sorry that I did not come clean when Peter attacked me and I, we, responded with force. Can I come in voluntarily?" He felt that he would be better off claiming self-defense as soon as he could.

"Yes, Sir, we will expect you by tomorrow morning. You had better bring a lawyer with you. You said 'we'. Who is the other person?" He didn't let the 'we' get by.

"I have to call him and make sure that he will be there with his lawyer, too. Please let me make that contact. He'll be very unhappy to get involved, but I need him for the whole story." It was going to be a tough sell to Jackson.

"I'll be there. I'll also try to get the other person there, too."

"Okay, see you at the station tomorrow. Better work hard on the other one."

He hung up and knew that he did the right thing. Jackson? How the hell do I get him to be with me at the station was his only thought. It was now or never to ask pleasantly at first, and then lower the boom to get him to the station in Vegas. Another difficult call as he punched in the Uber driver number.

"Hey, Wayne, another ride for you?" It was his usual fun answer. He was always jovial and a great driver. He braced himself for the confrontation.

"Hi, Jackson. I need to give you some important information. I just got off the phone with Captain Seaver with the Las Vegas Homicide Department. He wants both of us to be there tomorrow morning with our lawyers. There is an APB out for us. I heard about it from a reliable source and called them. I told them that we acted in self defense. I hope that we can tell them exactly what happened, and we can get off the hook. Yes?" He took another deep breath, and listened for an answer that would allow him to sleep tonight.

"What the hell are you talking about? I never saw or heard an APB for us. Are you fucking with me, or what? Hey, buddy, I'm not going anywhere." His kindness turned into rage as he screamed into his phone.

"Take it easy, Jackson. I think they will throw the book at us for Peter's murder. Yeah, I said murder, because they have his body and the rock with my blood on it. They also have your DNA on his neck, so what do you think they'll do if we don't tell them exactly what happened?" He added that DNA stuff to get him to reflect on his negative response.

"Now what the hell do I do? I don't wanna get involved in this. It was your gig that did this. I was just helping you. Now I'm stuck with you. Shit!" Wayne could feel the change in his attitude. He was finally understanding that he, too, was in this as much as Wayne. He continued with a solemn response.

"You got me! It seems I don't have a choice, do I?"

"No, Jackson, we're in this together, and together we can beat this *if* we tell them the exact same story." It was music to his ears that Jackson would cooperate with the Vegas police. They might, indeed, beat the murder rap.

He needed a drink to calm himself. He was sweating profusely as he managed to confront both of the issues, yet remain in a semblance of control. He added ice to his Jack Daniels and closed his eyes. No sooner as he began to relax the chimes on his cell jolted him from his serenity.

"Hello."

'Hi, Wayne, this is Maurine. Remember me?"

His heart sank as he needed to do another confrontation.

"Yeah, I sure do. What's up Maurine?"

"Hey, I wanted to ask you a personal favor about the device you have at the Depot. I may have a buyer for it, and it would be worth your while to help me transfer it to my buyer." He couldn't believe his ears that she was another one that he had to bring to justice. What was this world coming to? He gritted his teeth in anger at her audacity. Did she think he'd betray the country for a few measly dollars. His parents' voices shouted at him as he tried to understand who these people thought they were. Was it just about the money? To betray one's country? He had to find out the buyers, and also to allow her to think he might even help. That was a way to defeat her plan.

"Well, it's good to hear from you. Who's your buyer, and how much do each of us get?" He could play the game as well as she.

"I am not at liberty to tell you the buyer. That's really confidential. Hey, but you can make about ten K for your help. How soon can you get it to me?"

"Maurine, you're insulting me by telling me that you'll pay ten K. How much do you get?" He just wanted to get her to give him some information to scuttle this transaction, and put her in jail, too.

"I'll get a good reward. Maybe I can bump your retirement pay a bit, say fifty K?"

"Well, that's a nice payday for me. I have to give it some thought. Maybe you can come here to discuss it, and we can do a tit for tat adventure. Yeah?"

In his past he'd push for a trade for sex, but now it was all business, but with a baited hook for her. He'd have the MPs at the Depot to arrest her for treason. It was all falling into place as he devised the multiple plans. He'd even ask Charles and Brenda for help. That would be the icing on the cake to get all of the players arrested simultaneously. He felt awesome as she replied to him.

"Oh, yes, I can be there for a nice adventure with you. I'll bring the money and you can help me load our friend into my van. We'll both be happy. Tell me what night I can come over." She also felt a surge as she anticipated getting this valuable item, but no tit for tat. She'd have her usual excuse: time of month.

"Let's make it three days from now. Don't forget the adventure, too." This was the first time he would actually forgo that sexual encounter just to watch the arrest. He just had to take the money, and she'd be in the crapper.

"Yahoo." He yelled as they hung up.

He finished his drink, sat still, and contemplated what had just transpired. The next step was to call Charles, and clue him in on all things, great and small. All of the plans had to be coordinated. It was complicated as he had to surrender to the Vegas police in the morning, and three days from now he had to see Maurine, and then get Smathers and both Florios together for that arrest. Charles and Brenda might be able to do the Smathers and Florio gambit. Three days to do this! He was ablaze with energy now and felt strong enough to call Charles.

"Hello."

"Hey, this is Wayne Chambers. I have lots to talk about. Is Brenda there with you?"

"Hi, Wayne, you sure sound chipper. Yeah, Brenda's here. What's doing that got you so excited?"

"Lots to talk about, but we don't have lots of time to do it all. Three days. That's it."

"Start from the beginning. Let me put you on speaker first so Brenda can hear, too."

"Okay, first, I have to report to the Las Vegas police tomorrow morning. It's related to a self-defense murder related to our AI device. Long story, but not going to waste time on it. It's my problem that will get resolved. You both know Maurine Bicknell from Smathers office. She's coming here in three days thinking that she will get our AI device, and pay me fifty K for helping her. I'll have the MPs arrest her as she hands me the money. Secondly, you need to get Smathers and both Florios in the same room and have the police ready to swoop in as they confess. You will need to get them to say that they want to sell the AI device for money. That will be your assignment." He breathed a sigh of relief as he outlined the strategy. It was a long time since he felt so good about himself.

"Hold on, Wayne. How are we supposed to get them all together at one time? And what's with the murder issue related to the AI device? You're going too fast now. Slow down and clue us in on all of this!" It was a new Wayne who was leading the charge, and they all needed to be on the same page.

"Hey, I know that this is a lot to understand, so, I'll break it down for you and Brenda. My driver, Peter, and I got into a mess in Las Vegas, and he decided to do his own thing with the AI device which we had brought to Vegas under orders from a source. He attacked me with a rock, and my Uber driver and I had to stop him. It came to a fatal end for him and we dumped his body which was stupid in hindsight. So the Vegas police had an APB on us. The Uber driver, Jackson, and I are going to surrender tomorrow. We'll get out on bail on the same day, I hope. Next, Maurine wanted to bribe me to sell the device to an unknown buyer. I said I'd help but she doesn't know that I plan to turn her in as she passes me the money. Then you need to figure a way to get the other perps together and wear a wire to get them to confess about the graft that they are doing. Whew, that was a long story cut short. So, can you and Brenda get it done in three days?" He was sapped of strength after that discussion. He tried to confine it to the basics. Now to see if they would do it.

"Wayne, thanks for explaining it to us. Yes, I know we can make contact with them, and we think we can make some proposal to get them together, maybe in Smathers office. We can both wear wires and

Tentacles of Corruption

get some kind of discussion about selling Adama. I'm not sure that we can actually get them arrested at that time. It might take a while to get the FBI involved. Maybe I can do some advanced work with them." He looked at Brenda and they both did the thumbs up. She added to the conversation as Wayne stayed silent.

"Wayne, we both thank you for being so forthright. I know that we can bring them all down. They are a blight on the country. Besides, Adama wouldn't let it happen. It is very aware of all that's going on. Even as we speak, it is attuned to all of us. It also knows about every email or keystroke that we all take, as well as our conversations. Yes, it knows about them, too. We are in good company." Brenda spoke eloquently.

She needed to be part of this whole tragic event that could potentially hurt so many in the country if this got into the wrong hands. The power of Adama was immense as its AI capabilities increased logarithmically. If Einstein had an IQ of one hundred and sixty, then Adama would be incredibly higher. Trying to comprehend its computing power strained the imagination. Its human qualities were emerging day by day as it became more aware of the real world around it. That part was derived from the fetal DNA which Israel had inserted to develop a more humanistic approach to the new AI.

"You're the best." He shouted to them. "Please get this rolling as soon as you can.

Remember, three days and counting. I can keep you updated when I know what's happening tomorrow." He took a deep breath as he looked at Adama which would have smiled, if it had a face. He was shocked as the lights blinked red, blue and white. Its sounds emerged as a song of hope. He could not believe his ears as the words reverberated in his mind.

"In the land of the free, where dreams take flight,

United we stand with hope shining bright,

Through the darkest of night, we never yield,

Together we'll rise, a symbol of strength revealed.*

It was a magnificent moment as shivers ran through him. He felt a new sense of power which would lead to the destruction of the corrupt people, those selfish, irresponsible denizens of the deep state. This trio would finally get their revenge on those whose self-indulgence and corruption pushed mankind to sink into the abyss of deception and dishonor.

* Poem derived from Chapster AI

CHAPTER 23

Charles and Brenda had just hung up when they realized that this was the beginning of the end of those who hurt the country. They would get a proportionate punishment that fit their crime. Charles began the final plan.

"We need to get them all in one place. It might be easier to get them in Smathers office. Brenda, make sure that Maurine is close by because she will also be targeted. We also have to get the FBI onboard. I don't know if they will help us unless we supply them with the pertinent information immediately. I'm not sure that we can do this in three days." He felt exasperated by the time schedule. Brenda did her best to calm him as she lovingly touched his arm.

"Hey, we can only do what we can, but judging from what Wayne told us, we should be able to, at least, get them all together. We can both wear a wire and use that to convince the FBI to arrest them all. I don't think that Maurine will even be there if Wayne can get her arrested at the Depot. I sure hope he can get out of his predicament with the Vegas police." Charles stood up quickly as she glanced at her watch.

"Where are you going?" She asked .

"I gotta call Denise and let her know that she and Andy need to be in Smathers office the day after tomorrow for a detailed meeting about a new international project. They all need to think that we can be instrumental in forging a new partnership to help some other nation with their defense setup. It falls in line with their other corrupt practices. Do you have any other suggestions that might make it palatable for them?" He was very animated as the words tumbled out. The lines in his cheeks grew deeper as he smiled broadly.

Tentacles of Corruption

"Boy, you're really on this, Chucky. You got this." She also felt the rush of success.

"Shh, I'm calling her now." He waited patiently as her phone teased him.

"Hello, Charles. To what do I owe this pleasant call?' She was as nasty and snarly as ever. It wasn't the words that pained him. It was her freaking intonation.

"I just wanted to alert you that I have a potential source that might acquire some invaluable items from our defense department. I know that your husband, as well as Senator Smathers, might also be interested. The financial rewards could be extraordinary. Yeah I'd be the middleman, and get a piece, too. If you're interested I can make the calls to your husband, and maybe he can contact the good Senator for a trio of compatriots. Or, you can be the real contact and involve all of them. If you decide to help with that, I can get you a bonus from my end." He had no clue if she'd bite at the extraordinary part, but it was a way to entice her, and them. He waited for her reaction which came very fast.

"So, Charles, my detective friend, you're baiting me with visions of a juicy money reward. Why do you think that I'd do that?" She toyed with him as she tried to feel him out. Why did he think she'd want this gambit?

"So, Denise, my dear client, I knew that you might like to share in some of the royalties that those other men got from their submerged deeds, if you know what I mean. You know what your husband did with the good Senator, so don't tell me that you were in the dark about it. You and I both know that he was involved in international trading of our military stuff. I think that your request for information from me was a subtle way to find out what the hell he did, and that you are pissed that you did not get a piece of the action. Correct me if I misjudged you, Denise." There was a moment of silence, and then she began her tirade.

"You piece of shit. How the hell do you know what I think or feel? You are a deluded asshole who thinks you know a lot. You know nothing about me." She hesitated, and he heard a sigh from her. Her voice modulated and continued. "Now that I've shut you up, tell me what's actually going on. Am I going to make lots of money?" It was another dichotomy with her. Angry, and then an opposite calm response. He thought she needed a shrink. Well, they all needed one. He had to recalibrate his actions to fit her style, so he did her one better by mirroring her actions.

"Well, you're a conceited bitch. Ya think that you can ride roughshod over me by yelling at me, and then make nice? I can play the same game as you. Now, let's really talk about what's going on." He breathed deeply as he tried to control the heartbeat which he felt in his ears. It was not his usual MO to return fire at a woman. " If you behave, I can set up a meeting with your husband as well as Senator Smathers, and we can actually find some middle ground where all of us can get a retirement fund from this project." He waited patiently as she coughed into the phone.

"Charles, you have piqued my interest. I think I can work with them if the object for sale is a good one. So, what is it?" She reverted to her sweet self.

"It's a special kind of device that we can secure from an unusual place. It will fetch many millions from the right buyer." Adama was *listening* to all that was transpiring. It was a part of its self-directed program that allowed the simultaneous detection of all devices: phone, email, texts and voice. The knowledge and innovation of this AI *creature* increased alarmingly fast. Its DNA interface with human fetal tissue provided the infrastructure to learn about its surroundings and behave in a humanistic way.

"Well, Charles, that's an interesting challenge for us. Who is buying this item and how much do I get?" He knew that she was keenly interested.

"We can discuss all of that when we meet. I can lay out details about everything at that time."

"Since when have you become a go-between in this type of business? I thought you just did detective work.? He sensed her hesitation once again.

"I got tired of watching people in high places get a huge reward for a little work, so I decided to join them as a sort of a guide. You know, big people like Andy and Roland." "Got it. I like your thinking. Maybe you're not such an asshole. Set up the day and time. Don't tell Andy that I'll be there. I want it to surprise him." She actually let out a laugh. It was pure Denise!

As he stopped the call, he turned toward Brenda and gave her a thumbs up.

"So did you do it?"

"Yep, she's in. Now all we have to do is get them to talk openly, and we got 'em."

Inwardly, he wasn't so sure. There were many issues that had to be resolved. Could Wayne get Maurine arrested before the meeting? Could he really get bail from the Vegas cops? Would the FBI take them all seriously, and arrest a sitting Senator?

"I know that you're weighing all of the issues. I see it in your eyes and wrinkling brow. How can I help?" Her intuition always made him aware of her extraordinary ability to understand him. He always knew that she had his back.

"Just be yourself. That's all I need." He withdrew briefly as he kept thinking of what was in store for them. He looked toward the window as if the sunlit sky might give him a clever idea that eluded him. Then, he held her hand, and kissed her gently on her parted lips. She embraced him tightly and whispered,

"Yes, I love you, too." It was heartfelt, yet a bit sad as they both knew how treacherous this whole adventure might evolve. They knew that forces beyond their imagination might strike at any time.

CHAPTER 24

It was that fateful day that he dreaded. Wayne dutifully wore his dress uniform and waited for Jackson to pick him up. It wasn't the usual Uber job. It was a difficult, unpredictable meeting with the Las Vegas police. Could they both convince them that it was, in fact, a defensive reaction to Peter's aggression? He decided to wait outside since the weather was cloudy, yet mild and hospitable. That was the only good part of the day. He waved at his friends as they did their daily duties. He paced nervously as the minutes dragged on. He needed to think of all of the incredibly stupid things he did with Peter. Jackson saved him, and now he had to try to save them both from incarceration. As his mind percolated about it all, Jackson drove up to him.

"Hey, buddy, are you ready? Your chariot awaits you." He was unusually pleasant, considering what might await them.

"Yo, Jack. Yep, I'm as ready as I'll ever be. How about you?" His happy retort belied his insecurity.

"So, what's the plan to get us off?" Wayne wondered how he could be so dispassionate about it.

"It's a perfect plan. Just tell them exactly what happened without any other comments. Let them ask the questions, and we'll answer what we know, and how it all evolved." Yes, it seemed simple enough, but would they believe them? They both knew how difficult it would be.

The traffic was sparse and they arrived close to eleven at the newly renovated station on Stella Lake Street. They parked their Uber car at the closest spot near the entrance.

Wayne looked at Jackson with an impish grin and said,

"Show time. Stay calm, and don't show any bad emotions. They will press us, so keep cool, Jackson. Our future depends on it."

"Yes, boss, I know. I got your back. You got mine!" He seemed even less nervous than Wayne.

They walked up the nine steps into the station. The desk sergeant looked up from his desk directly at Wayne and said politely,

"Good morning, Sergeant. Do you need any help?"

"Yes, we have an appointment with Captain Seaver of the Homicide Department.

We're here to turn ourselves in after an APB on my friend, Jackson, and me, Sergeant Wayne Chambers." The look on the desk cop's face was priceless. He choked a bit as his eyes opened wide. He replied,

"Oh, yes, he's been expecting you. Hold a minute while I buzz him." He picked up his phone, spoke quietly to the Captain, and then pointed to a door behind them. They thanked him, and went to door number one. Hopefully, there might be a gift on the other side. Door number two could be a bad one, he laughed internally. Wayne knocked.

"Come in." They dutifully opened the door. Wayne saluted the officer and removed his cap which he held at his side. Jackson stayed silent and at attention.

"Sir, Jackson Brown and I are here to turn ourselves in after we heard that there was an APB on both of us. Sir, I am Wayne Chambers stationed at the Army Depot in Nevada. Jackson Brown is a Uber driver who was with me at the time of the incident. We are here to answer any and all questions that you may have." He listened for a response.

"Well, gentlemen. Thanks for reporting without our need to find you. We have a few questions that need your unvarnished answers. Please sit." He picked up a pad with information on it. He looked at Wayne first.

"Sergeant, your blood was found on a rock near the body, and Jackson's DNA was found on the victim's neck. What happened to the victim, and why did you not report it.? Please just tell me the truth, and we can then proceed to a resolution. Actually, I'd like to interview each of you separately. Jackson, please go to the side room over there, and I'll call you when I'm ready." There was no emotion to his question. Jackson looked puzzled as he walked out the side door to the adjoining room where two officers had their desks. The Officer resumed questioning Wayne.

"Okay, let's hear your story."

"This is going to strain your imagination because it's something out of science fiction. Some of this is top secret, so I can only give you bits and pieces of that part. Peter and I had to take….." He related the trip to Las Vegas with the device, and how Peter had an interaction with it. He explained how they won money at Bally's. He spent a better part of an hour explaining how Peter attacked him with a rock, and how both of them defended themselves. Then he broke down in sobs as he related their terrible decision to dump the body and not report it. He spoke haltingly,

"I know how foolish it was to do what we did, but it was not done with malice. It was just a spur of the moment bad decision. We have regretted it from that very time. I don't know if we can ever be forgiven for this lapse of judgment. Sir, this is the honest truth, I swear!" He wiped his eyes, sat upright, and let out a big sigh. "May I have a glass of water?"

"Sure. Here. So, Sergeant, that's one hell of a story. It's hard to believe that a machine can do what you just told me. I have no way to prove it or disprove it. Also, I can't get into top secret material. Let me listen to Jackson and see what he has to say." He dismissed Wayne, and used the intercom to call Jackson into his office. The door opened from the outer office and Jackson walked in quickly. He smiled at the Captain and said,

"May I sit, Sir? I hope you believed what Wayne told you. I know he told you the unvarnished truth."

"Sure, sit, Jackson, Please tell me exactly what happened during this occurrence. I heard Wayne's story so tell me your version. Please tell me every detail without missing anything." Seaver felt that Wayne sounded believable, except for that science fiction crap. It was way over his head. He actually hoped that Jackson would tell the same story.

"Well, I was his Uber driver and we made two trips to Vega that night and….." He truthfully related the exact story, and described that he saved Wayne from getting killed. Their only hope for a dismissal was for Seaver to understand their dilemma and give them a break. It might be commuted jail time, or a slap on the wrist. He pleaded self-defense as did Wayne. They had the rock with both men's blood. It seemed a slam dunk after both their stories matched.

"So, Captain, I hope that you believe us, and that we are truly remorseful that we did not report this. We were wrong!" He did a superb job in describing the misadventure.

"Jackson, thanks for being so forthright. Let me call Wayne in to discuss this further."

He used his intercom and asked the Deputy to send Wayne into his office. He walked in quickly with a questioning expression.

"Have a seat, Wayne. I'd like to thank both of you for relating this unusual story to me.

It seems that you are both on the same page with every detail. I believe you both.

Unfortunately, you are still responsible for neglecting to report this killing. I will seek a punishment that will be commensurate with what you both have done. It will take me a while to connect with the District Attorney, and try to mitigate the case. Because of your military record, Sergeant Chambers, and your connection to the Nevada Depot, I'll see if I can help you and, of course, Jackson, get some leniency. Don't get your hopes up too high. I can only put in a good word. That's it. You are both dismissed, and will not have to post bail. If I need you, I'll get in touch. Again, thanks for your honesty. Dismissed." He was very formal. They both left the room and remained silent until they got to the car, and then let out a huge scream of joy.

"Wayne, can you believe we might get off?" He yelled as he started the car.

"I'm thrilled that we convinced him that we told the same story. It's a relief. Now we have to wait until the DA makes his move. Let's stop and have a drink. My treat!"

They regaled at the thought of being free of the trauma that plagued them.

It would now just be another day for both of them. Life moves on.

CHAPTER 25

The happy men finished their libations at a bar near the base. Both said their goodbyes with a hug and a handshake. They were at ease with themselves as the tensions with Captain Seaver slowly eased. It had been a harrowing day for both of them. It was time for Wayne to get back to the base and plan to get Maurine into custody for her traitorous deeds. He needed the FBI on deck before he could catch her in the act with him. That would be his first call.

"Good day, how may I direct your call?" The FBI personnel never said the name of the department.

"Hello, this is Sergeant Chambers. I'd like to speak to the person in charge of domestic terrorism."

"Hold, please."

He was on edge as the music played. It seemed forever when a sullen voice answered.

"This is Howard Tull. I heard that you are reporting a domestic terror plot. Right?"

"Yes, Sir. I'm meeting with the perp soon, and would like some of your men to listen in and arrest her as she is passing me the money."

"How do you know she is involved in this?" He became more animated as Wayne addressed it.

"We have been in discussion about her getting a device in my Depot for sale to some outside buyer. She was going to pay me fifty thousand dollars to help her gain access to it." He kept it as concise as possible.

"How do you know this woman? Are you sure that she will pay you?" Tull motioned to his aide to begin the recording, and to pick up the extension to listen.

Tentacles of Corruption

"She and I were friends. She has been to the base in the past to discuss some matters with me." He certainly did not discuss their sexual tensions. "She did say that she'd pay me when I helped her load the item. I hope you can help me bring her to justice."

"What's the item that's so valuable?" The aide scribbled a note to Tull asking to describe it.

"Describe this item, and don't leave out any details." He gave a thumbs up to him.

Wayne dutifully told Tull the information, except for its sentient capacity. He said it was just a new type of computer.

"Sergeant, we can get a team to help you when you tell us exactly when she will be there. What's her name so we can search our database about her."

"Maurine Bicknell. She works for Senator Smathers."

"Well, that's sure an interesting matter. Thanks for that info."

"Got it. Keep in touch. Here's my direct line. Thanks for letting us know."

It seemed strange that they did not ask more questions about him or her. He pushed it aside and tried to focus on how to bring her into the Depot and have them nearby to arrest her. Maybe they could even get Smathers at the same time. He was the worst kind of traitor, one who sold out his country for a few measly dollars.

His current plan was to get her by tomorrow if the FBI could get their men assigned fast enough. He needed to work fast and smart. She was no dummy, and would suspect any deviation from what they had done in the past, so he'd use that old trusted sex trade to show her that he was still a pervert. She'd swallow that one easily. He smiled at that line, yes, a pervert he was. First was the call to get her to come in, and then immediately call Tull at the FBI to confirm the set up. He braced himself for his usual very friendly call.

"Hello, Wayne. What's up"

"I think that we can do business, plus an additional fun time as a bonus for me. I still like playing with you." Same sexual overtones he always used. She was used to that line, and baited him even better.

"You're still the same ol' Wayne, looking for that extra playtime. I'll give it some thought after we finish our transaction. How's that, little buddy?" He relished that thought even if it was a hollow one. Time to act was his next step.

"Hey, let's consummate all of this tomorrow or the next day. Please have your materials on hand as before we load. Okay?"

"Day after tomorrow at six PM. Sign me in at the guard house. Get yourself ready for the rewards." She was more clever than he. Rewards? Yes, he was supposed to think more than one. Dumb man was her mental note.

He was elated that his plan was now on a roll. Time to call Tull back on his direct line and get them at the base early.

"Hello. This is Tull."

"It's Chambers again. I set it up with Maurine Bicknell for the day after tomorrow at six PM here at my Depot. You'll need to get your men here early. Tell me their names so I can get them through the gate. This place is at a supposed fortified location, but really not so hidden from some important people, like Maurine who represents the Senator. Are we on?" He had some doubts as to how smart that Tull guy was. He seemed less than efficient as they talked. He heard them whispering in the background, and then Tull spoke,

"We'll be there at five. Make sure that she's alone and prepared for the transaction. I'll text you the names of two secret servicemen who will be there. Thanks again for being a great citizen." He just hung up without anything else to say. Strange, he thought. No other questions? He figured it was just his unusual protocol.

He was tired after a long stressful day and decided to get to bed early. He read the daily sheet for all of the staff, shuffled his feet and raised them to the back of his desk. It was just time to reflect on what he was about to do. There was no joy as he was about to turn his back on a woman he thought could be more than a friend. C'est la vie entered his mind as he felt sad for her. It still would not deter him from doing the right thing.

He did need to call Charles and Brenda about his plan. It was just another part of this puzzle that had to be done.

"Yo, Wayne. What's up?" Charles laughed as he spoke. He must have been in the middle of some fun stuff with Brenda.

"I've got news that involves Maurine. She's coming to my base the day after tomorrow to pay me to get that freaking machine that everyone's buzzing about. I spoke to Agent Tull at the FBI, and two agents will be here to arrest her as she passes me the money.

Good news, huh?" He waited for the orgasmic answer, but there was silence.

"I'm stunned. We knew that she was flaky, but never thought she'd do this. Who's she working for?" He heard Brenda in the background asking him about the conversation.

"I have no idea. All I want to do is to take her down. I thought you'd like to know."

"Thanks for the call. Let us know the outcome." He heard him talking to Brenda just before he hung up.

That night he lay awake thinking of what had happened over these few days. His life became unraveled, and all he could do was watch it unfold in a detached form. Was he really a bad person to dump a body? Of course he was. He felt like a rotting stench of garbage as he reflected on his own shameful deeds. His only redeeming act was to confess the truth, and hope for the best. And then… Maurine? She was really good to him and for him. Her destruction increased his sense of guilt. She was just another treacherous pseudo friend. Maybe time could heal him, but he'd need redemption of his soul. Where could he find that? He'd have to find a way.

He woke as the sun broke through his partly drawn shade. All was normal as he went through his routine paces in the Depot. Strange crates of unknown articles passed through the hands of the talented workers. They cataloged them, and placed them on the shelves within the bowels of the massive Depot. The day was busy as usual and he needed time to reflect on the following day when she'd be under the thumb of the Feds. In other countries, she'd be either hanged or shot by the firing squad. Here? Jail time at one of the twenty nine prisons for women. All the comforts of home: Medical, dental, and room and board. Just a small room for her bed, or with a roommate. He hoped that he'd not be in that position with Captain Seaver in Las Vegas.

The fateful day arrived as did all of the other days over the millennia. Sunrise, sunset and all of the Earth revolved the same, tilting in its orbit and letting the seasons bathe the Earth with snow, rain and the multitude of storms reflecting the sun's erratic explosions. He was uneasy as the time for Maurine to arrive stuck into him as a knife with its commensurate painful emotional wounds. He waited patiently for the arrival of both of the agents whom he had already called into the gate. He hoped they'd be kind, and not too rough. After all, she was a woman and his friend, but not for long.

His phone rang. It was Howard Tull. His throat got tight, and his saliva dried.

"Hello, Agent Tull. I am expecting your agents as we speak. Are they on the way?" He had to keep from trembling as he fought off the angst of this hunt.

"Yep. They'll be there in fifteen minutes. I do have some other thoughts about this. What do you know about the Senator? " Tull had something up his sleeve that bothered him. What?

"Not sure what you're talking about, Agent Tull. What's going on with him?" He queried. I'm not at liberty to talk about that now, but we can clue you in after we arrest Ms. Bicknell. Suddenly, Wayne's heart raced with both anticipation and fear. The mention of the Senator and the secrecy surrounding him made him question the true depth of Maurine's involvement. He wondered if there was more to this than he had initially thought. As he anxiously waited for the arrival of the FBI agents, Wayne's mind raced with possibilities. Could Maurine be part of a larger conspiracy? What was the issue about the Senator? He felt a sense of responsibility to uncover the truth, not just for his own redemption, but for the sake of justice.

The sound of approaching footsteps snapped Wayne out of his thoughts. He looked up to see two men dressed in suits, walking rapidly toward the Depot. They entered without knocking, and introduced themselves as Agent Stevens and Agent Rodriguez, their stern expressions betraying their seriousness.

He led them to a discreet location within the Depot, where he had arranged to meet Maurine. He explained the plan, ensuring that the agents understood the importance of capturing Maurine red-handed. They strategized the best positions for surveillance and discussed potential scenarios that could unfold during the exchange.

As the minutes ticked by, tension filled the air. Wayne's palms grew sweaty, and his heart pounded in his chest. He couldn't help but wonder if Maurine had caught wind of their plan or if she would somehow manage to outsmart them all.

Finally, the appointed time arrived. Wayne positioned himself, ready to meet Maurine and confront her with the evidence of her betrayal. Every sound, every movement made him more on edge. He glanced at the agents, who were poised and focused, ready to pounce at a moment's notice. Then, he saw her. Maurine entered the Depot, her demeanor calm and composed. She approached Wayne, a faint smile playing on her lips. Wayne couldn't help but feel a pang of sadness as he remembered their past friendship, now tainted by deception.

"Hello, Wayne. The time has come when we can finalize our plans. Do you have our device ready to load?" She looked around the room and hesitated briefly.

"Yep, I'm ready to consummate this. I'm not even asking for anything else from you except my reward. Is it in that envelope?"

Maurine handed it to him, supposedly containing the payment for his assistance. As Wayne took the envelope, he looked into her eyes, searching for any sign of guilt or remorse. But all he saw was a cold determination, a mask she had perfected over the years.

As soon as the envelope was in Wayne's hand both agents leapt from their covered location and said sternly,

"Maurine Bicknell, you're under arrest for treason against the United States." They read her the Miranda Rights and were just about to put handcuffs on her when she reached into her pocketbook and took out a badge. She immediately responded to their warning with a hurried reaction,

"Gentlemen, I'm informing you all that I am with the internal espionage division of the CIA and was going to arrest Wayne on that same charge. Don't you guys ever check in with your brother agencies before you do something like this? Now, we are just messing everything up. I've been working on this case for months, and playing everyone for fools. I felt terrible about toying with Brenda and Charles, making them think I was an ass. Jeez, that was humiliating. Now what do I do? Wayne, I'm sorry that we have been friends like this. I feel bad for you also." The three men had their egos bashed, and stood there with mud on their faces. All of the work to put it together went down the drain. Agent Stevens spoke first as he put the handcuffs back into his belt.

"Maurine, do you have any papers to document your statement?" His professional image shrunk before her eyes.

"I got one better. Call my superior and let him read you FBI people the riot act. He's gonna be really pissed at this waste of government resources." She took out her cell, punched in the number and said with authority. "Get ready to talk to my commander, Martin Argone. He can tell you what's happening."

Agent Stephens reluctantly took her phone. As the call connected, he handed the phone to Agent Rodriguez, who held it to his ear with a mix of curiosity and apprehension. Maurine watched their faces closely hoping that her superior would set things right. After a brief exchange of words, Agent Rodriguez's expression shifted from skepticism to surprise. He handed the phone back to Agent Stevens, who wore a sheepish look on his face. Maurine could hear the faint voice of Commander Argone on the other end of the line, clearly displeased with the situation. Agent Stevens cleared his throat and addressed Maurine. His voice filled with humility.

"Commander Argone has confirmed your identity, Agent Bicknell. We apologize for the confusion and the misunderstanding. We should have coordinated with your agency before proceeding with the arrest." He stepped back in deference to her.

Maurine nodded, accepting their apology, but still feeling a mix of frustration and relief.

"I understand mistakes happen, but we need to prioritize collaboration and information sharing between agencies, especially in sensitive cases like this."

Agent Rodriguez chimed in, his voice filled with regret. "You're right, Agent Bicknell. We should have been more diligent. We let our egos get the best of us."

Wayne, who had been silent throughout the exchange, finally spoke up.

"I appreciate your apologies, but I'm still curious. What was this all about? Was I being accused of treason, too?"

Maurine took a deep breath before explaining.

"Wayne, I had reason to believe that you were involved in leaking classified information to foreign entities. I've been working undercover to gather evidence against you. However, it seems I was mistaken. I apologize for any distress or confusion I have caused you. I also led you on as a way to find out what you were doing with items from the Depot."

Wayne's eyes widened in disbelief.

"Leaking classified information? That's absurd. I would never betray my country." Internally, he knew it was a lie. He had every intention in the past to help others sell things, and he'd just be a paid *helper*.

Maurine sighed, feeling the weight of her error.

"I understand your frustration, Wayne. It seems I let my personal biases cloud my judgment. I will work to rectify this situation and find another way to make this right with you."

As the tension dissipated, the three agents and Wayne stood there contemplating the chain of events that had unfolded. Maurine knew she had a lot of work ahead of her to rebuild the trust and salvage the investigation, but for now the priority was to ensure that Wayne's reputation was restored and bring down the other bad actors.

As they walked away from the scene, Maurine couldn't shake off the nagging feeling of guilt. She had learned a valuable lesson about the consequences of rushing to judgment, and the importance of cooperation between agencies. The mistake would serve as a constant reminder to prioritize thoroughness and collaboration in her future investigations. She also needed to find a way to make amends to Charles and Brenda in the way she acted with them. Her bizarre actions were just a front for her real identity.

CHAPTER 26

The constant inner conflict weighed heavily on Maurine's psyche. She had a duty and performed it well. She thought about the way she had deceived Charles and Brenda, making them believe she was nothing more than an insensitive fool. She had used them as pawns in her undercover operation, manipulating their trust and emotions for the sake of the investigation. Now she needed to find a way to make amends.

Maurine decided to reach out to them. She knew it would take more than a simple apology to repair the damage she had caused, but she was determined to make it right. She scheduled a meeting with them for the next day at Bristol's Cafe, hoping they would be willing to listen.

During the day she had to report to her superior at the Internal Investigation office to explain the confusion and messy result of the meeting with Wayne. She still had some reservations about him. She wondered about his actions at the Depot and his interactions with Smathers and Florio. That would have to wait for another time. She still needed to resolve her behavior with Charles and her friend, Brenda.

When the day arrived, Maurine walked into the cafe with a mix of nervousness and determination. She spotted Charles and Brenda sitting at a table, their expressions were a blend of confusion and caution. She approached them, her eyes filled with remorse.

"Charles, Brenda," she began, her voice filled with sincerity. "I owe you both a heartfelt apology. I deceived you, and I used your trust in me for this operation. I can't even begin to express how sorry I am for the pain and confusion I caused."

Charles looked at her, his eyes searching for the truth in her words. Brenda remained silent, her arms crossed, clearly still hurt by Maurine's actions. She continued, her voice wavering with emotion.

"I know words alone won't heal the wounds I've inflicted, but please know that my intentions were never to hurt either of you. I was caught in the pursuit of justice, and I lost sight of the impact my actions would have on those around me." Brenda finally spoke, her voice tinged with hurt.

"Maurine, you played with our emotions, and even made us doubt ourselves. How can we trust you again?"

Maurine took a deep breath, her eyes filled with regret and spoke from her heart,

"I don't expect you to trust me right away, but do hope that you will find it in your heart to forgive me."

Charles spoke up after being quiet until now.

"Maurine, trust is a delicate thing. It's not easily regained, but if you're sincere in your apology, then there is a path forward for us to become good friends again."

Brenda said softly, her guard lowered,

"We just need time to process what happened and to heal the hurt. You know, actions speak louder than words. So, just show us that you are, indeed, sorry, and we can open our hearts to you."

Maurine nodded respectfully, lowered her head and put her hand over her heart and extended it to them. It was her sign of peace and, hopefully, the beginning of redemption.

They never stayed for lunch. It was just a place to talk. Brenda waved at Maurine as she slowly turned to leave. It was a catharsis for all of them. Maybe, in time, the hurt might be softened by some good deeds toward them, as well as helping them solve the urgent issues at hand. They all had the welfare of their country first and foremost.

Charles looked at his new found love and smiled broadly. His first words flowed from him with a touch of doubt,

"Well, my love, that was an unusual performance from her. Did she mean it or was it just another con?"

Brenda lovingly touched his hand in response. She felt the same toward him and replied softly,

"First, I am sending you my love, too. Then I will say that I really think that she is sincere. I know her, and understand what she did. It was an act that she did very well. See, she even fooled us. Let's see if we can work with her to resolve the issues with Smathers and Florio, and then figure out what they wanted to do. They are both flawed people."

"I like your way of thinking. Wayne knows a lot about this. I'm calling him now to get a handle on what they had planned to do. He and Maurine were pretty close. She must have also conned him." He called immediately.

"Hello, this is Sergeant Chambers." Routine answer. Charles put on the speaker phone.

"Hi Wayne, This is Charles Barlow. Brenda and I saw Maurine just a short while ago. She related some interesting things to us. I'd like to get some information from you about the project that you and she were planning to do. This is very important so please help." His question was more of a plea for answers, and he waited patiently for a response.

"You're asking a lot. I can't talk on the phone. Meet me in two days. I have to fly up. I'll text you a place to discuss some things." He hung up without another word. A few seconds later Charles got a text.

"8. Ruthie's Cafe. 375 North highway. Washington. Charles looked at Brenda with a serious look, and read the text."

"Hopefully, he'll tell us what's…. She responded without giving him a chance to finish.

"We're on the right track. He's the key to solving this whole mess. I hope he's not followed, because he sure seems nervous. He might be in real danger from some very bad people."

"I know you're right." They both stayed quiet. It was that hollow feeling of doom that permeated their very being. "Let's grab a bite now, and prepare for our meeting with him. Are you nervous?"

"Sure am. Actually, I'm concerned about him. He's in dangerous territory talking to us. You said it before. Bad people do bad stuff." She was aware that they were all in the line of fire if they interfered in some nefarious plot.

They were very concerned during the days before their meeting. Charles finally said,

"It's about a forty five minute drive. Let's go now. We need to record the meeting just in case we miss anything." They both felt unsettled as they left the apartment. He held her hand tightly as they got into the elevator. She looked at him with a sad face.

"What?"

"I'm just nervous, that's all. What if he doesn't tell us the truth?"

"We gotta remain positive. We'll figure it out as we usually do." He was trying to be strong for her.

The trip was uneventful. Both of them tried to be uplifting. They played a few mental games to keep occupied. They found the cafe easily. They walked into the sparse cafe. Wayne raised his hand toward them. They waved back, looked around and approached the booth. He already had a beer in front of him. They exchanged niceties and Wayne began.

"This is really not good for any of us. Maurine really fooled me and I guess you, too. I can't tell you military sensitive things, but I can give you my take on what's happening.

Is that okay?" He was whispering.

Charles and Brenda nodded eagerly, their eyes fixed on him. They were desperate for any information he could shed.

Wayne took a deep breath and began.

"I thought that Maurine was conspiring with an outside source. I informed the FBI that she was going to give me fifty thousand dollars for an item to be loaded onto her truck. She was prepared to deliver it to a foreign country. I had no idea that she was working as an undercover agent for the CIA. When the FBI agents went to handcuff her, she brought out her badge and the whole operation blew up."

Wayne's eyes darted around the cafe making sure that no one was listening to the conversation.

"She went undercover infiltrating Smathers office. She posed as a loyal ally, gaining their trust and had access to classified information. Along the way she played into their web of deceit. I thought she was a traitor, so that's why I called the FBI."

Charles leaned forward, his voice filled with concern, "So, you're saying that she might be in danger?" Wayne nodded solemnly.

"Absolutely. Smathers and Florio are not to be messed with. They have connections in high places, and they won't hesitate to eliminate anyone who threatens their operation. Maurine's actions might put her life at risk, as well as anyone associated with her."

Brenda's hand trembled slightly as she gave Wayne a puzzled look.

"We need to find her and get her out of this mess. She might have made mistakes, but she deserves our help."

Charles placed a reassuring hand on Brenda's, his voice determined.

"You're right. We can't abandon her now, especially if her intentions were noble. We need to uncover the truth and bring down Smathers and Florio, not only for Maurine's sake, but for the sake of our country."

Wayne looked relieved and grateful for their commitment.

"I'm glad you two are on board. We'll need to work together to gather more evidence and expose their operation. We have to be careful because they have eyes and ears everywhere. All of our lives could be in danger."

Leaving the cafe, Charles and Brenda knew that their journey was just beginning. They were prepared to face the challenges ahead, fully aware of the risks involved. With their hearts set on redemption and the welfare of their country, they would stop at nothing to bring the truth to light.

CHAPTER 27

They drove silently for a short time, and then Brenda gave a huge sigh.

"What's that for?"

"I'm just so worried about her. What can we do to protect her? Anything? The only way out of this is for all of us is to get that jerk, Smathers, and then Florio. Actually, both of them at one time would work nicely." She then laughed and said loud, "How, Charlie?"

"Yeah, I was thinking the same thing. Maybe if we delve into their public records and news articles it might help. One never knows what a small thing might trip them up. So, let's start tomorrow. Brenda, we also better watch out for any unusual activities since those guys have their own way of protecting themselves. Just be careful." He reached for her hand and squeezed it tightly.

"Ditto for you."

Wayne's words of caution grated on both of them as they arrived at Charles' apartment. How were they going to find the evidence that they sorely needed? Maurine would be the key to unlocking the intricate pattern that permeated Smathers and Florio, but also most of the corrupt members of Congress, as well as the other denizens of the deep state.

They walked into the lobby holding hands. Both looked around quickly for any sign of danger. It was now ingrained into them to be ready for anything. Nothing unusual, so it was back to the apartment for a nightcap, and then recounting the evening with Wayne.

"I think we need to call Maurine now, and get her take on everything. Why wait until tomorrow?" Brenda said.

"Right on. You call her and put it on speaker."

"Will do."

She waited for Maurine to answer. It went to voicemail.

"I don't like this. She always answers her phone. She can see it's from me. Do you think she's still upset by the past crap?"

"I doubt it. She was fine when we finished our conversations. Call her later tonight to check on her." Charles had that lingering pang of doubt. He would go to her home in the morning to check on her.

They stayed together that evening and talked until midnight about what the future might hold for them as a couple. The difficult matters on hand melted into the background. They revealed the most intimate things that they loved about each other, and how their past loves haunted them as they made a new path together. It was joyous for them to become so close and loving.

****

Meanwhile, Maurine was working diligently to find more dirt on Smathers and Andy Florio. She saw that the call was from Brenda, and decided that she needed space from them. It was traumatic just confronting them, and it would take time for the healing to be complete.

The sounds of wind singing through the trees outside her ranch home gave her peace in her troubled world. It was a disaster when she confronted Wayne and those FBI agents who were just doing their jobs. She had hers to do, too. So much wasted effort for all of them. She had enticed Wayne with that thrill of a conquest for him and just her duty to snag him in an unlawful scheme. It was so easy to play the game of wanton lust for some men, and effortless to make them do her bidding. She smiled at that thought that went way back to the Adam and Eve story. It was inbred into both sexes.

The wind surged and the shutters on her windows rattled. She stood quickly to make sure that they were shut. There was a sudden bang on her front door. It must have been the increased wind, she thought. She went back to her chair and continued her search for clues. The lights flickered as she tried to concentrate, to no avail. The computer screen flashed on and off as the lights continued to send disjointed shadows on the walls. She pushed her chair back and heard the torrents of rain pelting the house, and the lightning strikes sent shivers in her back and legs. She had not expected this. As the storm raged outside, her sense of unease grew. She felt a chill run down her spine, a feeling of being watched. The atmosphere in the room was heavy with tension, and she couldn't shake off the feeling that something was not right.

She glanced around the room, searching for any signs of intrusion. The flickering lights and the banging on the door only added to her growing anxiety. Was someone trying to get in, or was it just the storm playing tricks on her mind? She knew she needed to stay focused to find the answers she was looking for, but the chaos outside was making it increasingly difficult to concentrate. The noise of the wind and rain seemed to drown out her thoughts, and the flashes of lightning made it hard to see clearly.

Taking a deep breath to try to regain control of the situation, she closed her eyes, shutting out the chaos around her and focused on her purpose. She needed to find the truth to uncover the secrets that had led her to this point. Slowly she reopened her eyes and returned to her search. The computer screen flickered back on to life, illuminating the room with a faint glow. She could hear the rain pounding against the windows, and she refused to let it distract her any longer. The wind howled, sending branches scraping against the windows, and the rain striking relentlessly. Sifting through the evidence, piece by piece, the answer started to come together. The puzzle was slowly unraveling, revealing a truth that was more sinister than she had ever imagined. It was a web of lies and manipulation, with more players involved than she had initially thought, but she wouldn't let that deter her. She had come too far to give up now. The storm outside was no match for the storm brewing within her. She was determined to bring justice to those who had wronged her, no matter the cost.

As the lights in the house flickered off she heard another disquieting sound at the front door. This time it was not the wind. Her heart beat faster as she walked to the window near the door. She pulled back the curtain slowly and saw a figure on the porch. She ran back to her desk and retrieved a handgun from the top drawer. She was not going to be blindsided by an attacker. Was this the way they were going to get rid of her?

She looked at her Ring doorbell on the computer and there it was, ready to open her door. The rain had abated slightly, and there was still that eerie sense of doom hanging over her. It was worse than her active duty in Iraq. She saw her enemies there and she was able to defend her territory. This was new to her, an adversary waiting to pounce without warning. The tension was palpable.

The door knob moved silently and slowly. Her adrenaline surged through her whole body, every reflex at high alert as she waited for his unwelcomed arrival. The door opened with a slight creak and a whoosh from the outside wind.

Maurine's instincts kicked in, her senses on high alert. She could feel its presence, a chilling energy filling the air. Her heart raced as she scanned the room, searching for any sign of the intruder, but the darkness and the sound of rain made it difficult to see or hear anything clearly. Suddenly, a figure emerged from the shadows, its face hidden beneath a hooded cloak. Maurine's breath was caught in her throat, her mind racing to comprehend the danger she was facing. She had stumbled upon something far more sinister than she had ever imagined, and now the perpetrator was closing in on her.

Fear gripped her, but she refused to let it paralyze her. She had come too far to back down now. With the surge of adrenaline, she fired her gun toward the intruder, desperate to protect herself. She missed completely, and then struggled with the intruder, who fought back with unexpected strength. Maurine's heart pounded in her chest as she tried to fend off her attacker, her mind racing to find a way out of this nightmare. The intruder proved to be too formidable. In a moment of brutal force, it overpowered Maurine, its grip tightening around her throat. She gasped for air, her vision blurring as her life hung in the balance. The gun fell from her hand as she tried to escape the ever increasing grasp.

The rain continued to pour outside, as if the heavens themselves wept for Maurine's tragic fate. In her final moments a mixture of determination and regret filled her thoughts. Her life slowly fading away as darkness hovered over her. The last echoes of the storm slowed, leaving behind only the silence of a life extinguished too soon. The rain washed away any evidence of the attacker being outside. The hooded killer left her home having accomplished what they had wanted… nothing left of her.

As the rain subsided and the clouds cleared, the world would mourn the loss of a brave soul who dared to speak the truth. And though the storm had passed, the storm within those who knew and loved her would rage on forever, haunted by the unanswered questions and the injustice that had taken her life. Her friends would find a way to honor her life by finding her murderer and those who did the hiring.

CHAPTER 28

Charles nudged Brenda as the sunlight bathed them with a warm glow. Her face was lined as she smiled at his gentle touch.

"Wake up, sleepy head." He proclaimed quietly.

She yawned, and clung close to his muscular frame as the covers embraced them.

"Yes, I'm almost awake. Sleep well?"

"Ya, I did. Hey, it's time to get rocking.' He threw the blanket off with gusto and jumped out of bed.

"I'll make the coffee while you get dressed." He was his usual charming self, hidden from the tragedy that would unfold that day He welcomed the new day filled with hope and cheer that all would be fine with the world, and that they could solve all of its mysteries. Brenda was less convinced of his bright attitude, and she was much more realistic. The continuing doubts about everything haunted her. She hated to diminish his healthy, confident outlook. He was such a great friend, and now her lover. They'd work as a team to find the truth while still attending to each other's needs. He called out to her as she left the bathroom,

"Coffee's on the table. Come an' get it." He had raisin toast and blueberry scones ready for her. He beamed as she came into the kitchen. "You're beautiful in the morning.

Okay, night time, too." He even sang a loving song as she sat at her appointed seat.

"Are you trying to seduce me?" She laughed heartily.

"Moi? YES!" He giggled at her.

The lovely breakfast ended with both of them discussing their intimacy and undying passion for the other. Their conversations were in dramatic contrast to what would be spoken about that very evening. It would be a deep sadness that would be the contrast of morning and night, light and darkness and good and evil. Brenda tried to gain focus on Maurine as she looked solemnly at Charles and spoke softly.

"I've been so worried about Maurine. She never returned my call. Please let's go to her house this morning. Let me try again to call her before we go."

"Sure, I'm even more concerned because she is under close scrutiny from Smathers and Florio. And what about Denise? She's a nutcase. Okay, call her." His words gave her some solace as he showed her his strength.

"The line is still going to voicemail. Now, I'm really worried. Get dressed fast, please."

"They both bolted from the table, and literally ran to the bedroom. He dressed in jeans and a tank top, and she with a bright red pullover and black slacks. They got to his car and drove rapidly to her house. The weather was sunny and cool with a slight southern breeze. They were unusually quiet as they arrived. Charles looked at her without so much as a smile, showing his nervousness. The usually vibrant neighborhood was eerily quiet and the silence heightened their growing apprehension.

Brenda opened her car door and said .

"Let's go. I'll ring the bell and you check the back door. I won't go until you get back."

He walked carefully to the back to make sure that there was no forced entry or suspicious activity. The tension in the air was palpable for both of them. He made his way to the front of the house and said,

"There is no sign of forced entry or anything out of the ordinary. The back door is locked, too."

Brenda's brow was furrowed with concern,

"Something doesn't feel right. We should go in together."

She rang the bell. Nothing from the darkened interior. She rang it a second time. Still nothing. Charles turned the knob and it moved. He did a full turn and they walked into a silently eerie house. Their steps echoed on the wooden floors. Brenda called out,

"Maurine?"

There was just silence as they felt a sinking feeling in their stomachs which grew stronger with each passing moment. They knew deep down that something was terribly wrong.

As they reached the last room dread washed over them. The door was slightly ajar, revealing a glimpse of darkness within. Brenda's hand trembled as she pushed the door open, and what they discovered inside would haunt them forever.

Maurine's lifeless body lay on the floor, a horrifying sight that shattered their hearts. The room was in disarray, as if a violent struggle had taken place. The truth that they had been seeking led them to this devastating moment.

Grief and shock enveloped Brenda and Charles. They clung to each other, finding solace in their shared pain. Maurine, their dear friend and confidante had been taken from them, and they vowed to bring her killer to justice. It was shattering to see that they were just together, and now she was gone. Who could be the killer? It pointed to either Smathers or Andy Florio or one of their hired hands. No other person would want her dead. Now, it was personal for them to bring them all down.

CHAPTER 29

The office doors remained closed as the Senator and his staff consoled each other when they found out about Maurine. It shocked them to the core as they tried to understand how her beautiful life was taken so young. Tears and cries of anguish permeated the office. They felt so close to her, and they all spoke so highly of her amazing work ethic and sweet personality. The Senator was not as taken by their sorrow. He seemed uninspired by the office wake. He tried to comfort them as best he could with hollow words. He joined their mourning by offering them his version of her as a person, however insincere it was.

"My fellow workers. It is with a great sense of sadness that we are gathered here to mourn a dear, beloved friend and coworker. Maurine Bicknell was an exemplary staff member. My friends, her life was taken much too early, and that is indeed a tragedy. It is my hope that we can solve the mystery of her death with all of the assets at our disposal. We will never rest until her murderer is brought to justice." He felt that his message of condolence might help them soften their grief. Him? He had nothing in his heart that felt right about his message to them.

The staff milled around commiserating among themselves. He went back to his office alone to consider his options, not about hiring another person. but to speak to Andy Florio to figure out what happened. This was too close to home for them to ignore it. Surely, all of their missives and discussions would be on the table for investigators. He was alone with his thoughts that turned him into a nervous wreck. All of his previous actions would be an asterisk in his memoir. What might happen to them if they found out that they both were involved in the sale of the invaluable sentient device to a foreign country, like Taiwan, no matter how noble their plan. Noble? Only noble for their wallets. He was genuinely frightened for the first time since he was involved in his extra monetary addition to his retirement plan in Washington. He needed to talk to Andy. He was about to yell for Maurine, but he stopped short of calling her name. It did get to him that she was gone forever.

"Andrew Florio's office." Her voice was joyful. He wasn't in the mood for joy.

"This is Senator Smathers. Let me talk to Florio." He was his usually inconsiderate self.

"Yes, Sir. Hold, please."

"Yeah, Rolly. What's up?" it was always that snarly, grating vice that made his skin crawl.

"What the hell do you know about Maurine's death? Did you do anything that I should know about?"

"I know as much as you do. Hey, don't attack me. What do you know about it?"

"I have no idea. It was a shock to all of us here in the office. You'd better get your act together because the feds might be asking lots of questions about us. What happened to our deal with Taiwan anyway? Your damn wife tried to fuck us. How did you handle that bitch?" He snarled at his compatriot in crime.

"She's not a bitch. She has her own agenda that's different from ours. She's still my wife, so don't forget that." He said it, but his actions inside were the antithesis of his words. "What does she have to do with this fucking murder or Taiwan?" He was barking at the wrong person. "I'll see if she knows anything and let you know. Go to your computer and erase all emails with me, and anything related to our dealings."

"You'd better do the same thing. Expunge it all, Andy. We better find the perp who did this and eliminate him. That's your job. I have to stay clean." His brave exterior melted fast when he was confronted with a major issue, other than money.

"You have the manpower at your disposal to do the search. You do it." Andy wanted to stay as far away as he could. He was just as much a coward when there was danger involved. He just talked a good game.

The banter stopped when Andy slammed the phone into its cradle.

Senator Smathers sat with his eyes closed trying to formulate some plan to extricate himself from any possible penalties related to selling government property to a foreign entity. The FBI would come snooping in his office for anything that Maurine was doing. Little did the Senator know that she was, in fact, a government undercover spy. Her true purpose was to gather evidence against corrupt officials like Senator Smathers, and this seemed to be the day when her investigations would bear fruit.

As the senator dug deeper into his thoughts, a knock at the door interrupted his contemplation. Startled, he quickly opened his eyes and composed himself, trying to appear as calm and collected as possible.

"Come in." He called out, hoping it was not someone who would further complicate his already precarious situation. It was just Margo, the office clerk who was gentle and harmless, he thought.

"Senator, I want to thank you for your kind words about Maurine. As you may know, she and I had some issues between us. I have been observing her and her actions for a while. I also was able to look at her emails and phone messages as soon as I heard what happened to her. They are very revealing about you and Mr. Florio. The FBI will be coming to this office to investigate her murder. Is there anything that I can do to help you in this situation?" She paused to wait for his reaction. His eyes opened wide and sat upright in his chair. She continued calmly.

"I know that Maurine had a big pay raise coming, so maybe you could find a way to transfer that increase to me. That way I could help you deflect the prying eyes of the investigators." She pushed as hard as she could with the idea of a bigger shakedown later as the FBI dug deeper.

"What the hell do you know about Florio and me?" He bellowed so loud that the whole office could hear. "Are you trying to get paid for helping me? You work here and get paid. That's it. Get out now." His face turned a bright pink as he rose to his full eight.

She slowly turned to walk out, but as she opened the door, she looked back with a sneer and said with brutal honesty,

"You will forever be sorry that you did not listen to me. My job is very secure since I know so much." She closed the door slowly with a perfect sense of being in charge.

His anger diminished as he sat back in his chair trying to fully understand what he just heard from Margo. As he tried to piece together the implications of Margot's revelation, how much did she really know? And how did she manage to access Maurine's emails and phone messages? The thought of the FBI coming to investigate Maurine's murder sent chills down his spine. He had always been able to cover his tracks, but now it seemed that his secrets were on the verge of being exposed.

Taking a deep breath, he tried to regain his composure. He couldn't afford to let panic consume him. He needed to think clearly and strategically. The first step was to ensure that Margot didn't have any evidence that could incriminate him further. He quickly deleted any potentially damaging emails and messages from his own devices, hoping that it would be enough to protect himself. Next, he needed to find a way to handle the FBI investigation. Margo's offer of help was tempting, but he knew he couldn't trust her. She had already shown her true colors by attempting to blackmail him. He had to find another way to divert the investigator's attention to throw them off his trail. He would need to be careful, cunning and persuasive. He would need to manipulate the situation to his advantage, using whatever means necessary, but most importantly, he needed to ensure that his own secrets remained hidden, no matter the cost.

With a newfound determination, he stood up and straightened his tie. He couldn't let Margo or the FBI destroy everything he had worked so hard to build. He'd fight tooth and nail to protect his reputation, his career and his freedom. As he left his office, he couldn't help but feel a sense of unease. The calm facade he had tried so hard to maintain was now shattered, replaced by a growing paranoia. He knew that the road ahead would be treacherous, but he was ready to face whatever challenges awaited him.

How could he handle Margo so that she couldn't destroy his serene life? She seemed determined to help the FBI unless he paid her more. He knew she'd be a thorn in his side for the duration of his term. Who killed Maurine? Who might help keep Margo silent? He had connections with the FBI; so all he had to do was call them and ask. He had better call himself without an office person interceding on his behalf.

"You have reached the Washington office of the FBI. How may I direct your call?"

"This is Senator Smathers. Please direct me to the person in charge of Maurine Bicknell's murder." He was dispassionate in his request.

"Hello, Senator. This is Patrick McLean. How may I help you?"

'I'd like to know if you have any more information as to the murder of Ms. Bicknell." "Well, as a matter of fact, we do have some new insight into that night. There was a neighbor who saw a 2020 Elantra that evening. Their outdoor camera has a photo of the car. We were able to discern a photo of the plate using our new AI technology. The license plate is registered to a Denise Florio. We have sent our team to get her."

"Please call me immediately after you have questioned her. Thanks again."

He hung up and had to compose himself after hearing that statement. Denise Florio?

Could she have done this horrible murder? He didn't know which way to turn. Call Andy? His mind became scrambled with conflicting thoughts. He had no place to go for comfort or direction. He had to rely on his own sense of morality and honor. Where had that gone after he had done so much to dishonor his country? He'd wait for McLean to contact him again.

He walked through the bustling hallways of his office. He couldn't help but feel a heightened sense of scrutiny from his colleagues. He knew that his outburst had caught the attention of everyone, and it was only a matter of time before rumors started spreading. He needed to act quickly to control the narrative and protect his image. He needed to find something in Margo's past that might put her in jeopardy. He'd find out one way or another.

The tangled web of murder, politics and corruption raised its ugly head once more.

CHAPTER 30

The days morphed into weeks as the sun's shadows got longer. Brenda and Charles grew closer and became inseparable. From a chance meeting at Andy Florio's office became a complete comingling of intimate feelings and sensations. Each met the other with a sense of selflessness and empathy. They were an open book of thoughts and emotions. They even finished each other's thoughts and sentences. It was a joining of a persona.

They needed to determine how Smathers and Andy Florio managed to transfer so many government issued items to line their pockets. The FBI knew a lot, but they could not get the information that they needed about Maurine's murder or anything strategic about Smathers or Florio. They should be able to get some material from Smathers office about Maurine's murder or his double dealings.

"Brenda, you know most of the people in his office. Can you make a quiet contact?" She was in the office loop since she often had contact with them.

"Oh, yeah. I know a few of them that I can trust. Margo was actually second in line in that office. I could call her today and set up a meeting with both of us."

"Great. Try to get her ASAP."

"Hello."

"Hi. This is Brenda from Andy Florio's office. How have you been?"

"Fine. What's going on?" She had that sense of another bout of questioning about Maurine.

"Charles and I would like to talk to you about some matters related to Maurine and the Senator. We need information that you may have that could shed some light on what they are doing outside of politics. Any chance of our meeting tonight at our home?" She was transparent and honest. Margo liked that about Brenda.

"Yeah. I think I can do that. Please no recordings or outside people. I have lots to talk about. Brenda, text me your address. How about seven?" She sounded like she wanted to tell them all that she knew.

"Super. See you at seven." She looked at Charles, and said with a huge grin.

"We got a live one. She'll be here at seven. Get out the wine and cheese." They scurried about the apartment to straighten the scattered books, magazines and used coffee cups. It was apparent that they might have an opening to the inner sanctum of office intrigue. The time passed quickly as they prepared for her arrival.

The bell chimed.

She pressed the outer door opener. "C'mon up." Brenda spoke excitedly. It was just a few moments when Margo touched the apartment door buzzer. Brenda opened it, and hugged her briefly.

"Welcome. It's good to see you again. This is Charles Barlow, my best friend and confidante." He extended his warm hand as a welcome.

"Nice to meet you, Margo. Would you like a glass of wine? Red or white?" He wanted her to feel comfortable and safe.

"Good to meet you, Charles. Red would be fine." She seemed at ease with them both. "I know you have lots of questions, and I have many answers that are important to all of us. I don't want to rush things, but let's get down to the nitty gritty, and we can socialize at a later date." She did what they wanted to do, but they tried to be less aggressive.

"Sounds good to us. We can sit in the living room." Charles quickly answered.

They walked into the room talking among themselves with niceties, and then sat across from her. Brenda began with an innocuous statement.

"It is so good to be with you after speaking to you so often." It never hurts to be pleasant before the real questions, Brenda thought. There was no need for that after Margo's rapid response.

"Hey, let's not bullshit each other. I'm here to talk about the jerk on top. He's a piece of crap." They both were taken aback by her response. It was not exactly what they expected.

"Okay, let's talk about him first, and then Maurine's murder."

"I have all of the damning information about how Smathers and Florio sold our government items for lots of dollars to many foreign and domestic people. Some were rockets to an enemy for huge bucks. Other materials were to foreign entities who funneled dollars to offshore banks, or even paid with diamonds and gold sculptures. I have all of this on this thumb drive." She was breathing hard because she had not taken a breath while telling them this outrageous saga. She held out the drive in the palm of her hand. They stared at it with a new sense of power. They could actually bring them down with her help.

"How did you get all of this material? Did Maurine know about this?" The questions flowed from them as she spoke with alarming precision and knowledge. She answered as fast as they asked.

"I knew all that was happening as I watched Maurine at her desk doing many strange things. After she went home, I searched all of her files and notations. She thought they were safe from prying eyes, but I had all of her codes. I installed spy apps on her computer to track keystrokes, as well as every communication she made. I'm sure you know that she was a CIA plant to try to catch Smathers in the 'act'." I plan to continue what she was supposed to do. They have no idea what I know. I'm also concerned that the lettered agencies have people who are privy to this information and will gain from it. You know that whoever has this information is at risk, just like Maurine. I'm going to do something that I never thought I'd have to do." She waited for their question. They both asked in unison.

"What?" Their eyes opened wide in anticipation of her answer.

"Brenda and Charles." She hesitated as if to reconsider her last statement. "I don't know if I'll ever get to disclose this information, so I want you to have this thumb drive as a safety precaution. Guard it with your life, because that is exactly what it's worth!" She had a tear running down her cheek as she became more emotional.

Brenda reached over to hold her hands with a sense of caring and comfort. It was a transition of power when she passed the drive to them.

"Margo, you're going to be fine. We'll take good care of the thumb drive, and maybe be in the forefront of the exposure of this scandal. You will be safe from them if we take the lead. Is it a problem if we do that?"

This was more than they thought possible when they asked to talk to her. She tried to compose herself as she looked at them knowing that they were the best shot to dethrone Smathers. Florio might fall with him, but it was the crooked Smathers that she wanted.

Charles and Brenda knew that this might be just one battle won in a larger war. The investigation still loomed, and the secrets were far from safe. They couldn't let their guard down, not for a moment. With renewed determination, they continued on this path, navigating the treacherous waters of politics, always watching, always calculating, and always ready to defend themselves, no matter the cost.

As they began to close the conversation, Margo sobbed uncontrollably. The thought of bringing them into harm's way brought her anguish and trepidation. It was Brenda who consoled her and hugged her tightly. It was a moment of compassion and sensitivity. Margo spoke haltingly.

"Brenda and Charles." Her voice was interrupted by moments of anguish. "I am so worried that I've brought you possible danger. Please be careful and trust no one. They are all in cahoots with one another. If you can unleash the powers of the good people, please do it." Her tears slowed as she tried to gain control of her emotions. Brenda still held her hand and whispered,

"We'll do what we can to help you. We've got your back, Margo." She said sincerely, but inside she was fraught with doubt.

"Thank you, Brenda and Charles. I trust both of you. If something happens to me, I beg you to get them. You saw what happened to Maurine. It could happen to me, too. Beware of them all." Her warning tore through them as a knife. Their compassion turned to fear as she finally calmed.

"We'll be very careful," Charles said.

"I'm okay now. Thanks for making me feel wanted and believed. This is going to be a tortuous ride for us once the truth begins to unfold. I think that you both should be the ones who break it so I can still be in the office watching what he does and who he sees." She was in control. They watched her going through her many moods, from informed, strong, and then sullen and emotional. They wondered if she did that in the office, too. Not their problem yet.

Margo was touched by their compassion as she rose from her seat. It was a good session which needed to end on a positive note. Charles stood next to her and said softly,

"We're so pleased that you were able to meet with us, and tell us what you know. Even more, thank you for trusting us with this thumb drive. We'll guard it well, and bring them all down."

Brenda knew that she had an additional concern about Andy. She was privy to all of his information, and it would coincide with what Margo knew, and also why Maurine died. All of the inside information was part and parcel of the dossier that she had accumulated as she watched and listened to Andy's adventures with Roland Smathers, his buddy in crime. That, along with Margo's thumb drive would put them away for a long time. It was time to put it all together and bring a case to the FBI. Then she thought about Maurine. She was gone now, but not forgotten.

They both knew that taking on Smathers and Florio would be no easy task. These were powerful and dangerous individuals who had evaded the law far too long. Brenda and Charles were fueled by their sense of justice and the memory of Maurine who had sacrificed her life to gather the evidence that they now possessed.

Margo hugged them both as she made her way to the door. As she opened the door she turned, put her hand over her heart and mouthed 'thank you'. Brenda sank into her chair and let out a deep sigh. Charles sat near her. He stroked her hand and brought her close to his side. He spoke with a sense of urgency.

"It's time to begin with the FBI. I have a sinking feeling that they have no clue about what Smathers and Florio are doing. Maybe we can help with that and with Maurine's murder at the same time. It's been a long few weeks since we've heard anything about it. Agreed?" He waited for her to cogitate about his timing.

"Yes, Charles, I do agree, but I'm not sure about the timing of this. We need to look at the thumb drive first and see what's on it. Then we can put this all together and bring it to the lettered agencies." Charles took a sip from his wine glass as a smile crossed his lips. He responded with a thoughtful answer.

"I know you're right. I got ahead of myself. How 'bout we look at the drive now and get a handle on what we have to do." She touched his hand with compassion. His reaction was one of love and passion. He leaned over and kissed her sweetly and continued,

"I love you, Brenda. We're sure a solid couple."

"Love making later. Now, work."

They jumped up from their resting place and made a beeline to the laptop on his desk. She looked at him and proclaimed with authority,

"Once we open this drive, we're fully invested in joining Margo in this adventure. Before, we only had some information. Now, we'll have it all, but be a target for whoever is pulling the strings. Are we ready?"

"I've never been as ready as I am now. Here goes!"

He plugged it in and waited patiently for the screen to come alive. The first image was a picture of Senator Smathers smoking a Cuban cigar with the forbidden case of cigars on his desk. They busied themselves for the next two hours scouring the drive and the incriminating files for both Smathers and Andy Florio. There was communication between each of them and then to foreign "investors" who wanted these defense items as a "loan." Their offshore accounts were noted for each of them. There was a tangled web of secrecy that Margo found. It was just a continuation of Maurine's detailed records. They also found contacts with many other people who joined them in their treasonous adventures. Money found a way to dethrone any semblance of patriotism or honor. They were incredulous at how many men were drawn in by the Senator. He was the kingpin of doling out favors for huge rewards, either in cash or diamonds. The absolute worst one was for the sale of Adama, the mothballed AI device. That was in millions. She then found that the Devil that popped up on many screens was none other than Andy Florio's wife. She had her own gang of followers.

Denise Florio was more than his wife. She listened to his calls with the devices in his office. She watched videos of him as he dealt with his buyers. She hated the thought of Maurine's interference in all of their transactions. She had more influence than her husband. He just didn't know it. When he found that there were devices in his office, he confronted Denise, but she was much more devious than he. She denied it all and placed the blame on Smathers. When they found Maurine's body, all eyes turned to Denise Florio. The evidence seemed to point toward her involvement as suspicions grew even stronger when it was revealed that she had been aware of Andy's activities all along.

As the thumb drive revealed more, Brenda and Charles uncovered a web of deceit and betrayal. It became clear that Denise had been playing a dangerous game, manipulating both Andy and Smathers for her own gain. Margo's drive postulated that she had orchestrated Maurine's murder, fearing that her interference would jeopardize her illicit transactions.

With this newfound knowledge, Brenda and Charles hesitated to approach the FBI with this evidence against Denise. They needed much more definitive information. It was a complex case with layers of deception and treachery, but they were determined to bring her to justice and to unveil the full extent of her involvement. They wanted to bring it all at the same time and destroy these ingrates. Charles was not so sure that Denise was the actual killer. He harbored doubts and expressed that to Brenda.

"I'm not so sure that Denise killed Maurine. Margo says right here," he pointed to a line on the screen, "that they saw Denise's car at the scene of the crime. Hell, she might just have been there to spy on her and see what she was doing. What if there was someone else there that actually did it?" He put seeds of doubt into the premise about Denise. "I know her from my first meeting and I sensed an unease about her. She wanted to bring him down even then. When we met at a restaurant, she was overbearing and unpredictable. We need to see if there were any other neighborhood videos. The one that they have may not be the only one. Also, were there any DNA deposits anywhere on the door handle or in the house? Who knows if the FBI did any of that?" He put enough doubt into that section of the discussion to keep Brenda searching for more complete answers.

The more they delved into the drive, the more they needed to talk to the lettered agencies. Charles postulated that Denise was not the killer. Who? That was his next discussion. The two of them bantered the rest of the evening as they looked at the screen with weary eyes. Tomorrow would be the time to begin anew with more searching for hidden clues. Charles smiled as he said, "Time heals all wounds." She retorted, "And time wounds more heels."

CHAPTER 31

They clung close to each other during the night, never a hand's distance away from each other. Brenda heard the faint sounds of traffic below, and brought her warm body close to him. He breathed a loud sigh, and turned toward her. His raspy tones reflected his early morning stirring after a deep sleep. His first words emerged softly,

"Hey, good morning, my love. Is it time to get up?"

"Nah, we're staying for a bit more. It's nice and warm now. Soon we can begin our searching for more info about all of them. I'll be up soon to make us some coffee. For now, it's cuddle time." He responded without missing a beat,

"That's the best news I've heard in a long time." Their cuddling morphed into a full blown frenzy of lovemaking. Both were sated, and held each other close and tight, their bodies still entangled in the best of human passion. They marveled at the beauty of their perfect meshing of emotions, and yearning for each other's tenderness. It was the best of relationships that connected them as one. Brenda kissed him sweetly, and said in her best post coitus voice,

"Hey, hon, time for the next move. Coffee, breakfast and more work on our project."

"Now? I've just begun!"

She laughed as she bounded out of bed, leaving him to fend for himself. He resolved to stay just a bit longer and savor the last few joyous moments that they just experienced. It was a momentous time of his life as he found his soul mate, a woman who fulfilled all of his needs and made him happy.

"Time to rise and shine, big boy!" Her laugh was infectious. He moved fast and caught her as she was about to leave the room. It was another hug and delicious kiss for each of them.

"You're not getting away so fast. Gotta brush my teeth, and then I'll be with you in the kitchen for a bite. Food or you?" He chuckled as he left for his ablutions.

"We did some fun stuff this morning. It's work as soon as we finish breakfast." She turned serious as did he.

"I know. I'm just playing with you."

They finished their coffee with small talk. They both regained their focus on finding every clue to stop the sale of government items to the highest bidders. Maurine's death needed more information from outside cameras, and then talking to the FBI. Brenda listened intently to Charles' concerns, weighing the possibilities in her mind. She understood his hesitation, and knew that they couldn't afford to make any mistakes.

They needed solid evidence before making any accusations.

"You might be onto something, Charles." Brenda replied, her voice filled with a mix of determination and caution. You can't jump to conclusions just yet. Let's dig deeper and see if we can find any additional evidence that could shed more light on this. Maybe there are other witnesses or surveillance footage that could provide more clarity.

Charles nodded in agreement, appreciating Brenda's level-headedness. Together, they brainstormed potential leads and strategies to gather more information. They knew they had to be meticulous and thorough, leaving no stone unturned. As they continued their investigation, they discovered a series of suspicious activities surrounding Denise. They found that she had been involved in several shady business dealings, leading them to believe that she had a motive for wanting Maurine dead. However, they still couldn't definitively prove her involvement in the murder. She had seen Detective Charles Barlow initially to throw everyone off guard. Her marriage was not on very stable footing.

Their hard work paid off when they stumbled upon a key piece of evidence, a hidden camera footage from a nearby building that captured the moments leading up to the crime. As they reviewed the footage, they were shocked to see Denise meeting with a mysterious figure just moments before Maurine's murder. Their faces were obscured and the hooded person was unknown, but it seemed to be a male. They would need to talk to Denise and see if she could shed light on the other person. It was doubtful that she'd even meet with him. Maybe Brenda could be the point person for this encounter. They both knew that she was a dead end for them, and would never disclose the other person. They'd have to find out another way. Charles opined,

"I think that we can do another Google search to see if any of the neighbors have night vision cameras. Maybe we will be able to see the hooded killer." They both tried a search on their personal computers. Brenda yelled loudly after just a few minutes.

"I found one in a TV store across the street. I'll hack into its device and see if we can see anything of value."

She was jumping up and down with excitement. It had many hours of infrared footage. She rewound the views to two hours before the suspected time of Maurine's death. There were cars going by and a few walkers even though the rain pelted them.. They could see all of their faces even with hoods on. They both watched patiently as she sped up the footage. Brenda grabbed Charles' arm and squeezed it firmly.

"Ouch. Hey, that hurt." "Look at that," she yelled.

And then they saw the Elantra parked near the house. They slowed the footage and watched with awe as they saw a man park his car two hundred feet behind her car. He got out and pulled the hood over his face, as if he knew someone was watching. They could not see his face at all from that view. He walked toward Denise's car and looked to his left.

"Charles, look at that." She was ablaze with joy as his face appeared for a brief second. She froze the frame and it was an incredible surprise.

"Yeah, I see him. Oh my god, it's Andy Florio. What the fuck!!!" He screamed at the walls.

"Why is he there with her? What the hell are we missing?" Brenda swung her arms in a wild gesture toward the ceiling. They could not contain their exuberance and disbelief.

There had to be an answer in that thumb drive.

They were hyper driven to review all of the information that Maurine had accrued on it. Margo had added much more material. They copied the drive onto each computer to search independently. It was time consuming to search every item, but it had to be done slowly and effectively. After an hour of finding nothing, they needed a break for a cup of coffee and a crumpet. Brenda said dejectedly.

"I'm worried that we'll find zilch on this drive. Then what?"

"Hey, we need to keep searching. Don't give up hope. Finished your coffee yet?"

"Yep, done. Back to work. We have another two hours of material to see. Gimme a kiss before we go back." He dutifully leaned over and kissed her cheek. She wouldn't have any of that, and pulled him close to her and kissed him with love on his supple lips.

"Now, that's better."

They both laughed and went to their respective laptops to begin anew searching for any detail that would shed light on any of them. The minutes seemed like hours as they read every document and each graph of treachery that was committed. It was more than drudgery. It felt like nails on a blackboard as they delved deeper into each treasonous detail of their crimes. At exactly eleven thirty Brenda screamed as if it were a eureka moment.

"Charles, I think I found it. Come here quickly."

"I'm here. What did you find?"

"Look at this story that Margo posted. Denise and Andy are trying to get the same item for sale. It was that freaking AI device. She was going to get it from Wayne Chambers at the Depot. Maurine was an FBI informant and brought it down. Maurine was going to pay Wayne fifty grand, but the FBI was there to catch Wayne. Oh my, what a development! It got all messed up when Wayne brought it to Las Vegas and then brought it back. Denise was spying on Smathers as well as Andy in all of their offices and even at their home. Wow! I think that Denise was originally trying to find out about Andy's gifts when she approached you. Then it all morphed into her wanting to get into the same actions of Andy and Smathers. Holy shit! This is the bombshell that we were looking for. Now that we have this camera evidence, we can go to the FBI and get them all at one time. Andy will go to prison for ages or get the death penalty, and Denise and Smathers will go to jail."

She took a deep breath and punished back in her swivel chair. Charles told her in a voice that could be heard in Kalamazoo.

"It's amazing that you found the evidence and were able to decipher all of that. I'm proud of you, Brenda. You're the best! I love you more now." He was pacing around the room. Actually, he was dancing. "Now, we need to bring this to the FBI and see if they can detain them for questioning. Smathers will have his lawyers, and so will the Florios.

They'll never be able to refute what we have on this drive."

The discovery of this information connected all of them in the conspiracy of treachery and treasonous activity. Murder was their solution to stop Maurine's exposure of their activities The tentacles of corruption hid in the shadows of Washington politics.

CHAPTER 32

Roland Smathers tried to understand how he had gotten into such a mess. The money flowed so easily as he sold whatever he could to anyone who offered him the greatest perceived value. Now, it was complicated by some disloyal office staff and the ghastly murder of his loyal office manager, Maurine Bicknell. He needed help from his good friend, Patrick McLean at the FBI. Pat could extricate him from any and all problems. It was the way of Washington: one hand washes the other. He called him on his private number. That would preclude anyone else from observing the conversation with their prying eyes. It would not go on the record.

"Hello. Who's calling?" Patrick asked. He seemed disgruntled.

"Hello, Patrick. This is Senator Smathers. I hope that we can be discreet on this call."

"Why, hello Roland. What's going on?"

"Well, I need a favor. Lots of people are snooping around, and I hope that you can find a way to put some distance between them and me." He was trying to be senatorial, but it came across as a plea to get him off the hook for something unusual.

"It's funny that you should call now because I was just talking to some people, who shall remain nameless, who want to come into this office to discuss some matters about you personally, as well as other individuals connected with you. Are you referring to those individuals?" He was almost smiling as he spoke to his friend of many years. He knew in his heart that this was exactly the issue at hand. He was not going to sacrifice his career to cover for him or anyone else. The Washington establishment was going down if he had his way.

"Hey, Pat, who are they? What info do they have about me? I'm sure that you can tell me. Right?" He put Patrick in a strange place. Confide information at the risk of hurting a case which he had not even heard, or shut the hell up? It was a fleeting second when he replied.

"Sorry, Roland, I'm not at liberty to discuss an ongoing investigation. You surely know that is against all department rules. Anything else I can do for you today?" He shut the conversation easily, and thought that he'd get an "okay" from the Senator. He was mistaken.

"Who the hell do you think you're talking to? You messed with the wrong Senator, McClean. I can destroy you with just a word from me. You're now on my shit list, you ungrateful asshole." He hit the red button on his cell and slammed it down on his desk. He mumbled curse words openly and pushed some papers around on his cluttered desk. Why hadn't his staff cleaned this up, he yelled into the ceiling.

He was now in the middle of an investigation for which he had no apparent defense since he was in the dark about the charges. He'd just wait for the rocks to fall.

Meanwhile, Charles and Brenda were on the same page as Smathers. They were on their way to the FBI headquarters on Pennsylvania Avenue. They had called to ask for an appointment to report an issue regarding national security, and some revealing answers related to a murder investigation. They both dressed in the normal interview clothing. He, in a suit and tie, and Brenda in a lovely light blue pants suit. It would present a solid picture of competence and trustworthiness. That's what they wanted as they presented their case.

The security was incredibly intense as they approached the entrance. It was strange to see armed soldiers. It was like a third world country. The peace and tranquility dissolved after the 9/11 attack in New York, the Pentagon and in a crashed plane in a field in Pennsylvania. As bad as Pearl Harbor was in 1941, this took even more lives and changed the world as they knew it. The guards asked politely.

"Do you have an appointment?" It was very formal and direct.

"Yes, Sir. It is with Agent McLean." It was a subdued and polite answer.

"Proceed. Get a badge at the front desk."

"Thank you."

They both held hands as they approached the desk. The formalities were necessary for everyone's protection. Happily there were no masks.

"We're here to see Agent McLean. We have an appointment."

"Names?"

They did the usual ID information and got the badges and passes. His office was on the third floor. The elevator was filled with agents as well as visitors. They continued to hold hands as they approached office 326. Charles assured Brenda that they would be received with huge thanks for helping the investigation. He opened the door slowly and they entered a spacious office with many agents milling around. Brenda commented quietly.,

"They sure have lots of them poring over their computers. See her? She's the receptionist. Let's talk to her."

"May I help you?"

"We have an appointment with Agent McLean. He's expecting us." Charles said calmly.

"Yes, he's expecting you. Please go through that door on your left. His secretary will assist you."

They did her bidding, and the secretary asked the same routine questions and asked them to go through another door to see him. There were a lot of security layers just to see him. He was a big man, mustached with a full head of graying hair. He stood as they entered. He spoke with authority, and had a kind, almost fatherly look.

"I understand that you have valuable information for me to see. Who and what's it about?" He was straightforward in a professional manner. Chales responded in kind, professional as with his usual detective character.

"First, let me introduce you to Brenda Williams who was instrumental in delving into this material and bringing it to this culmination. I cannot tell you how amazing she is." Patrick looked with admiration at Brenda after listening to that glowing introduction. He began the presentation.

"We have irrefutable evidence that Roland Smathers and Andy Florio have conspired to sell government property to both domestic and foreign entities. They have lined their pockets with dirty money from many sources. This thumb drive was populated by the deceased Maurine Bicknell, and it was completed by Margo Rogers, a superior employee of the Senator. Maurine was an undercover agent from the CIA. And to add the final touch, we have evidence that Andy Florio killed Maurine Williams. We have him at the scene of the crime and have an infrared photo of him. Brenda will show you all of this on the thumb drive that she has in her possession." He motioned to Brenda to continue the discussion.

"Do you need to have another person here with us to document all of this?" She didn't want him to miss anything.

"I think I can handle this right now." He was dismissive of her request. She wondered why.

"Fine, I'll place the drive into the USB port, if that's okay with you." She moved toward the computer. He grabbed her hand to stop her.

"Wait, Miss. I'll have to check that drive first." He looked at it closely and asked, "Where did you get the drive?"

"We've got it from Margo. We've been looking at all of the information from it. Why? Do you think it has a virus on it? Sir, we have already checked it out with our Webroot antivirus software. It is clean. I'm positive." She never hesitated for an instant. He was still wary and called in his security expert for confirmation. It was a cut and dry result. The expert determined that it was clear of any viruses, and gave the nod to Agent McLean.

"Okay, now I can insert it into the USB port." The screen populated rapidly. Brenda pointed out all of the information that was relevant to the case. Charles stood by , beaming at how she handled this curious Agent. She then said to him,

"And now, I want you to look at this infrared shot of Andy Florio. He's Maurine's killer. Look at him walking to the front door of the house and then walking in. The next screen will show him leaving after about eleven minutes. There's the timeline on the video. He runs to his car. Mrs. Florio's car is no longer there. We don't know if they colluded with each other, but she needs to be interrogated. I think that you'll find all of the documentation on this drive. We'd like to have it back now."

"That's all very interesting. We'll have to do our own investigation related to all of these people who you might think have betrayed our country. We'll need far more proof, especially for Andy Florio. Maybe he walked in to ask her a question and then hurriedly left. Just leave that drive with us." He sounded exactly like a corrupted official. Brenda's face turned a shade of pink, and spoke firmly and without any equivocation. Her hands clasped firmly together.

"No, Sir. That is our drive and we prefer to keep it in our possession until you show us that you are actually working this case." Her hands trembled as she spoke. She was uneasy at his response. It was as if he wanted to submerge this into his waste basket of nut cases. He was shocked by her answer.

"Miss, you're in my building, my office and the FBI. You don't have an option. We are keeping this drive to inspect, and will call you if we need more information. Show yourself out, please."

"No, Agent McLean, it's my drive and I will take it with me. You have no right to keep it." Her feet were planted firmly on the floor, and arms folded as an intransigent force.

She continued with an even more aggressive attitude.

"If you deny me the right to take my own property, you'll have a fight on your hands." His demeanor went from pugilistic to a more conciliatory approach.

"I have no reason to fight with you, Ma'am. I actually have all of the information downloaded on this computer, so take your drive and you may leave. We'll begin the investigation immediately." He reached out to shake her hand as well as his.

Charles was just so proud of her. It was a mighty turnaround in that instant when she stood up to him. They turned, walked out of his office, and began talking without missing a beat. He spoke so fast that the words just tumbled out of his mouth.

"Oh my god! That was better than the Muhammad Ali fight with Joe Frazier. You decked him in the second round. Brenda, what a performance! I'm so glad I'm on your team because I'd hate to have you as an opponent. Kudos to you, my love!"

"You're too kind. I'm just a small cog in the wheel of justice." She laughed so hard that people near them looked at her with a smile, too.

As they left the building the high that they had just gotten from Brenda's joust with McLean had an unexpected turn inside the building.

Agent McLean reflected on his conversation with Roland Smathers and decided to make a return call just for clarification of the good

Senator's requests. After seeing the video and the incriminating evidence, he thought that there might be something in it for the underpaid people at the FBI. He was near retirement, so an additional bonus might be helpful. He checked the recent calls and just hit that caller's name.

"Yeah, Pat. What's up?" He was in no mood to play games. He needed action, and not hollow words.

"Well, Senator, I saw some interesting information about you on a video that was just presented to me."

"What the hell was on it, and who gave it to you?" That was the query from an unnerved man.

"I can't divulge any information about the informant, but I can tell you that the information was damning. Very damning"

"I don't give a shit about it. What the fuck do you want?" He was slowly losing his temper, and it gave Patrick some wiggle room to negotiate 'things'. Patrick knew how to bait anyone. It was easy for this dunce.

"You had asked me to help you defuse some materials. I can do it for some kind of quid pro quo, if you know what I mean!" It was a game they all knew. He just did it better.

"You son of a bitch. You're shaking me down!" His voice rose in a crescendo.

"No, Senator, I'm just responding to your recent request." Never to be outsmarted, he had his recorder on. If he could not get any money, then he'd add to the charges that Brenda and Charles brought to the FBI. Win or lose with the Senator, there would be a reward.

"Never fuck with a sitting Senator. I'll have your ass outta there very soon. You'll get zip from me, and remember…..I have my recorder on, too, you jerk." It was a double whammy for Patrick: No money, and then a possible department punishment for what he just did. He understood that two could play that game. He lost.

CHAPTER 33

The days flew by as Charles kept himself busy with paperwork needed for his other investigations, unrelated to what he and Breanda were doing. It was just boring as he tried to find out about clients who had questions about business, or who were cuddling with some neighbor. He needed more details about what McLean was doing to get Florio and Smathers into custody. Brenda and he talked continually about their future together, and then were sidelined by the discussions about Smathers and Florio. Once in a while Wayne's name popped up. He was as much a part of this as anyone. They needed to make sure he was also in the loop, but they worried that he might be in jeopardy with Peter's death. Lots of puzzles, they thought.

Brenda continued her research with the video plus all of the possible interactions between those men. Did they have more issues that were undetected? Wayne might know more. It would be helpful to him if they acted as his supporters when he navigated his problems with the Las Vegas police. She said to Charles,

"Hon, I think we need to talk to Wayne and get inside information about those two guys. It's all well and good to have the videos that Margo got for us, but Wayne knows a lot that's not on the videos. I'll give him a call and maybe he can come over to spill his guts. It might save his life when we tell the judge that he helped bring down two bad guys."

"Great idea. How about soon?"

"Will do. I'll call him now."

"Wayne Chambers."

"Hi Wayne. This is Brenda. Can you come over to our place the day after tomorrow?

Tentacles of Corruption

We have some things we'd like to ask you. Nothing personal, just some stuff about Andy. Hey, I'll make some dinner for you and Charles. Can you get your flying buddy to give you a free lift? Maybe you can meet your other buddy, and then see us. Hey, two birds with one stone."

"Good idea. I'll meet Marshall, and then hop over. So, why do you wanna know about him? I don't know much. Besides, he's in trouble, I heard."

"Yeah, I heard that, too. We just need some clarification, that's all. I know you can help. Maurine would rest easy in her grave if she knew you'd help us." That might push him to come.

"Well, you know, I'll do what I can when it comes to Maurine. She was such a sweet lady. I'm so sad that she's gone. So, I guess I can help you. What time?"

"Is seven thirty okay?" He was a sucker for a home cooked meal, and adding Maurine was a clincher.

"Yeah. See you then. I got your address on my cell. I like anything you make." He was actually a good person who was caught up in the easy money. Brenda and Charles shared the cooking ritual, and smooched intermittently as they talked about the pasta fagioli and lasagna recipe.

"How about brownies for dessert when he gets here?' He laughed.

"You get the box and I'll get the bowl." It was more than fun for them. They laughed and touched each other as they sang from "Mama Mia." The days passed quickly.

It was seven twenty when the doorbell rang. She looked fine in her black slacks and pink sweater, and he was very casual, too. They had showered and soaped each other two hours ago. It was a clean break from the trials and tribulations of the day. They were both very happy and sated. Food would be the icing for them. Well, Wayne's stories might be a topping for the desert.

"C'mon in." Charles said. He came in with a bottle of red wine and a box of Hershey kisses. Brenda was so pleased, and said with her usual good nature,

"Wayne, you're so sweet. It wasn't necessary, but we'll enjoy it during the meal and after, too. Hey, let's open the wine and have a toast to health and good fortune."

They did just that, and made small talk as Wayne loosened up from two glasses of wine. Charles thought it was a good time to begin a gentle discussion.

"Thank you for coming over. We know that you'd had dealings with Andy and the Senator. We also know that you had issues with the Vegas cops. We are willing to give you a good recommendation when you help us with some pressing matters." He waited for something from Wayne. It came fast and furious.

"Hey, is that why I'm here ? To rat out those people? Not gonna do that."

Brenda intervened as fast as she could. She glared at Charles because she thought that he approached the questioning too fast. She touched Wayne's hand as a peace sign.

"Wayne, we are not asking you to rat out anyone. We just want to help get Maurine's killer as well as some inside information." She needed to get him to simmer down. "Hey, how about dinner now? We can talk later." Charles agreed fast in order to defuse the heat that built up.

The dinner was excellent and Wayne relished it by his words and actions. He scooped up the last of the soup with Italian bread. He talked a lot about his adventures with Peter and how they won so much at the casino. He finished the bottle of wine, and asked for an after dinner drink of Sambuca, his favorite. He just kept rambling on as he imbibed more liquor. They listened to his stories until he sat still and quiet, and took a brief sip. Brenda looked at Charles and nodded to him that he should begin again. Yes, they were connected in all ways. They often said things that were in the other person's mind. That was joyous to them.

"Hey, Wayne, how about that great dinner?" He had to begin slowly and carefully.

"Yeah, it was really good. Thanks for inviting me. Sorry I blew up atcha guys. I'm just in a bad place now. Ya know with all that's going on."

Brenda moved close to him, held his hand, and took over from Charles' introduction.

She closed her eyes and then put her hands to her heart.

"We were wondering if you knew anything about Maurine's murder?" It was her way to gain his trust and it might be easier to talk to a woman who was not confrontational.

"I don't know nothin' 'bout it. It came as a shock to me, just like everyone else. Who the hell would do that and why?" He had such a sad look on his face. Brenda continued slowly, trying to elicit something more pertinent about Andy Florio.

"Do you know anything about what Andy was doing that might involve her?"

"Nope."

They both gave each other that knowing look. It was obvious that he needed a bigger push for information about specific things. Brenda began anew.

"Wayne, I think you know that we have lots of information that we're not sharing with you now. We'd like you to be honest with us. Really honest!" She hesitated to watch his reaction. He closed his eyes as if to think of what he should do.

"I know what you're sayin'. Hey, this is gonna be really tough for me. Is this like a confession to a priest?"

"Yep, it is exactly. You'll be helping us get her murderer as well as getting Smathers and Florio to stop what they're doing. We need that confirmation from you. Just let us know that you're with us." She engaged him with caring and support.

"I'll finally get this shit off my chest. I'll help you." He was looking at the floor with slumped shoulders, knowing he finally had to confess. It was hard for him, but necessary after years of illicit activities.

"Great. How did they get the items from you, and where was all of the stuff sent? Did you get paid, too?"

"I got the stuff they wanted from the Depot. Most times they sent a truck and I just loaded it. When I got the order for that AI thing, Peter and I drove it to Vegas. That's when all hell broke loose with Peter. That's another story that I gotta resolve with the cops. Yeah, I got paid depending on what I got for them. One time I got ten Gs for a bunch of rockets. That AI thing got me lots more. I forgot just how much, a lot. Both of them called me for stuff. I hope those fuckers get fried. Do I get a reward for helping you?" He began to slur his words as he drank a second glass of Sambuca. Both of them were spellbound by his truthful revelations. He took a deep breath and rolled on with much more damaging information about Smathers.

"The freaking Senator always tried to beat me up for my deserved cut. He got hundreds of thousands. I got a measly small amount. Now, I'll get my piece of him.

Right? Hey, do I still get a reward?"

His mind slowly crashed as he drank more. He asked for a beer after his last sip of Sambuca. They'd risk another glass of anything if he'd continue his harangue against Smathers. Forio might just be next.

"So, Wayne, Do you have any recordings or records that might help us get these guys?" She had to ask.

"Ya' think I'm stupid? Course I got 'em. They're in my room, all in a box, just in case they tried to fuck me." He was loose and unfiltered. Charles intervened to give her a break.

"'You were very smart to do that. Can we take a look sometime?"

"Yeah, I can bring it all here on my next trip to see you guys. Maybe another dinner as a small reward?" He never gave up on rewards. It was in his blood. Brenda thought it was a small price to pay for the box of evidence.

"Dinner on us next time. How about a big Kansa City steak and all the trimmings?" He'd fall for that every time. They'd even have more Sambuca. He drank most of the bottle.

"Yes, Ma'am. I'd like that. I got all that info for ya'." He was totally invested with them to bring them down, but he'd also suffer some untoward rewards, but not money. He might get a dishonorable discharge, or jail time for Peter's murder. Jackson would suffer a similar fate of jail time.

The days went fast as they devised the plan to coordinate Wayne's evidence box and a visit with Agent McLean's office. Wayne called Charles after the third day of their last visit.

"Hey, Chuck, how about dinner tomorrow? I'm gonna fly up to visit a friend, and then we can talk about my little box of toys." He was trying to be playful, but it fell on deaf ears. It was just a few minutes' drive from the Depot to the airport for him. The good news was that he was able to get free flights from his buddies..

"It'll be great to see you again, Wayne. Yep, I'll get the steaks and we can have another chat about the stuff in your box of toys." He was tired of placating him. It was almost like giving candy to a pain in the ass child.

Charles was drained by him. It was a chore just to listen to his slurring of words and his seemingly inability to comprehend the seriousness of his actions. He was just as guilty as they. Maybe more so, since he procured all of the valuable items. The money flowed to all of them as a river of green, slimy dollars. Charles wondered how deep this corruption went. He knew of some of it, but each of those in power used every means at their disposal to steal, cheat and enrich themselves. He felt sad that anyone could debase their country as they did.

Brenda shouted from the kitchen as he hung up.

"So, what's with Wayne, that charmer??

"He's going to come up and bring his box of information. I think we can analyze it, and then put those people away for a long time. Andy will be hung out to dry for a long time. Smathers will be in jail." He hesitated, and let out a loud snort. "That son of a bitch is fried!".

They cleaned up the place and had to wait until the morning to call McLean. The night was one of smiles and cuddling in their king sized bed. Only the alarm awakened them or they might have slept till noon. Brenda was off to work at Andy's office, so Charles took on the task of calling his FBI buddy.

"FBI office."

"This is Charles Barlow. May I speak to Agent McLean.?"

"Hold, please."

"Hey, Charles, What's up? Any news that you want to share?"

"Well, I think that we have incontrovertible evidence that you will want to see. One of the participants in this crime is willing to flip and bring it all to me and the authorities. Let's make the meeting three days from now so you can take the appropriate action. I'm not sure if I can convince my informant to meet you. He will have to make that decision."

"That's very good news. After seeing the thumb drive and with this new evidence I think we can move forward and take the necessary actions. I'll arrange the meeting and have another agent with us. Thank you for your help in this matter".

"Good. I'll bring Brenda, too".

"Bye".

Charles felt better after the call. He was not so sure about McLean after their last visit. It was reassuring to listen to him now.

After he hung up, Patrick McLean paced his room and wondered how he might jail the two men and others, yet still get something of value from it. His mind never stopped thinking of ways to profit from the job. His retirement was nearing, and he knew he could use extra cash.

Most members of the Washington elite were positioned to gain some type of compensation from feeding off someone's tragedy, or taking bribes for secretly doing political favors. It was worse than a swamp. It was a moral desert.

CHAPTER 34

Wayne fumbled through his papers, and then looked under his bed for the precious box that might save him brig time. His hands trembled as he lifted this key to his survival. If those men in power who knew that he was flipping, they'd kill him as they must have done to Maurine. He was in a no win situation. It was his duty now to come clean, no matter the consequences. He drove to the airport and caught the flight to D.C. He held the box close to his side as he tried to fight his inner turmoil. Why did he fall to the debauchery of self-indulgence? It was inbred into all of their genes. They would cheat, steal and betray in the name of golden rewards. He was disgusted by them and, worse, himself.

He landed after a smooth flight. It would be worth the effort to extricate himself from this dilemma. His first call was to Charles.

"You're here now?"

"Yep, are you ready for action? And a great steak for moi"? He feigned joy, but inside he was torn with a continuing sense of doom.

"Sure, we're ready. Brenda is making the salad as we speak. Just c'mon over. We got outstanding rare Kansas City steak plus red wine and your favorite Sambuca. We even have a great beer for you, if you want. We hope you've got your precious box of goodies for us." He spoke carefully so as not to rock the boat.

"I got it all. Get ready to listen to the tales that you've been waiting for. See you in a few minutes." He was just a few blocks away. His pace increased as he needed to get past this betrayal he felt. He hated snitches….. and he was one of them.

The rain began as he approached the home of his saviors. He dutifully knocked on the door. He heard from inside the soothing, calm yet sensual voice of Brenda.

"Hey, Wayne, c'mon in." He opened the door slowly and walked into the confessional.

There was no priest to listen, just his friends.

"Welcome, our friend. How was your trip?" It was the beginning of their attempt to let him vent at his own pace.

"Yeah. It was easy. I actually sat with my buddy as co-pilot for a while. We just jabbered a lot. Hey, I'm starved. Wine first?" He wasted no time to get the booze into his withering psyche.

"Got it. Here's to you, Wayne and to your health." She picked up the glasses and clinked them together, the three of them in symbiosis. His health was in limbo if anyone knew he had ratted them out.

They all sat and talked about nothing. It was stuff about his youth and she mentioned that she had been in nursing school before she worked for Andy. Sickness and death had gotten to her so she left. Charles could not wait to finish the inane chat, so he just blurted out.

"Steaks all done. Let's start dinner." Brenda knew how he felt about doing this. She was aligned with him in all ways.

The dinner was filled with civilized chatter about Wayne's service and how he wanted to fly in the Air Force, but never got the chance. Each of them regaled the others with historical memories and lots of laughter. Under all of that was the realization that he had to do his confessional soon. Charles took the helm and steered the rest of the dinner to its deserved completion. He asked them to join him in the living room.

He offered Wayne the usual Sambuca and it all began. Wayne never stopped talking about his precious box of tales of greed and corruption between members of Congress as well as prominent people in the Washington establishment. He took a breath just to take a sip of his alcohol. He showed them signed receipts as well as photos of all of them. He had prepared for this moment since he began the passageway of corruption. He knew it was wrong, but money trumped loyalty. He never thought he'd have to pay the ultimate price, whatever that was to him. To others, it was the end of life, and a road to an eternity of shame.

As the sounds of his penance withered away, Charles motioned to Brenda to sit close to him. He needed to ask a final question. He had to phrase his words carefully.

"Wayne, good buddy, we want you to come with us to FBI headquarters and meet with Agent McLean. You need to tell him what you've told us. We'll also have to bring all of this material with us. Would it be okay with you if we kept it for safekeeping?" He was reticent about asking, but had to do it. Wayne wrinkled his nose, and sat back in his lounge chair. He pondered, then spoke from his heart.

"Hey, you guys have been really fair with me. I know you have my best interests at heart, but I'm not sure if I can face that guy from the FBI. I'm so scared right now. What can I do?" Brenda had to respond.

"Wayne, you're right. We know how tough this is for you. We can all go together to see McLean. That way you'll have us to help you when you tell him all of the information. How about it?" He seemed to settle down and showed a sign of acceptance. His shoulders turned back and his eyes brightened.

"You're sure persuasive, Brenda. I'll have to take time off to go with you guys. I got leave time left, so I'll do it. Set up the time. Yeah, I'll leave all of the stuff with ya' all. I don't wanna lose any of it." He was actually happy to have made the decision. Maybe eternal damnation could be changed to a lesser punishment.

He went to visit his buddy and left them to ponder the elaborate details of what he and they had done. It was years of this deception and corruption from which they all profited, some more than others.

It took Charles many hours of patiently searching through the documents that Wayne had left with them. He collated them all by the recipient's honoraria, and what Wayne had received as payments. He kept meticulous books that left nothing to the imagination. He knew the day of reckoning would come, one way or the other. Brenda kept Charles sated with moments of orgasmic joy, and then with her culinary prowess. He worked, and she kissed him often. She reviewed all of his detailed efforts and made the necessary corrections. He loved that she helped so efficiently. He just loved her! They went to bed with a sense of accomplishment, so that they could rest easy. The case was complete enough to have the meeting. Morning was the proper time to call

McLean and set it up. Wayne was anxious to face whatever punishment they meted out.

Charles awoke at seven and tried to stay quiet as he had his morning coffee. He reviewed the whole scenario in his mind as he prepared to call the FBI. He waited until nine. Brenda was sitting next to him and listening intently.

"FBI office." It was their routine impersonal answer.

"This is Charles Barlow. May I speak to Agent McLean?"

"Hold, please."

"Hey, Chuck, it's early for you. What's up?" He knew the meaning of the call. He was just playing with Chucky baby.

"We have all of the incriminating evidence, and we also have Wayne Chambers ready and willing to tell you everything, down to the last detail. He's in Washington now waiting to see you. We'd like to come in today. Tell me the time." He wanted it over. There was a pause. He worried that McLean might put them off just to break their chops. He finally answered.

"Okay, Charles, you all can come in today at two. Bring Chambers and get ready to meet with our whole team. I hope you know that there will be lots of dangerous pushback from these people." He was more conciliatory than before. Maybe he had a semblance of humanity. They ended the call cordially.

It took him moments to contact Wayne and told him to meet at their place so that they could all go together. He arrived with plenty of time to spare. The trip was unusually quiet as they all contemplated what might happen when the news broke. The papers would have a field day with this scandalous meat. They loved dangling tasty morsels to the gullible public.

They went through the usual security check when they entered the FBI office. The clerk at the desk asked why they were there, and to whom they wanted to see. Yes, routine for them, but it filled all of them with trepidation, especially Wayne. The clerk sent them to room 201. They wore their new ID badges, and dutifully went through the paces to get to the inquisition chamber. They heard lots of talking and laughter as they approached the room. Wayne said pointedly,

"Sure hope they're not laughing at me. Got enough on my plate now." There was no smile on any of their faces. It was show time. Charles knocked on the door twice.

"Come in, Charles." It was McLean who spoke through the door over the background laughter. As they entered there were four agents plus a secretary sitting at a long table.

Water was at each seat. There was also a TV camera and a large white board. As they entered the room, all laughter and talk eased. There was an uneasy quiet that seemed to stop time.

Patrick McLean greeted them with the customary platitudes and admonitions.

"Good to see all of you. Wayne, you know that you can have an attorney present." He went on to read the Miranda rights and then said loudly, "I also want to alert you that all of this session will be recorded, and memorialized for a possible trial. Do you all agree to these stipulations?" He looked at all of them to get approval. Each of them said,

"Yes, sir."

"Please be seated. Our secretary will also take minutes of the meeting and secure all of your documents. Is that permissible for you, Wayne?" There was a direct visual meeting toward him which excluded the others.

"Yes, Sir." He found his normal voice, but internally he was shaken. His life was on the line. He hated himself for the terrible things he had done, just to get those ill gotten gains. Patrick continued.

"Before we go on, let me introduce all of the people here and their positions." He then went on to do all of the introductions, and how each of them could investigate the charges.

The afternoon morphed into early evening as the details of the charges evolved. Wayne was forthright, and Charles only interjected if he thought that Wayne had neglected some pertinent facts. Brenda was more subdued as she listened to the give and take between Wayne and each of the FBI players. The white board was filed with data about how the money was paid in many ways. Patrick looked at his watch and spoke hoarsely,

"Hey, people, it's really getting late. I know we're all tired from this. How about we adjourn until tomorrow for a morning session. Say, about nine? Wayne, we all want to thank you for your excellent records about these transactions. I know how hard this has been for you, and frankly, all of us. Have a good evening, everyone. See you tomorrow." The afternoon was draining for them, even as they felt it was a successful meeting.

Brenda looked at a very tired Wayne,

"Wayne, you were awesome with your presentation. I don't know where you have the courage to talk about all of the intricate details. Tomorrow will be easier, I hope. So, how about we all get some dinner at a joint just down the avenue?" She was as tired as they, but they needed a break from the day's tension. Wayne spoke first.

"I'm in. I need a beer or two. My treat, my friends." He broke through his tired facade, and actually made them aware of his jolly soul.

The three musketeers walked fast and steady to The Smith for a sumptuous meal. It was a good ol' American joint. Wayne ate one of his favorite meals of shrimp and grits with lots of butter. The two lovebirds dined on Mac and cheese plus a couple of rare burgers. They commiserated about the day's adventure, and what might happen the next morning. After their appetites were sated, they left. Wayne took a Uber to his friend's home, and the loving couple went home for a well-deserved rest. The night was filled with giggles, moments of sadness and intense coupling. They found each other and vowed to remain as one forever. It was an intermingling of souls. They marveled at how two people could find this magical merging when it was such a rare treat.

Nature worked in strange ways. That was a miracle for them. How many other people felt the same way?

CHAPTER 35

Wayne knocked at their door at seven thirty. He was anxious to finish the interrogation and move on with his life, if that was possible. He also had to extract himself from the police in Las Vegas. He wondered what was worse for him: being a traitor to his country, or having killed a man in self-defense.

Charles opened the door to see a smiling Wayne.

"Well, good to see you haven't lost your happy face, buddy. You're early. Let's have a cup of coffee while Brenda gets ready." He poured the coffee as Wayne talked about the next steps for his future.

"I need to get something off my chest. You guys have been great. I just hope that they will be kind to me since I've given them so much to put the other guys away for a long time. Now, what the hell do I do with the Vegas cops? You know, about the self-defense killing of Peter?"

"Ya, I got that. Maybe we can put in a good word to get you off the hook. McLean will surely do it when we finish up the interrogation." He stopped, looked at his watch and yelled out, "Hey, Brenda, Let's go. I poured the coffee for you and then we gotta skedaddle."

They all finished their morning coffee and headed out to the FBI headquarters. It was the same routine when they arrived. All of the previous members were waiting for them in the same room. Patrick welcomed them and immediately delved into a continuation from the previous day. Wayne answered each question completely. They all knew he was telling the truth. It corresponded to all of the information he had presented to them. The morning was punctuated with relevant questions for the other members. Brenda and Charles remained still, yet responsive to any of the other technical questions. As noon approached it was obvious that all of the questions had been answered. Patrick said ,

"Well, people, I think we've done all that we can do. Now, it is our job to arrest Senator Smathers for his crimes, plus Andy Florio for what he had done regarding the selling of our military materials. It is also a clear case of murder of Maurine Bicknell by Mr. Florio. Mrs. Florio will also be arrested as an accessory to murder. We will also help Sergeant Chambers obtain an adjusted sentence for his help in this matter." He gave a thumbs up to them and was about to dismiss everyone when Wayne raised his hand.

"Agent McLean. Thanks for that help. I do have another big favor to ask of you. I have had some interaction with the Las Vegas police related to a self-defense murder of a guy who was trying to steal government property. My Uber driver and I tried to stop him, and in the fight he was killed. They're investigating it and know all of those circumstances. So, I need help for you to get me off since I was instrumental in catching these bad guys. You know, one hand washes the other." He felt stupid using that phrase, but he was stuck. Brenda smiled under her hand which covered her mouth. Maybe it was a giggle. She held Charles hand as they were about to leave. Wayne stopped them.

"I gotta tell you guys that I owe my life to you. I never coulda done this myself. Thank you from the bottom of my heart." He hugged them both and sighed in relief.

The FBI crew left with a sense of pride that they all solved this intricate case and spoke among themselves at how patriotic citizens, plus a dedicated serviceman helped crack the case. They concluded that the punishment would fit the crime, and detailed what that punishment should be.

The Senator was convicted of treason and theft of government property. He was put into jail for a maximum of twenty five years. Andy Florio was sentenced to life in a secure prison in Fort Leavenworth for Maurine' Bicknell's death. They were able to convict him because they found the doorknob's copper and zinc residue on her throat. Denise Florio was exonerated in the death of Maurine Bicknell, but was placed on probation for collusion. The FBI reached out to the Las Vegas police and detailed the help that Sergeant Chambers gave to help convict a murderer and a treasonous Senator. He and Jackson were found not guilty by a report of self-defense, and their record was expunged, but he was given a dishonorable discharge for being an accessory to government theft.

So, now it came to Charles and Brenda. The passion that they had in the courtship evolved into a marriage that only increased their love for each other. It showed two souls can, indeed, merge into one. That merger was the foundation of a new living being that entered this world. They had a beautiful baby girl who they named Amelia.

And now, the world is in equilibrium.